DAVID JACKSON AMBROSE

UNLAWFUL
DISorder

DAVID JACKSON AMBROSE

UNLAWFUL
DISorder

JADED IBIS PRESS

Ambrose, David Jackson
Unlawful DISorder / Jackson Ambrose

Cover Design by Crystal J. Hairston

Published by Jaded Ibis Press.
http://www.jadedibispress.com

JADED IBIS PRESS

"If I had a world of my own, everything would be nonsense. Nothing would be what it is, because everything would be what it isn't. And contrary wise, what is, it wouldn't be. And what it wouldn't be, it would. You see?"

—The Mad Hatter, **Lewis Carroll**, *Alice in Wonderland*

"I just want to take time. To tell you. A story. About a man called Shout'n' John."

—**Shirley Caesar**, "Shout'n' John"

He didn't really remember what going crazy looked like. What he remembered was that one day, a day without the sun, he went to his mother's job to ask for his money, and then he knew he had to kill her. So he reached across her desk, plucked the cigarette from her ceaselessly moving mouth, and tried to squeeze all the air from her. Next thing he knew he woke up in this dark place, with cold concrete walls and reverberating voices.

He could not determine if the voices were in the hallway or in his head, but he wanted them to stop. He wanted to sleep. He curled under the threadbare blanket on the narrow cot, hearing the sibilant rasp of his dry feet snagging on the much-laundered sheet.

The door to the tiny room banged open, and the reverberations grew louder. He peeked over the edge of his blanket and saw shadows unfurl toward him, then felt a draft of cold as the strip of wool was yanked away. Shadows grasped his arm. There was the sound of paper tearing and the waft of alcohol. Brisk, terse rubbing against his arm. The brief, bright sting of steel struck his olfactory senses. He jerked—the only power of protest that was able to swim to the surface through a smog of Benadryl. He could smell the comforting antiseptic scent of a bandage. It was followed by a light pressure on his arm, a balm meant to soothe in the wake of the hypodermic burn. Then darkness fell like a slowly lowered window blind and the shadowy figures retreated.

He might have slept for one day, or it could have been one month. Benadryl fog made time an abstraction in places like this. But when the small-boned, white woman with the flowered skirt and tight gray bun introduced herself as Dr. Herrera, he knew he had slept for three days.

Psychiatrists never introduced themselves until day three, after the initial intake. The initial intake where they had made him wait hour after hour in a small, windowless room, without radio, or television. Where two large Black men in sterile white scrubs had stood by the door, silent like death, only speaking when he asked, "How much longer do I got to wait here?"

"The doc will see you as soon as she's done. There's people waiting to be seen before you."

After the tenth hour, he did what it seemed they had been waiting for. He leaped up, screaming, and threw a chair. They descended like night, pinioning him beneath their weight, ignoring his outbursts, his demands to go home.

Now, Dr. Herrera watched him with kind and cold eyes. There was a hiss of nylon as she crossed her legs.

"Do you know why you are here?" she asked.

"Where am I?"

"What is your name?"

He rose from the bed to sit on the edge. He noted that the doctor sat back, more erect as he rose. He placed his feet on the cold floor, looked down. He noticed the sheen of gray on his skin, a sign that he needed lotion.

"Bowie. Bowie Long."

She began to ask the next question, but he cut her off. He had been in and out of psychiatric facilities all his life; he knew the routine. "DOB: Christmas 1984. Residence: 1400 Maple Leaf Street, Norristown, PA. It is the year 2010. A Black man rules the world."

He huffed a laugh, short and powerful, like steam from an engine, before continuing, loud and unmodulated, "First time I was in a place like this, a comment like that would have sealed the deal that I'm bonkers. Where am I?"

"You're at the state hospital."

His shoulders slumped defeatedly. Jesus, it was worse than he had thought. He ran a hand through the tumultuous tufts of his hair. He noted he needed a comb and some shea butter when his fingers snagged in the tufts. He was accustomed to privately run facilities. The state hospital was the place of last resort. The place for the true loons. Or those that didn't have insurance to pay for anything else.

There were no perks here. The state hospital was tantamount to being at the county jail. A lockdown holding cell where you were remanded by the decree of a judge, under petition, and you were expected to get yourself together before the week ended. He had seen the result of longer stays. People roaming the streets with dead eyes, rooting through dumpsters, congregating at the McDonald's to beg for loose change, police chasing them away like errant pigeons.

He felt something burning in his eye.

"How long I been here?"

Dr. Herrera looked up from her clipboard. Her gaze was steady and astute. "It is better to focus on recovery rather than how long you have been here. Don't you think? If you are able to comply with treatment modalities, cooperate with your treatment team, attend all group sessions, take all prescribed medications and adhere to your treatment plan— show that you are no longer a danger to yourself or others— you will be able to go home upon judicial review of your original 302 petition. You have a therapist on the outside, correct?"

He nodded.

"Do you know what brought you here?"

"I tried to kill my mother?"

Dr. Herrera sighed, clicked the tip of her pen; it scratched the paper on the clipboard. "Is that what you remember?"

He nodded again.

"Could you describe that moment for me?"

"She wouldn't stop talking. I wanted her to stop talking."

"Why did you want her to stop talking?"

"Because she's full of shit."

He thought back to that day. It now seemed so far away. He couldn't remember anything other than her voice telling him he was hearing things, asking him through lips clenched tightly around a cigarette if he was hallucinating.

The word terrified him. He didn't want to hear her saying that word. It brought back memories of another time. Made him think of other things. Sitting in the back seat of her car. Watching the back of her head, her hair missing in spots—nerves, she said, from constantly worrying about him. She was driving him to Horsham Clinic. The nice place. It was like a rich man's mansion out in the bucolic countryside, with actual sheep grazing in front of the massive stone structure. He heard her voice asking him if he was sick. He saw the car mats spinning around in circles. He saw the back of her head, the missing spots. They were moving. It looked like a dark face, watching him. There was a curve in the sparse hair near the base of her neck grinning a malevolent grin, laughing, laughing at him while her voice echoed above saying those words: *sick, seeing things, godogod.* The grinning thing released a tuft of smoke. He had kicked the seat, screaming.

"She said I was trying to kill her."

Dr. Herrera nodded, looked down. "What do *you* say?"

"I waited all day. Waiting for my check. I wanted to get my money, buy something to eat. Maybe get a cheesesteak. Maybe take the bus to Atlantic City. She knew I was waiting on my check."

Dr. Herrera looked up, as if waiting for him to continue.

When the mailman had finally gotten there, incensed, Bowie roared out the door to meet him at the curb, furious he was late.

The mailman looked at him bemusedly, shrugged, unbothered by the short man flaring up, speaking with the rapid-fire dialect of the hearing impaired.

He told Bowie that the mail from social security had come the day before, that he had given it to the woman who was sitting out front smoking a cigarette as though her life depended on it. Bowie ruminated on the information for a millisecond, then he stormed off down the street, leaving the door to 1400 Maple Leaf Street wide open, the television blaring inside.

The mailman chuckled, shaking his head as he dropped the mail into the slot of the screen door.

While he was running down Maple Leaf, thoughts were running through his head. She had known he was waiting for his check and she hadn't said a word about it coming the day before. He heard thoughts in his head, and he didn't like what they were saying. He thought if he could run faster he could make the voices go away. He could outrun them.

Dr. Herrera scratched a few notes on her clipboard. "So you went to your mother's job to ask about your check?"

"Goddamn right."

"Do you think it might have been a better idea to perhaps call her rather than show up at her job?"

"I knew she had it. She always does this shit, acting like

my money is her money."

"Do you think, in hindsight, that if you had first changed into street clothes and a coat before you showed up at your mother's place of employment, that you might have gotten a better result? I mean, let's think about what people seeing you on the street, your mother's coworkers must have thought when you appeared in your pajamas."

He tried to recall the emotions he had been feeling at that time. It was hard to access memories through the fog of constant medications in his bloodstream. He knew he had been angry, tired of his mother always treating him disrespectfully. The people in town were so used to him, to her as his caretaker, he knew she would have had no problem cashing his check.

Bowie shrugged. "Why should I care what people think?"

"Well. Is it possible that had your first impression been less out of the norm to others, they might not have called the police? Or that you and your mother might have been able to reach a more agreeable solution without leading to a situation that resulted in a police escort to our evaluation facility?"

Bowie realized he didn't know how to "reach a more agreeable solution." His mother would always talk louder and louder until he eventually gave up. She always got her way. He didn't have an answer for the doctor.

"Why you asking me these questions, anyway?"

"Does it bother you? My asking you questions?"

"These ain't the normal questions. Like, 'do you feel like

harming yourself, do you feel like harming others, how many days have you missed taking your meds.'"

"Those questions are part of regular assessments, yes. But so are the questions I am asking now."

"They never asked me questions about why I ended up in the hospital before. All they ever do is ask about what outpatient treatment I go to, if I been taking my meds. Even when I tell them I been taking them, they look at me like I don't." Bowie shifted back on the bed, resting his back against the cement wall and lifting a knee, resting an elbow there. "I just wanted my money. The cops saw me and they brought me here. I just wanted them to stop talking, too. Talking to me like I was already a patient, like they know me. Telling me to calm the fuck down. They act like you can't see them laughing at you like everything is a joke. I said I would break out their windows, but I was bullshitting. I just wanted them to know what time it was."

The hiss of nylon as Dr. Herrera uncrossed, then crossed her legs. "And what time was it?"

"I ain't afraid of no cops. And if they was going to get in the way of me and my money, they can catch some, too."

SOUTHEAST STATE HOSPITAL
PSYCHIATRIC EVALUATION

PATIENT: Bowie Long
DOB: 12/25/1984

IDENTIFYING INFORMATION: The patient is a thirty-two-year-old African-American male. Patient is a well-built, muscular male of dark complexion. Five feet, four inches in height, one hundred fifty-five pounds according to nursing assessment. Patient admitted on transfer from local police dept. where he was apprehended in response to 911 call from County Administrative Building in psychiatric crisis/act of aggression against mother: Magdelene Long. He was uncooperative with responders, threatening to break car windows (criminal charges pending).

Patient is not employed. Patient resides with maternal parent, who is divorced (per patient self-report). Patient receives disability related to diagnosis of bipolar disorder.

Admission information obtained from court petition documentation, which contained input from parent, describes patient as stubborn, defiant, argumentative and prone to violent outbursts. Patient unable to self-regulate upon presentation to district judge, resulting in order for involuntary commitment. He is documented to have been assaultive during intake process, throwing chairs and attempting to attack orderlies. Three-person supine restraint applied for twenty minutes, followed by two-hour mechanical restraint with wellness checks at thirty-minute intervals, as mandated by state guidelines. Intramuscular sedative applied to alleviate patient's stress and subdue presentation of aggression.

"During your stay here, we want to give you tools for recovery, to help you manage your emotions in less combative ways," Dr. Herrera said. "What would you like your life to look like when you go home?"

Bowie frowned, watching her mouth with a piercing, almost threatening glare. "Say that again?"

"Certainly. What do you want your life to look like?"

He laughed, as if the answer were obvious. "I want her to stop acting like I'm a kid, running after me when I leave the house, asking where I'm going. I want her to give me my money. She knew, just like I knew, she already spent it. Stayed out all night at the casino, balling with my shit."

Dr. Herrera tried to interject but Bowie kept rambling, as if on a stream of consciousness, "Then she was telling me about how I have to pay rent and buy groceries. Pay my fines and my phone bill. Her usual bullshit. Meanwhile, her phone is in my name because she didn't pay her own phone bill. So I just wanted to stop her talking, stop her bullshit."

"Have you been violent with your mother before?"

He shrugged and brought a hand to his mouth, absently biting a fingernail and spitting it onto his shirt. "She says so."

"What do you feel about paying rent, your bills? How is that usually handled? A representative payee can help you manage your finances."

"I don't need no repa—what? That payee shit. Why don't you ask her how she feels about paying *her* bills? The electric and cable is in my name because she don't pay her own shit. Why don't we get a rep payee for her?"

"You have a lot of anger when you discuss your mother. Are the things you mention, the utilities in your name, money issues, are they the reason for this anger?"

He stopped chewing his nails, baffled. "What anger? I'm not mad."

Dr. Herrera smiled. "You might want to tell that to your face. Because it looks like the Incredible Hulk."

Bowie started, then laughed: brief, staccato, loud.

"Do you have any struggles with hallucinations?"

She watched him shrug, look down into his lap. The doctor's shift had been swift. Bowie was impressed: disarm, then go in for the jugular.

"Nah. I had them before, first time I got sick, I was eighteen. She told me she was taking me to Brookdale. That wasn't a shithole like this place. Sorry, Doc."

She nodded in acquiescence. "Tell me about that."

"She said I heard people whispering to me. I was in the bath, and she heard me talking and she came in, and I was bugging. The towels was spinning in circles on the rack, just round and round, all by themselves." That moment burst fresh in his mind, releasing the smells from that time, the smell of bar soap and towels overly saturated with fabric softener, the reek of stale tobacco smoke as Magdelene burst into the bathroom.

"She said I started screaming, climbing around trying to get out of the tub but I couldn't get traction. She had to pull me out."

"Can you describe this?"

"I just did, didn't I?"

"And what about now? Are you hearing voices?"

Hallucinations. He didn't have hallucinations. But when he was lying on his back, reflecting, or praying, or sitting cross-legged on the floor, or shitting on the toilet, and he looked down, with his eyes closed, the darkness wasn't exactly dark. It was a kaleidoscope of grays, blacks, and lavenders, shimmering like soot falling from a chimney. And in between those hues of monochromatic colors, sometimes, he could see, tucked away in a far-off corner, a face smiling maniacally. Nothing terrifying, nothing that he could say was a hallucination. It was too small to be frightening, but it was there, like a sentry, watching. Grinning. He wondered if the doctor would call that a hallucination. Keep him in this rathole longer.

"No."

SOUTHEAST STATE HOSPITAL
BIOPSYCHOSOCIAL HISTORICAL
ADDENDUM

PATIENT NAME: Bowie Long

Original psychotic event reported by maternal parent to have occurred at age eighteen. Diagnosis of bipolar schizotypal with delusions of religious nature. No reported psychiatric family history, no reported family history of substance abuse. Patient reported to have received special education due to partial hearing loss, severity undetermined at the time of this assessment. No particular supports given for hearing loss. Patient declines use of hearing aids. Maternal parent reports no current hallucinations. Parent reports ongoing delusion pertaining to having a paramour that parent states does not exist.

The center hall was the interior unit of the hexagonal facility where those in the throes of the most challenging psychosis were placed: closest to the bulletproof nursing observation pod. Bowie's initial presentation of destructive behavior and the subsequent mechanical restraint had indicated that the center hall, where shouts and curses bounced off the walls in long echoes, and the smell of urine and feces reverberated as though it had sound waves that glommed onto sinuses and clouded thoughts like a constant weight, would be the most appropriate placement for him. But, really, all those familiar with the facility knew that it was also the location where most Black people were admitted, and remained, until they proved their behavior was acceptable for placement in a less restrictive setting.

Once Dr. Herrera deemed him appropriate, he was moved to the north hall, where those moving toward recovery were placed. In the north hall, instead of screams bouncing along the walls, light laughter merged with quiet conversations amidst a low and steady drone of people whose brains were muted with Cogentin, Haldol, clonazepam, lithium.

There were fewer aides on the outer halls. Patients were free to roam to the dayroom, shuffle along the halls to chat with the orderlies sitting in chairs, monitoring from the corners, or peer into the window of the med administration office, like pigeons in search of feed.

Bowie waited in the line for phone access. He ignored the threatening leers from much older men looming close, eyeing him calculatingly. He was accustomed to the lascivious gaze of men in places like these, where his diminutive stature placed him in the category of prey to those that were taller, broader, more aggressive. He growled, cursed, when a hand grazed him, drawing attention from the orderlies.

He listened to the phone ring. Five, six, seven rings, then the manufactured sing-song voice, "Please try your call again later."

He dialed again, listened to the ringing. He tried to ignore the gray feeling that washed over him, that feeling of being abandoned. He knew she wasn't home, or she would have answered right away. He longed to hear the nicotine burned rasp, the comfort he gained from its familiarity.

He dialed again, then an orderly descended through the cacophony of angry voices that demanded he give up the phone and let others use it to call people that were available. He banged the phone into the cradle. He knew where she must be. He could almost hear the bells and ringing in his head, see the rapidly spinning numbers, the flashing lights. He could almost picture her looming over her favorite machine, Double Down.

His discharge papers crackled in his fist like unruly cockroaches. He sat in the lobby, a dim reminder of his wait during intake. He had been waiting for hours. This was unlike her. She was usually hours early when he was discharged, pacing through a cloud of cigarette smoke, just as anxious for his release as he was.

He looked at the paper prescriptions, attached to his other papers, that the social worker had inserted into a plastic baggie.

Depakote, a.m. and p.m. Of course. Depakote had always been there, from the very beginning.

Risperdal, a.m. and p.m. For anxiety and obsessive-compulsive tendencies.

Abilify, a.m. An antipsychotic to treat bipolar disorder symptoms and depression.

Benadryl, p.m. To help with sleep.

Nothing new.

By sunset, as he continued to wait with visibly increasing agitation, the hospital staff met to discuss the next course of action. Bowie struggled to maintain his composure. He ignored the voice in his head telling him she must have decided this was the final straw, that she was going to leave him to live permanently at the hospital, or a group home, like a discarded piece of garbage. He knew if he showed any anger the orderlies would return, their broad bodies filling space like liquid insulation filling attic rafters. Luckily, the residual Benadryl, running through his blood from the previous three days of intramuscular injections, allowed him to rest his fury and anxiety behind a shadow of calm. He could feel it back there, though, undulating like a warrior in a video game, waiting to be activated. But he was able to let it stay in its place, behind the smog of chemically induced ennui.

He picked up the baggie filled with personal effects that had been taken from him at intake. There was a dollar bill and a quarter and one dime, a broken cigarette and a hairbrush, along with the pajamas he had been wearing when the police brought him in. He removed the cigarette and brought it to his nose, inhaling. He didn't smoke, but he usually carried a pack of cigarettes in his pocket for when his mother inevitably ran out. Then, he would sell cigarettes to her for a dollar. He felt weird, but smelling the rich, earthy tobacco made him think of his mother, made him feel a little calmer, somehow connected to her, even when she was nowhere around. He pulled out the brush and dragged it through his hair, the sound of static erupting around him like fireworks.

When he finished he put the brush back in the bag, removed a torn strip of napkin, and peered at the phone number written in faded ink. The number was not familiar to him. He put the scrap in his pocket and removed the last item from the bag. It was a business card with a black triangle at the top, a glaring eye in the center. Lightning bolts shot out from the eye. It read, *SPIRITUAL HEALER—MOM BIRDIE—ALL THINGS ARE POSSIBLE THROUGH CHRIST!*

He crumpled the card in fury. Magdelene must have put that card in his pocket during their confrontation. He remembered her beseechingly telling him to calm down, telling him to call Mom Birdie so she could help remedy his problem. Pray with him. Him praying instead of her giving him his money!

He threw the card into a corner, then, looking up at the camera welded to the ceiling, he retrieved it and walked in a pantomime of politeness out of the small holding room into the central lobby, where he threw the card into the wastebasket.

Turning from the trash can, he was confronted by an old Black woman with a mass of tangled, gray dreadlocks sitting on one of the Ultrasuede lounge chairs. She was mumbling a stream of curses in time with the musical clinking of the cowrie shells in her hair. He laughed quizzically and sat down beside her.

"Mom Birdie, what you doing here? I know that crazy bat didn't send you here for me."

The woman looked over at him with clouded eyes. "What you think I'm doing here, fool?"

"I don't need no guidance. I'm about to get out of here,

and if you know what I know, you'd get out, too."

The woman cackled in amusement. "You think you don't need no guidance, huh? Young, dumb and full of cum. You think you can just get out of here by walking out that door? You still locked in this white man's prison no matter you on this side of the wall or the other. Dumbass."

Bowie smacked a hand over his eyes in derision. "How you going to cuss me like that, old lady? I thought you was a woman of the Lord."

"God know you a dumbass just like I do"—she laughed high and piercing—"but don't worry, I'll be here when you get back. Maybe you'll be ready to know what you already know by then."

Bowie stood. "Only way you'll be seeing me is if you walking through those doors, just like I'm about to do."

The administrative staff watched him through the plexiglass that divided the lobby from the gatehouse and on the monitors that fed the cameras at each corner of the outer room. They wondered who Bowie was talking to, but they decided talking to himself was more self-stimulation than hallucination and allowed him to be discharged into his own custody.

He walked out of the clanging metal doors with two bus tokens, the barely perceptible nod of good riddance from the receptionist trailing him from behind the gray, scuffed plexiglass.

The house at 1400 Maple Leaf Street sat above a cluster of rowhouses at the very top of the hill leading out of Norristown. It perched there, singular, like it held a secret. The house rested a slight distance away from the street unlike the other structures, whose thresholds sat close to the narrow pavement that wound steadily upward, crouched in the shade of a cluster of oak trees that darkened its doorstep. It boasted gables and cornices, rather tawdry when compared to the simplicity of the shotgun structures, and contained abutments that housed an additional, separate apartment behind a low picket fence where a lean, brown woman sat at a low window absently blowing cigarette smoke through the screen.

In summer, people along Maple Leaf would leave their doors open, allowing any random breeze to waft through. Inhabitants would sit out on the spare stoops, smelling one another's day-old food, listening to one another's conversations and fornications while observing who sat in the cars that zoomed past.

Those stoop sitters observed Bowie walking hastily up

the hill, his bag of belongings clutched beneath his arm, but few spoke. Even when he greeted them at a decibel slightly higher than needed, most just nodded, eyeing him with predisposed eyes.

Bowie was able to read their judgement. He knew what they thought they knew. It was part of the impetus that compelled him to shout out *hello.*

They watched him ascend the hill, his bowed legs arching efficiently, until he grew vague within the shadows of the oaks hovering above 1400 Maple Leaf. He agitated the doorknob, shaking it within its housing. He banged on the door, unaccustomed to it being locked. He leaped from the stairs and zipped around the chain that barred cars entry from the property next door. He passed the large two-level garage that was not in use, felt the milkweed brush coyly against his pantleg as he passed through to the back door.

He entered the silent threshold into the pantry. Cans of food sat in the shadows on shelves that lined the wall from floor to ceiling. He liked this room. Even though it was always dark, its small space was a comfort. The freezer sat in the corner, humming busily. The noise filled the room—other sounds barred, unable to permeate. This was a safe space.

He entered the kitchen with trepidation. The smell of cooked animal fat from bygone meals tweaked his nose. He walked swiftly through, almost turning his body away from the scuffed door that closed off the basement as he passed it. The door seemed to vibrate as he moved by. He struggled to listen to the freezer's engine from the pantry. He didn't want to hear the voices that were muffled by the scuffed wooden door. As he darted past, sensing a presence, the whispers grew louder, accelerated. He burst past the alcove into the living room and shouted, "Mom!"

The shout was to blot out the sounds behind the door. He didn't intend to summon his mother. He knew, from the quiet, from the locked front door, that she wasn't there. He stood in the dim light that refracted through the verticals in the bay window and spun around. All the furniture was new. Burgundy velour replaced brown leather. Round glass table tops and steel bases replaced square Cherrywood. A large armoire held a new television amidst globes and owls and vases, all emanating the scent of manufactured lemon. Even the smell shimmering in the room was different than before.

He darted up the stairs to her room and flung open the door. New furniture filled this space, too. A large brass canopy stood in the spot that had once housed a large pine Queen Anne. The bed was still unmade. A tall pine armoire spewed handbags and clothing onto the floor. He looked around in amazement. It felt like he had walked into the wrong house. Even the window dressings, billowing sheer, burgundy panels floating on the breeze sneaking in from the windows left slightly ajar, were different.

He made a one-eighty, flung open the door to his room. It smelled familiar. The stagnant odor of fried foods that had permeated old clothing, the lingering staleness of soap and cologne mixed with hair gel and sweat. His bed stood at the far end of the room, nearly lost under a mound of clothing,

24

haphazardly stacked furniture crowding it. All the castaways of the house had been tossed inside so the other rooms could assume their new identities.

An old picture tube television perched precariously upon a stack of old shoes and coats thrown over a wingback chair. The chair had been downstairs before he was taken to the hospital. That chair and the other pieces of furniture overtaking his room were the only items of furniture that had not been acquisitioned from Rent-A-Center. He imagined, from past experience, that Magdelene had sold the rental furniture and reported it stolen in some scheme to get gambling money.

He cursed under his breath as he climbed over the detritus on the floor and struggled to maintain his balance as his foot snagged on a hard object. Was it a vacuum? He made his way to the dresser standing before his bed. He yanked open the drawer, searching for his phone. He found it under a mound of unmatched socks. He thanked God she hadn't pawned it.

He tried to ignore the voices.

He asked himself if the voices in his head, telling him that his money had paid for all this new furniture, could be considered hallucinations. He wondered if Magdelene had sold everything that had been rented, including the washer and dryer. That would have required going into the basement.

He wondered how they had gotten past the shimmer.

He ran, found his charger and plugged it into his phone, then threw all the crap from his bed and lunged across its length to plug it into the outlet behind the bed. He called her phone.

"The number you have dialed is not in service. Please check the number and dial again."

He called around the network of people that customarily had weekend card games. No one had seen her. So he knew where she must be.

He pulled the scrap of cocktail napkin from his pocket and dialed the faded number.

E den was sitting at a table in the rear of the Norristown Public Library blearily reading the assigned chapter from psychology when his pocket vibrated. He wondered why anyone would be calling him when everyone knew he studied from three to five every evening. He slid his phone from his pocket but did not answer. Not recognizing the number, he placed the phone face down on the table and continued reading.

Two minutes later, when the phone vibrated again, the same number as before filling the screen, he had a sense who it might be. Over the past two years that he had known Bowie, he'd had at least four different phone numbers.

He silenced the phone, placed it back on the table.

He looked at a group of young boys walking noisily through the stacks, laughing at some remark, throwing their bookbags onto the table across from him. There was an older woman hunkered down behind one of the index card holders. She peered over her glasses, then let out a loud, "Shhhh!"

One of the boys piped, "Shut up, old, white bitch!"

They tittered laughter but also quieted down.

Eden raised a brow in surprise. Perhaps they wouldn't be so loud that he'd have to find a better location, wouldn't have to move the carrels against the back wall.

A flash of copper caught his eye as the security guard, who was usually posted at a desk at the entrance, stalked past and banged a fist on the table where the boys were seated. The tittering stopped. They watched him, sucking their teeth.

"Listen up, boys. This is a library. There's no talking in the library, right?"

"We ain't talking."

The guard was an older man, his hair graying at the temples. He placed his hands on his hips, hooking his thumb underneath his belt and flexing his fingers, and glared at the boys. "You're not running around your house, or running around the streets here. You want to act like monkeys, you go home."

Eden closed his book with a loud thwack, glared at the guard when he looked over, then stood up, dropping the book into his backpack and picking up his phone, once more vibrating.

He heard one of the boys: "We ain't bothering nobody, old head. We got homework. We got a right to be here like anybody else."

"Yeah, just pipe down. You're not in Elmwood Zoo."

Eden walked to the benches in the lobby, counting the vibrations of his phone. One, two, three, four. On the fifth and final vibration, he tapped the green button, listening for a moment before speaking.

He heard the echoing sound of silence, then a splash of water. "Where you at?" Bowie asked, his voice slightly hollow.

Eden huffed, speaking in subdued tones even though he was not inside the main sanctuary of the library. "I've told you before, don't start off a conversation by asking me where I'm at. Where I am is none of your business, first of all—" Eden listened to him laugh, loud and unmodulated.

"I'm sorry—"

"And I also told you," Eden continued, "if I don't answer when you call don't keep calling me back-to-back. That shit's annoying."

"Yeah, sorry."

"Come to think of it, where've *you* been? I haven't heard from you all week."

"Yeah. You miss me?"

"I'm glad for the break. I got shit to do." Eden laughed to soften the impact of the words, even though he meant what he said.

"I was in the hospital. If you want to call the state psych hatch the hospital. Nut can is more like it."

Eden sat on the bench, dropped his bag from his shoulder and leaned back against the wall. "Why were you in the psych hospital? You lost your shit?" He was joking, but he wasn't.

He heard the water. He pictured Bowie in the bath. Many of their phone conversations took place when Bowie was in the bath. He said the water calmed him, kept wild thoughts at bay. Eden pictured his lean, compact body. His well-muscled calves, his broad feet, dark as ebony against the filmy, soap-smeared water.

"The cops came. They took me there."

Eden looked up as the door to the men's room creaked. A tall white man walked out, tucking a shirt into the back of his pants. His eyes fell upon Eden, held his gaze. Eden recognized the look. The hound dog merge of lust and melancholy that white men used when cruising. He quickly dismissed him, but then looked again. The man, misreading his reconsidered gaze, backed into the restroom door, re-entering, holding the door ajar for a count longer than normal, mashing his lips together hungrily.

Eden watched him, surprised that the public library was still being used for impromptu sex. He thought Scruff, Grindr, Jack'd, all those other options for random sex had made tearoom sex obsolete.

"The cops don't just take people to the nut house. Do they?"

"You want to see me? I'm home now. You can pick me up."

"I'm doing homework, then I got to go home and make dinner." Eden really did want to see him. He missed him, the easy way he offered himself.

"What about after that?"

"What did the police pick you up for? Are you in the tub?"

"Huh? My mom pissed me off. You should see this shit. She got all this new shit, spent my money while I was in there. I'm glad I choked the bitch."

Eden slowly shook his head, thinking he had misunderstood. "You tried to choke your mother?"

Bowie laughed, water splashed. "I should have choked her bald-head ass. She ain't even come pick me up, probably at the casino."

"But who chokes their mother? What is wrong with you?"

"You know what's wrong with me; I'm crazy."

Now Eden was angry. "Don't give me that shit. You had a psychiatric issue, you told me, when you were eighteen. That was then. I have people with psychiatric issues in my family. My dad was bipolar and he never tried to choke out my grandmother. And trust me, she had it coming. You act just like those people want you to act."

"You coming to see me or not? I can wait around the corner at the top of the hill just like I always do."

Eden paused, pondered whether it would be rude to ask. "How was it? How does it feel to be in a place like that?"

He listened to water splash, listened to Bowie breathe powerfully, pictured his beautiful, prominent Aztec nose.

"You don't do shit most of the time. Walk around bored to death. But it's good enough, though. You get to sleep most of the time, doped up on Benadryl."

Eden hummed an acknowledgement. He recalled visiting his father in psych wards, how he walked around in a haze of drug-induced calm.

Bowie continued, "I guess that's really what people

need when they go to a place like that: some rest. You get to just sleep, with nobody bothering you, and your thoughts aren't always running, running . . . . You know, it's not bad once you get used to it"—he laughed—"except for them burly niggers giving you the toss around."

Eden said, "That would be my fear, getting used to it. That kind of place should not be gotten used to."

Bowie sat up, bored by the topic. "You coming to get me, yes or no?"

Eden considered it. He thought about the person he had thought Bowie to be and weighed it against this new information: someone that assaulted his own mother. "I'll call you tonight, after I take care of everything, and let you know."

"Come on!"

Eden laughed. "Come on, what?"

"Come and see me." The urgency in his voice aroused Eden.

"I can't, man."

"Why?"

"Where's your boyfriend?" Eden countered. "Why don't you call him?"

"I did. He says I can't come see him until I get a haircut, and my mom took all my money. The bitch ain't even here. She ain't even come pick me up. Now I'd be wrong if I tracked her ass down, wouldn't I?"

"Hold it. He doesn't want to see you until you get your haircut?"

"Huh? Who?"

"Your boyfriend," Eden repeated.

"That's what he said," Bowie went on, "but I'm 'bout to drop his bony ass anyway."

"Does this guy really exist? I mean, who says that—I can't see you cuz your head is woofin? That's crazy."

"No, *I'm* crazy," Bowie laughed.

"That's not cool. Don't call yourself crazy. What you claim will become your truth."

"What's that mean?"

"I'll call you tonight."

"Okay. I love you, man."

Eden hung up, thought of the man waiting in the stalls. That quickly, Bowie left his thoughts. He considered the lure of getting his dick sucked. While there was never an occasion that he would not want his dick sucked, he was long past the days of public sex. For some reason the thought of getting caught flagrante delicto, while exciting in one's twenties, was somewhat sad when one reached their forties.

Saving him the need of making a decision, the door to the men's room banged open and the man stormed out, glaring at him as he passed. Eden chuckled, shrugged, then stood and entered the restroom. He walked into the last stall, clicked the latch, hung his bag on the hook of the door.

He unzipped and relieved himself.

He heard the door open and footsteps click across the tiles, towards the sink. He listened for the sound of water but heard none. Eden zipped up, loudly clicked the hardware of his belt. There was silence on the other side of the stall. He turned and sat on the seat, peering beneath the doors. He saw deeply polished work boots standing in the corner of the restroom. They were facing outward, which struck him as odd. The man was just standing there, not peeing, not washing his hands, not walking towards the stalls.

Eden sat on the toilet seat for a few beats, watching the shoes, trying to see what would happen. There was no sound, no movement.

When Eden opened the door to the stall, he looked directly across the bank of mirrors lining the wall above the sinks and saw, off in the corner, the security guard standing with his arms folded in front of him, glaring authoritatively at him. Eden moved to the sinks and turned on the tap, ignoring the man. He lathered his hands briskly, ran them below the water, then turned to the paper towel dispenser and dried his hands, acting as though the guard was not in the room.

When he passed, Eden cast a withering stare at him and moved towards the door, flinging it open with a loud bang.

D r. Herrera sat in the cool of her vast office entering her notes into the electronic system that the facility had recently mandated as the only acceptable method for transcription. When she heard the knock at the door, she sighed in annoyance and bade a terse acknowledgement. She could picture her before she even entered, the much harried, minimally experienced social worker, blond and waifish. So thin she appeared to be constantly leaning forward.

She looked up as Meghan partially entered, hiding halfway behind the massive oak door. "I'm sorry to bother you again, Dr. Herrera, but Mrs. St. Charles . . . well, she's still here . . . ."

The doctor glared above her reading glasses. "Don't stand there behind the door like that, my dear. Step forward."

She watched bemusedly as the girl skittered into the shadows of the potted palms that grazed the vaulted ceiling. "Mrs. St. Charles, Doctor. She insists on seeing 'someone in authority,' she says."

Herrera nodded. "She said that over an hour ago. The woman is still here? You must be firm with these people. You cannot allow them to bulldoze you."

The girl nodded. "Ma'am, if you could just speak with her for a moment. She won't leave. And she's upsetting the patients sitting in the lobby waiting for intake assessments."

"Well, we can't have her doing that, now can we?" She tried to mask her annoyance. "Bring her up."

Dr. Herrera took her glasses from the bridge of her nose and rubbed her eyes. She asked herself, for the millionth time, why she had not yet retired. Every year, the employee pool grew younger as she grew older. They came with their shiny, new MSW degrees and a knowledge of behavioral health gleaned from textbooks and case studies but scant real-world experience. The field had once been flooded with burly, silent Black men, some with high school diplomas, many without, some military vets, all with few other options when it came to job security. Men that had been groomed to be efficient at addressing the most pressing psychotic presentations. Governmental reformations had changed the requirements, and now thin white women were the norm. Women who usually fled the first time they were faced with the real threat of escalating decompensation and resultant aggression, or, worse, had the audacity to press criminal charges; all their high-minded ideals of "making a difference" jettisoned overnight.

She stood, running a hand across her tightly pulled French braid. She always preferred to be standing when people entered her inner sanctum. This way, she could direct them to take a seat on the sofa pushed against the far wall before she seated herself in one of the two chairs that accompanied a small, round table. The chairs had a higher seat than the sofa, allowing her to peer down at the person sitting on the sofa.

She quickly assessed Magdelene St. Charles as she strode briskly, almost agitatedly, into the room. She was tall and lean, dark as stealth, with a short cap of wooly hair that clutched an angular face and framed piercing dark eyes.

She watched Magdelene watch her, sizing her up, before the woman extended a skeletal hand toward the doctor, shook quickly, then released.

"Miss Long, is it?" She knew it wasn't. She didn't know why she had asked.

"St. Charles, Mrs. St. Charles," the woman quickly corrected her. "I am Bowie Long's mother. And I want to know how the hell you people let him out on the street without my supervision or say so."

Dr. Herrera smiled, a barely perceptible grimace, and waved a hand toward the sofa, indicating she should take a seat. "My apologies if there is some discrepancy. Discharges are the purview of our social workers, not something that I handle, But I do apologize if there has been some miscommunication."

Magdelene looked toward the sofa that the doctor's hand still pointed toward, a small look of confusion clouding her features, then shook her head, dismissing the furniture with a wave of her hand. "Miscommunication my ass. I expressly told you people that Bowie was to sit here until I am able to get him. Then I come and you people tell me that he's already been discharged. So you just let people out into these streets at random?"

"Random? Mrs. St. Charles, while I understand you might have a concern for your son, he has been deemed acceptable for discharge. He has met all his goals, he is his own representative, and so, ma'am, to keep him here longer than the stipulation of the court petition would be illegal."

Magdelene jammed a hand into her large handbag, rooted around, dug out a pack of cigarettes and looked around the room before going back into her bag for a lighter. "How have you deemed him ready to leave without anybody consulting me?"

"Ma'am, I spoke with you myself to ascertain Bowie's psychiatric history. The social workers invited you to participate in family therapy while Bowie was in treatment . . . ."

Magdelene flung up the hand gripping her cigarette to stop her from speaking. "Who the fuck can take time off from work to come up here to chitchat about feelings? Do you offer a stipend to make up for the loss of pay I would take to sit up here with you headshrinkers?"

Dr. Herrera's head began to throb. The woman's voice was low and gravelly, the nicotine morphed baritone of someone who had smoked for many years.

"I understand your dilemma. This is a challenge for many family members trying to support their loved ones. Please, I have to ask that you not smoke in here. These are smoke-free facilities."

The woman put her hands on her hips, scoffed at her, clicking her dentures in annoyance. "Trying? I am the only support my son gets. I don't *try* shit! I do the work. Every day. So I don't need nobody trying to question what I do or don't do for my kid."

The doctor eyed her with droll compassion. She tried to keep her mind clear from judgement, but she wasn't sure how successfully she was doing so. "Why don't you take a seat on the sofa, Mrs. St. Charles. We can still discuss whatever things you know that will be helpful for Bowie moving forward. Just because he has been discharged does not mean he wouldn't benefit from any additional information you want to provide. He absolutely has aftercare providers that I'm sure would appreciate any additional information for a more informed global picture."

Magdelene backed toward the door, laughing harshly. "I need to get home to my kid. And pray that he's safe and sound. If anything has happened to him, you can bet your ass you'll be hearing from my attorney. So you have a blessed and prosperous day."

Dr. Herrera looked at the huge oak door as it slammed into its housing.

Yeah, she needed to look into moving back to the home she had so meticulously restored in her beloved Venezuela. Retirement was looking better by the second.

After he got out of the tub, he swiftly dried off and walked to his room, tugging on his dick distractedly. He lay on the mounds of clothes on his bed and stroked himself. While doing so, he kept looking towards the door, expecting Magdelene to come bursting through, hurling accusations. After a while, his thoughts drifted to where she might be.

He got up, dressed himself, and, taking the two tokens he had been given at the hospital, he took the bus to the Valley Forge Casino. He felt the rush as he passed from the vestibule into the lights and sounds of the casino floor. The scent of revelry was a combination of carpet cleaner and money. He walked the floor, eyeing overdressed women perched on golden high- heeled shoes, hunched over slot machines. Fat men of every shade wearing slouchy sweat suits and basketball shoes hovered nearby—close enough to allow a clear vantage point of both the slot machines' digital displays and the sweat glistening on the women's cleavage, visible over low-cut necklines.

He saw the back of her head, gleaming under a strobe

light as she manically swiveled on a chair in front of Fred Flintstone. He stood behind her, watching her shoulders hunch as the display spun to a stop, then watched her press the blinking button again. He moved closer.

"What you win?"

She flickered a look over her shoulder, then turned back to the display. "These motherfuckers holding tight to their shit tonight. I only won fifty dollars."

"Let me hold twenty-five."

She quickly became annoyed. "I don't have no money, Bowie. I put it back in here trying to win big."

He shrugged, began to walk away.

"Where you going? You stay right here. Don't go roaming off."

"Why? I'm not going to stand here watching the back of your neck all night."

She swore, dug a hand angrily into the handbag hanging on her shoulder, then crushed twenty-five dollars into his outstretched palm.

"I'ma go to the cashier's window and see if I got any comps."

"And you come right back, too." She didn't look at him; her focus was on the spinning wheels in front of her.

Bowie darted off, looking for his favorite machine, or one that sent him good vibes. He was lucky. Had always been lucky, even when he was first taken to a casino as a kid. Adults felt it emanating from him. The small boy with the head shaped like a warrior from a lost tribe, winning big money at casinos, at card games, even bingo. Money came to him as if he were a magnet.

Before long, his twenty-five dollars had ebbed and flowed. First he had fifty dollars, then twenty, then he had three hundred, then half that, then five hundred, then twice that.

Magdelene could feel in her bones that he had struck. After making sure that her machine wasn't going to turn good, she quit it and went in search of him. It didn't take long to find him: When he struck five hundred, his shout filled the room, followed by a loud clapping of hands. She went over and demanded her cut. She had groomed him, from his very first hit, that you have to share your good fortune in order to keep good fortune shining favorably. Bowie always gave her half his winnings.

She felt his energy, his good luck vibrating off of the money he handed her as though it were a living thing. They both walked away from the cashier's window, heady from the power of winning. Her shoulders were no longer slouched. Her eyes beamed excitedly. He saw how he looked through her eyes, how he became a valuable, prized thing. They nodded knowingly to one another, walking toward a new bank of slots.

This day, their luck did not multiply from staying together. They quickly found out that they were not winning as a unit, so they swiftly parted, looking to find the elusive chimera of luck and stay within its aura.

Bowie realized he had made a mistake. He should not

have split up his winnings quite so soon. He had disrupted the continuum. Now, his winnings were rapidly dwindling, and he was not recouping any of it.

Time folded in on itself, and in the blink of an eye, he had nothing, and he felt like nothing. He searched the room for her. Found her toward the wall along the back of the room. She was winning. She waved him away, agitated.

"Let me hold twenty-five dollars."

"Come on, now! Not now."

"Give me twenty-five. It's my money."

She ignored him. He walked away, watching other players laugh or swear while others were just glaring at the flashing displays with their arms folded across their chests. Hostesses darted through bodies holding trays of pastel-colored spirits aloft. He passed the restrooms, noticed the older man standing by the door with his hands jammed deep into the pockets of his suit jacket. Bowie recognized the look in the man's eyes. It was the same expression the men had given him at the state hospital. Hungry and curious. Lost and questioning.

Bowie nodded as he passed into the restroom. The man smiled fleetingly, his melancholy changing to hope. The restroom was crowded. He pushed through the men to the sink, washed his hands without soap. He looked at his reflection in the mirror. He watched the man enter the room, locked eyes with him through the mirror.

Bowie walked to the stall at the very end of the room, entered, pulled the door behind him, leaving it slightly ajar.

He moved his legs back against the toilet, unbuckled his pants and gently brought out his dick, dark and resplendent against the checkerboard pattern of his boxers.

He knew this demographic. The old men lurking in the shadows of casinos with hound dog expressions. He was not surprised by the look of joy that flashed on the man's face when he pushed open the door to behold Bowie's phallus. He was accustomed to the look of covetousness that befell men when they first saw him exposed. It was almost like they didn't even register that what they held in their gaze was attached to a person, to him. There was no need for small talk, for pretense that they wanted to know his name. The exhibition of his dick cut through all niceties.

As the man reached forward, fell to his knees, Bowie looked him over, noticed the ticket stubs sticking from a back pocket. He sat back on the toilet, groaned to distract the man, pressed his hands against the back of the man's head, mashing him into the glory of his scent. He leaned forward, tentatively reached two fingertips toward the tickets, and slipped them from the man's pocket with barely a rustle. The muffled sounds coming from the stranger's throat echoed out into the murmured sounds of the casino proper.

Magdelene had moved on to The Dukes of Hazzard. Thinking maybe her luck would hold under the tutelage of Bo and Luke Duke. A shadow fell over her shoulder. She looked back to see Bowie standing behind her. He sat in the vacant chair next to her and placed a ticket stub into the machine.

She looked as the machine began to blink animatedly.

"Where you get those from?"

He kept playing. "Huh."

She looked at him. "You been in them bathrooms."

He ignored her.

"How much you get?"

"Thirty."

She shook her head. "You do dumb shit. If you going to do that, you should be getting some real money, not that bullshit ass shit."

The machines throbbed and blinked.

Magdelene stood up and watched over his shoulder. "I know you got more than one ticket. I can feel it. You ain't splitting your wins?"

"I already gave you a split. I been noticing something. It seems like anytime I hit, you got your hand out, but when you hit you give me some chump change."

"I'm your mother," she snapped. "I do for you twenty-four seven. I don't only give to you when I hit a number. You don't ever have shit to give but when you hit."

Bowie jumped out of his seat but made sure to stay close enough to the machine to claim use. "Are you fucking joking? What about my fucking check? Where the fuck is that?"

Magdelene waved a hand in front of him. Her face was a black cloud. "I don't want to hear that shit, Bowie."

"I bet you don't," he leered. "A house full of new furniture, top to bottom. But nothing new for me. And all your old shit thrown in my room like it's the city dump. Was you expecting to leave me in that hospital for good? We know how good you are at forgetting people, right?"

People turned to look. Magdelene noticed the stares, the laughter and sidelong looks. Bowie did not.

"Do you have any idea how it feels to be in my skin? To worry about you day and night. Try to keep you safe. Stop you from getting sick. I was nervous. I had to do something. I couldn't stay in that house, all alone, hearing all that commotion . . . ."

He paused, watched her. Then, he nodded. "I don't like to be in there without you home neither. I try to keep myself busy, run a bath, turn the radio real loud, but it's hard. I know."

He rubbed her back, glared at a woman that approached his slot machine until she faded away. Magdelene shrugged his hand away, readjusted her bag on her shoulder. "I'm going to go smoke."

He nodded. "I'm going to finish with this machine."

"You don't go nowhere."

He had already climbed back onto the seat. He shouted over his shoulder, "Where I'm going?"

He thought she had walked away, but then he felt body heat and a shadow over his shoulder. He looked back and saw the flash of a security badge, then, two men in dark blues with their arms braced in the combative stance he understood quite well.

"We're going to have to ask you to come with us."

PSYCHIATRIC EVALUATION
BEHAVIORAL HEALTH COURT

PATIENT: Bowie Long
EVALUATOR: L. Dopinger

This evaluation has been requested by the County Behavioral Health Court to determine mental competency and suitability for consideration of inclusion of individual into Behavioral Health Court.

Behavioral Health Court is a collaboration of the county court systems, the police department, and the Office of Mental Health. The purpose of the program is to ameliorate legal and criminal charges for persons with a diagnosis and history of mental health challenges who have come into contact with the law. It is hoped that the program will divert persons with certain diagnoses from serving time in prison, or at the very least, minimize prison stays.

Applicable persons, once released from jail, will have supervision from the Office of Probation, case management from Mental Health Services, and regular appearance at court before a judge to ascertain level of compliance to the program and compliance with developed treatment plan.

Noncompliance with treatment plan can result in discharge, and resumption of the legal proceedings heretofore interrupted by Behavioral Health Court.

IDENTIFYING INFORMATION: The patient is a thirty-two-year-old African-American male that appears to be younger than his years due to his small stature. He appears to be in his teens. Patient is rather thin, and appears to be malnourished. He is nondescript in appearance with a combative effect. He answers questions grudgingly, and appears to be an unreliable historian, based upon references to persons that do not exist.

Appears restless. During the interview, patient seemed to be unable to remain seated. Particularly when his mother relayed information, patient would pace the room, looking out the window, and returning to his seat to ask the evaluator to repeat the information the mother had conveyed.

Mother is primary caretaker of patient. She reports that diagnosis of bipolar d/o was determined at age eighteen.

Patient reports that the initial presentation of diagnosis was related to response to a bad breakup. Reports this event as a "nervous breakdown."

Mother minimized this event. Evaluator was unable to delve into specifics due to Mother's interruption of this line of questioning. She refers to these events as corelated to delusions. Patient became visibly agitated with Mother at this implication. Evaluator will explore this topic at a later date.

Patient was arrested by Upper Merion Police upon report of robbery from Valley Forge Casino. Member was apprehended by casino security upon report of pick pocketing of customer at the venue.

Patient spent two months in county jail while Mother and Case Manager advocated for acceptance into Behavioral Health Court.

Based upon Mr. Long's extensive involvement with outpatient hospitalization services, where he has received medication management since age eighteen, it is my recommendation that Mr. Long be fast-tracked into the program and immediately discharged from jail.

DIAGNOSTIC IMPRESSION:

Unspecified Bipolar Disorder

Reactive Attachment Disorder
Oppositional Defiant Disorder
Post-Traumatic Stress Disorder, Chronic
History of Parental Neglect

RECOMMENDATIONS:

Participation in Behavioral Health Court.
Participation in Individual and Group Therapy to develop ability to better express self and self-advocacy. Control anger, conflict resolution skills, develop empathy, prosocial relationship skills.
Medication Management to maintain baseline mental health.
Family Work is indicated to work on tools for better cross communication and improve self-advocacy.
Mr. Long has been banned from Valley Forge Casino. It is recommended that he be responsible for restitution of any and all monies he appropriated.

At eleven at night, when his phone throbbed, Eden knew who it was. He readjusted himself, got up from the chair where he had been reading Morrison, checked the prostrate form in the hospital bed to be sure the ringing had not awakened his father, and verified the number on his screen. He swiped it to end the call.

The phone rang again. He cursed under his breath, silenced the phone and began to swipe the screen.

busy. cant talk right now. what do u want?

dont you went to see me tonight

I cant

way not?

taking care of my dad

way cant you pick up you phone baby?

i just told you, I'm sitting with my dad

you didn't say that you was setting with you dad way cant you come get me later will be waiting. dont you went this ass?

stop the bullshit. you know you ain't ready to give up no ass.

u say that every time and then you don't do nothing

I mean it this time baby. Am ready for you

maybe I can see you around twelve?

ok baby

Eden shook his head. He walked back to the bed, pulled the blankets more snuggly to the slightly snoring man before mashing the off button on the remote and closing the door as he left the room.

He sighed in annoyance as his phone rang.

"What?" He heard water splashing in the background.

"I'm washing up for you, boo."

Eden barked a laugh. "Don't call me boo."

"Why not?"

"It sounds corny. I'm not one of your jump offs."

"You don't want me to tell you how much I love you?"

"You should tell that to your man, right?"

Bowie sucked his teeth. "Fuck him. He ain't about shit," his voice dropped a register, "I'm washing my ass, baby . . . ."

Eden laughed again. "Since you're in the tub, I would assume your ass might be included in the process. What is wrong with you, anyway? All your conversations don't have to revolve around sex, you know. Did you think you called the sex line and dialed me by mistake?"

Bowie laughed. "No. I'm just horny."

"What's your address, again?"

"You can just meet me around the corner, at the Family Dollar, like we always do."

"Okay. Hey, what happened that day you called me when I was at the library? I told you I'd call you back, but I never heard from you."

"Huh? What day?"

Eden entered his room, lit some candles and began to change his sheets. "I called the number from my queue, and some lady answered and said you don't take calls from men."

"That crazy bitch. So you was looking for your man, huh? I knew you like me."

"Of course I like you, silly. If I didn't like you I wouldn't be allowing you to waste my time. Especially since you don't like to do all that much."

"What you talking about? I like to do much."

Eden laughed. "Man, all you do is jack off for forever, like, for thirty minutes, and you don't even bust a nut."

"You full of shit, man. I bust crazy nuts."

"Are you for real? You haven't bust a nut ever. And we been knowing each other for what, a year now?"

"A year? You been my man for way longer than that."

"Your man. You crazy. You got a man. And, so do I. Remember?"

"Then what you seeing me for, since you got a man?"

"I ask myself that every time I drop your ass back home!"

Eden thought about those nights. Smelling Bowie in the candlelit darkness of his room. His smooth, hairless body, so dark he seemed to meld into the night, smelling like freshly milled soap. The cave of his armpit, damp with lust. "You are the most beautiful thing I've ever seen. I love your bullet-shaped head. Your soft lips, your smooth skin."

"You like this dick."

"See, that's what I mean. You are crass as fuck. You always talking like you think you're in a porn clip, but you don't even sixty-nine."

"What's sixty-nine?"

"EXACTLY! That's what I mean!"

"Sorry, boo."

"Didn't you hear what I said about that boo shit? Anyway, you know what I like most about you? You're not full of shit."

"Damn right."

"You were up front from the very beginning. You told me about being in the psych hospital. Having bipolar disorder. Even about being on probation. Most people would have kept that shit secret."

"This Norristown. Ain't no secrets. So anyway let me tell you about how I'm in Behavioral Health Court for this man lying, saying I took some vouchers out his back pocket while he was pissing at the urinals at the casino."

"Urinals? Was you cruising the tearooms?"

"The what?"

"Come on, Bowie. Don't act like you don't know what I'm talking about."

"What's a tearoom? I told you it was in the bathroom."

"Do you troll the men's room when you're at the casino? I mean, you get disability, right? So, where do you get money from to gamble?"

"If some dumb motherfucker wants to give me money, you think I'm not going to take it?"

"I think you're not being *given* money if some faggot expects something in return, is all."

Bowie laughed at the word. "Faggot."

Magdelene walked through the open door into the bathroom, a burning cigarette dangling from her mouth. "Who you talking to?"

She pulled down her pants, her underwear, sat on the toilet.

Bowie said, "I hope you ain't shitting. I don't want to smell that."

"Shut up, boy. You came out these parts."

Eden said, "What?"

Bowie said, "Huh?"

"What did you say?" Eden asked.

"I didn't say nothing."

"I asked who you on the phone with?"

"Grandmom."

Eden said, "Huh?"

Magdelene nodded approvingly. "You been in there long enough. The water's going to get cold."

"I'm getting ready to get out. You can get in right now." He stood up, water dropping smoothly. Magdelene flicked ashes into the water. "Mom!"

Eden said, "Is your mother in the tub with you?"

Bowie said, "I'll see you later." He hung up.

Whenever she saw him nude, Magdelene could not help but be overcome with a sense of pride for a job well done. His skin was unblemished, from his broad, well-formed feet, to his muscular ass, high and firm. His shoulders broadly tapered down to a trim waist. He grabbed a towel and wrapped it around his narrow hips, and dried off on the bathmat while she wiped herself and flushed the toilet.

"You missed your back. Let me get it."

He backed toward her, allowed her to remove the towel from him and dab it at the water on his back. "You want me to put lotion on you? You getting ashy."

She stood and pulled up her pants. He said nothing as she took the bottle of lotion from the nearby vanity, and began to rub it in circular motions along his back, down his strong thighs, curved calves. "I got you some nice new pajamas. You can put those on to sleep in . . . ."

He took the towel from her and walked toward his room. "I'm going out for a little bit. I'll put them on when I get back."

She jumped up and followed down the hallway after him. "Going where? You don't need to be going out this late at night. All that's out there at this time of night is trouble. Haven't you been in enough trouble already?"

He pulled open a drawer, tugged a pair of boxers up his legs. "I'm not going to get in no trouble."

"What you going to do, then?" Her voice was strident. She folded her arms across her hollow chest.

"Mind my own business."

"See, you wasn't on the phone with Grandmom. If you were, you would be in a calmer state than this and wouldn't want to be running around the streets all night."

Bowie pulled an oversized shirt over his head, answering in a muffled voice from beneath the shirt, "I'm calm."

He brushed past her and walked down the stairs into the living room. He could hear the voices from behind the door in the kitchen. The television was not loud enough to mask it. He guessed that Magdelene had turned down the volume to try to eavesdrop on his phone conversation.

"I can't keep going through this shit with you! You want me to sit in here all by myself?" Her voice was so loud it cracked.

"You'll be all right, Mom. Just turn on the radio in your room and go to sleep. I'll be back in the morning."

"You know what I should do. I should call your PO. That ought to take care of you running the streets. Tell her about you and your shit."

Bowie stood in the doorway. He grabbed his head with both hands, his back to her. "Stop it!" he screamed, his tongue thick in his mouth, as it usually was when he grew agitated. "Stop it. Go the fuck to bed! And leave me alone!"

He banged out the door, but Magdelene opened the screen, yelling up the street at his retreating figure. "Don't look to me to get you out of your shit, now, you hear? I'm done with your bullshit!"

Magdelene turned back into the room, raced over to the TV and turned the volume as loud as it would go, then scanned the darkened room for her cigarettes.

Eden saw him pacing in the darkness at the edge of the intersection they had agreed upon, talking animatedly on his phone. He pulled the car up to the curb and smiled through the window.

Bowie stood crouched over the phone. "This is what I'm talking about with you. I can't go nowhere without you thinking something is wrong. You always think something's going on. You need to fix your mind. I think you need some meds. I seriously do."

He looked up into the beam of Eden's smile and his face broke into a large grin of his own. He bounded from the curb, yanking the door open.

"Watch the door!" Eden screamed. "Don't be yanking on my shit!"

Bowie hopped up into the seat, slamming the door, talking on the phone. "It's nobody. I gotta go. Yeah, I'll talk to you later. I told you, it's nobody!"

He ended the call, looked over at Eden, smiling mani-acally. "Hey young head."

Eden tried to frown, but he loved when Bowie called

him young head. It was an acknowledgment of their age difference but it also turned it into an irony. "Who was you on the phone with? Giving your man a bullshit excuse?"

Bowie slouched down, reaching around to recline the seat, not bothering to respond to the question.

After a beat of silence, Bowie said, "You look good, you been working out?"

He reached out and caressed Eden's arm. Eden exaggeratedly shrugged him off.

"I'm driving here. Don't distract me." He looked over, his eyes burning bright. "You look good, too. You don't need a haircut at all. You got some pretty little curls."

When Eden reached out to touch Bowie's hair, he leaned into it, like a puppy getting attention. Bowie closed his eyes, seemed to stretch his neck out. "You like my hair. It's good, huh? I put some gel in it. I used to have waves when I was in school."

"You got that good shit. Your man was tripping that time he told you don't come down to Philly until you get a haircut. It must be something else that's bothering him."

"Something's always bothering him." Bowie reached across and massaged Eden's crotch. "That's why I'm here with you."

Eden removed his hand. "THAT'S probably the problem. Being with another man."

"Oh, I can't touch you?"

"You can touch me. But you always seem to only touch one place. Guess what? I am an entire person. I got arms, legs, a brain . . . ."

Bowie nodded, grinning. "Yes you do, boo."

He reached over and placed a warm hand high on Eden's thigh, close enough to his crotch that Eden could feel his body heat. "Cut it out, would you? And didn't I tell you not to call me boo? All that means is a niggah forgot your name cause he out getting his slut puppy on."

"Sorry, boo," Bowie shifted in his seat, pulled his flaccid penis from his pants. He began to stroke himself.

"The fuck are you doing?"

Bowie looked off in the distance, his eyes moving back in his head. "I'm getting ready for you, baby."

Eden stopped at a traffic light, looked over nervously to make sure the car idling beside him could not see inside. "Put your shit away. I told you before I don't fuck in cars."

"You didn't say that when you first met me."

"What you mean?"

"We had sex in your jeep when you rolled up on me at the bar. The first night we met."

"Uh, no we did not. You pulled your shit out, just like you do every time you get in this car. And just like every other time you pulled your shit out, I told you I don't fuck in cars. You have a very vivid imagination, or your memory is fucked up beyond belief. I can't be fucking in cars, dude. Do you see me? I'm too goddamn big, and too goddamned old to be trying to maneuver my ass around in a car. I'd be done kicked out a windshield. Plus, I like to be able to relax and take my time."

David Jackson Ambrose

Eden reached under Bowie's shirt and laid his palm on his stomach. He loved the way his belly felt, so smooth and warm.

"Besides, I keep telling you that the bar was not the first time we met."

Bowie tucked himself back in his pants, but loosened his belt buckle so that Eden could caress the entirety of his abdomen. "Bullshit. You took me to your house and we fucked."

"What are you talking about! We've never fucked. You never let me. I'm starting to think maybe you've never done it."

"Man, I've been fucking forever. You ain't my first boyfriend. I had two boyfriends before you."

"I'm not your boyfriend. You claim to have one in Philly."

"Yeah. He's my second one. Then came you."

"I'm not your boyfriend."

"What you call it then?"

"Well. We're friends, I guess. But let me get you straight about how we met. You were working at the supermarket, right? That night when I came in. And you left your post at the self- checkout and followed me around the store."

"Bullshit. You followed me!"

"Uh. Every time I went to one aisle, you would stand at the end of the aisle staring at me. So when I checked out, I expected you to make your move, but you didn't do shit. So I had to come back in and pretend I lost my license."

61

Bowie laughed. "You was bullshitting? You didn't lose your license?"

"No! And while we were looking for it, I expected you to start a rap, but you STILL didn't say shit. So I wrote down my number and told you to call me if you found it. AND YOU NEVER FUCKING CALLED ME."

Bowie laughed. "I'm sorry, boo."

"You forgot all about me. I guess you just stand at the endcaps for every man that comes in your store. I thought I was special."

"No. You are special." Bowie rubbed Eden's arm. Now it was Eden's turn to feel like a puppy.

"But you never called. And then, a few weeks later, when I see you dancing with fat ass DeeDee Whitney at the 404, you walked past like you didn't even know me."

"I'm sorry. I probably lost your number."

"Or your man ran them pockets and threw it out."

As if on cue, Bowie's phone rang. He huffed angrily, reaching into his pocket.

"What? I already told you. No. Bye!"

"Wow. You talk to your boy like that?"

Bowie sat silently, bristling with fury. The phone rang again.

"What? I didn't say goodbye. Oh, sorry about that. Later."

He hung up. Eden looked over. "What was that?"

"My mom don't like me to say bye to her. She likes me to say later."

62

"That was your mom on the phone? Why's she calling you? You just left the house. Is she all right?"

"That bitch is fine. She's just a pain in the fucking ass."

"Wow. What a gentleman."

"Huh?"

"Nothing. The way a man treats his mother shows a lot about who that man is as a person."

"You don't know this bitch."

Eden shook his head.

The phone rang again. Bowie held the phone out to Eden, the light blazing in his face.

"See what I mean? She's crazy."

"She's calling again. What's she want?"

"She don't want nothing. She wants me to be home. She always calls me like this. Over and over. That's why I usually leave my phone at the house when I'm with you. She drives me crazy."

"You know you don't have to answer, right?"

"If I don't, she'll just keep calling."

"You can put your phone on silent, though."

"Yeah. But I'll *know* she's calling." He answered the call. "What now?"

Eden watched him curiously. He was so odd looking that it was beautiful. His face was like a painting by Modigliani. His large, soulful eyes, his nose prominently extended from a smooth, flat forehead. He had a wisp of shadow above full, brown lips, and skin the color of the darkest chocolate. His head was shaped like a dorsal fin, held up with a thick, muscular neck above broad shoulders.

He laughed into the phone. "You sound stupid." Bowie looked over at Eden. "She says she doesn't know who I'm with and that you might kill me."

"Hmmmm."

"What? She said she followed me around the corner and she got your license plate number."

"Did you tell her that we've known each other for a long time. That I'm not just some crazed serial killer. If you explain that to her maybe she won't be worried."

His arm lunged out in front of Eden's face. "You tell her."

So he did.

When he finished talking, there was silence on the other end. A silence that seemed fraught with displeasure. Then, a voice spoke. It was deep, raspy, as though rarely used. "Thank you." Then the call ended.

"Wow. Real personable."

Eden could feel Bowie watching him closely. "What? Didn't I tell you that bitch was crazy? What did she say? She cuss you out?"

"She didn't cuss me out."

They drove in silence for no more than what Eden imagined to be thirty seconds before Bowie's phone began ringing again. He just sat there glaring out the window while it rang five times. Eden laughed, which made Bowie laugh, and then he dug into his pocket for his phone.

Eden couldn't hear what was being said, but he could

hear the voice speaking on the opposite end of the phone. The voice was deep and raspy. He wondered if the caller was really a male. The modulations and pacing of the speech sounded more masculine than what he imagined an older Black woman would sound like.

Bowie listened intently, then said, "I'll take them when I get home. Don't worry ab—"

There was more yelling from the opposite end, then Bowie hung up. He moved his fingers to the side of the phone, then Eden heard the sounds of the phone shutting itself off.

"What's up?" Eden asked. "You forgot something?"

He sucked his teeth. "Now she's going on about did I take my meds."

"Did you?"

"Now you think you're my mom? I'll take them when I get home."

Eden sharply turned a corner and circled the block, driving up Maple Leaf Street. "You just got out of the hospital and already you're not taking your meds at the time you're supposed to?"

"Where you going? I said I can take them tomorrow."

"What's your house number? I'm taking care of my old man now, who's laying catatonic in a bed twenty-four hours a day, and you know what? He never thought it was a big deal to take his meds whenever he was feeling good. And then suddenly he wouldn't feel good anymore, and he would disappear for days while we sat waiting for calls from the police.

And they were never good calls."

"What are you talking about? I don't hear what you're saying."

"If taking your meds every evening at the same time helps you stay out of trouble, out of the hospital, why would you not just take them? What's your address?"

Bowie jabbed a finger out at the large, dark house looming on the left. "Right here." Eden skidded efficiently to a stop. "You know how that shit makes you feel? Like your mind is being sat on by a fucking rhinoceros, and you see people with this little thingy around them like an angel's light. You reach out to pick up something with your hands and it's not right there, it's like a trying to pick up a quarter and it's really a fifty-cent piece."

Eden put the car in park and turned to him. He reached over and grabbed his hand. It was warm and trembling. "Well, what does your brain feel like without it? Is that any better?"

Bowie didn't answer. Instead, he pulled on Eden's hand and moved closer. Eden abruptly put up his hand to flag him. "Go, man."

"You going to wait for me?"

Eden smirked. "Depends how long you take."

Eden laughed as Bowie pushed away from him, turned and jumped out of the car, and darted around the side of the house as if his pants were on fire. He turned up the radio, then turned down the visor to peer at his reflection in the mirror on the back side. He frowned as he noticed an errant gray hair sticking obnoxiously from the deep forest of browns in his eyebrows and plucked it with a whispered curse, "You raggedy bitch, you."

He caught movement in his peripheral vision and turned as Bowie walked out of the front door and down the steps, grasping a phalanx of amber vials in his arms. Eden reached across to open the door for him.

"Shit, you have enough there to fell an elephant."

"What?" Bowie threw the bottles into the back seat and hurriedly closed the door behind him. "Go, go, go."

Eden looked up and saw a dark silhouette standing behind the screen. It was too dark to see anything other than a lean, dark shape backlit from the interior of the house. As he shifted to drive, he took a second look at the house. A plume of smoke billowed from the screen. Eden blinked as he saw the overhead light behind the shadow fracture into splinters of shimmering daggers, and then he pulled away from the curb.

S he couldn't stay in that house alone. It made her restless. So, after she ended the call with Bowie, she grabbed her purse and her keys, and walked out past the blaring television, out to her car. She headed to the Chester Park Casino, a cigarette jammed between her teeth and a wary eye on the gas gauge, bobbing alarmingly close to the *E*. She prayed to the God of small miracles that she did not run out of gas along the highway. She also prayed to that God for a bit of luck, so that she'd be able to maybe win some money and be able to put maybe five or ten bucks in the gas tank for the ride back home.

God must've put her on call waiting, because her thirty dollars did not expand to anything beyond thirty dollars. She roamed through the flashing lights, through the mediocre band playing a tad too loudly, past the women dressed for either church or a bordello, and men strolling in clothing far more casual than the ladies on their arms. She spent some time out on the smoker's deck chatting up fellow smokers, reminiscing about days when they were flush, their biggest winnings, their biggest losses, and how many cities they had chased after an elusive winning.

When the night grew blackest and she could no longer be distracted by all the engineered distractions and machinations of her surroundings, and her pockets remained empty, she skulked back through the cavernous parking lots, squinting through nondescript late-model vehicles until she found the familiar shape of her own car. She lit her last cigarette and headed home, her car puttering along on fumes as much as petrol.

She dragged herself into the house, past the television, and up the creaking stairs. In the upper hallway, she opened Bowie's bedroom door, hoping against hope that he might have returned home. She then opened her own door, looking amongst the tangled sheets for his darkened form. She dug in her bag for her phone and dialed his number. It went directly to voicemail, most likely dead.

Shrugging her dress over her shoulders, she let it fall to the ground. She stepped over it, leaving it in a puddle on the floor. She turned on the radio sitting on the dresser and fell into bed, staring up at the ceiling until her exhaustion lulled her into a fitful sleep full of lights, full of numbers, full of fruit, full of revolutions. Her sleep was a scrim of blackness, large and all-encompassing, punctuated by a cacophony of voices saying both nothing and everything.

She didn't know how long she had slept when there was a loud roar blasting in her head, booming against her tympanic membrane. She sat up with a gasp, her hands stretched out in front of her protectively. She looked out at the darkened room and whispered, "Bowie?" She heard a million voices as one audible exhalation, then nothing. She climbed from the bed, her hair an angry tumult on her head. She grabbed blindly for her robe, covered her nude form and walked through the black toward the hallway. She descended the stairs, feeling a noise she didn't hear, sensing an unrest swarm around her. Her feet felt the cool floorboards giving slightly beneath her weight.

She looked into the living room that was bathed in the indigo of television light, the TV blaring innocuous garble. She then turned on her heel and walked into the kitchen. She sensed the difference before she saw it. She looked out at the tall table and stools in the center of the room, at the stove and refrigerator against the far wall.

She gasped when she saw it. The door to the cellar was standing wide, revealing gaping blackness. She grabbed at her clavicle, clutching her robe to her chest, and lunged forward, toward the door, and flung it shut, leaning against it as though some unseen force would hurl it open. That space, where unspeakable things had happened all those years ago. She tried to wipe the memory of those mold encrusted stairs. The old man tumbling silently down. Her one child curled in a corner. Her other child standing at the landing, a hammer dripping crimson from its claw hanging by his side.

She grabbed at the hardware, pressed the clasp of the metal lock through the opening and into the strike plate with a loud, satisfying sound.

She then looked at the wall on the corner to her right,

where there was another door. She stepped forward and banged on that door, screaming. "Bitch!"

She ran through the room to the pantry, out through the back door and over to the small structure that abutted the main house. It had once served as a garage and storage room but was now an apartment. Magdelene banged on the door and shouted obscenities all at once. The woman that opened the door, glaring, looked like a younger, smaller version of the woman on the other side. The familiar tinge of sulfur burned Magdelene's nose.

"What the hell is all this noise? It's past three in the morning."

"I told you before not to be coming over into my house!" Magdelene yelled.

"Wha? Ho, hol, hold it. Wasn't nobody in your house. What you mean?"

"Cut the bullshit, Lilith. I told you last time Bowie's shit went missing if you ever step foot in my house again I'd bring the police in here and haul your crackhead ass to jail, didn't I?"

The woman laughed, leaned against the doorjamb, blocking entry that Magdelene was not attempting. "Your house. When's the last time you paid Mama rent? Your house."

"Don't you fucking worry about what I do and don't do with Mama, hear? You worry about your own shit and paying your rent in food stamps. You was over in my house and you fucked with that cellar door. It was wide open."

Lilith fell away from the doorjamb, back into the apartment. "The door was open? Why you think I would do that?"

"You tell me? Who else would do it?"

"How 'bout Bowie? You ask him?"

Magdelene put her hands on her hips. She wished to God she had a cigarette. "He ain't crazy enough to be doing shit he ain't never done before. And he ain't home, anyway."

"Where is he? Why ain't he home?" Lilith looked back behind her, into the apartment, then moved out toward her sister, closing the door behind her, speaking in a low voice. "He in the hospital again?"

Magdelene shook her head. "No. They let him out."

"Well how you let him go running around these streets? The police just looking to lock his black ass up."

"You think I don't know that, Lilith?" she shouted, then lowered her voice. "He's a grown man. You think I can just hold him here in this house?"

She nodded. "I know. I'm just worried." Lilith could see that she had softened Magdelene. She put a hand on her forearm. "I swear, Sister. I wasn't over on your side. And I would never open that door. You know that, don't you?"

Magdelene shook her arm off, watched her coldly. "I don't know that at all." She walked away from her, back to her side of the building and slammed her door. She noisily clicked the lock, then, thinking that Bowie might lose his key, as he always did, she quietly unlocked it and crept into the kitchen, watching the cellar door as she passed.

She climbed back up the stairs and she, who did not

permit closed doors in her house, closed the door behind her and buried herself beneath the blankets, trying to muffle the unrest that permeated the air around her, that seemed to shift around like some sort of living thing.

Eden knew from previous experience that he would regret having Bowie stay the night. Well, maybe regret wasn't the right word. He always enjoyed his sheer physicality. The feel of him, his scent. His exuberance, however, was a bit distracting. For Eden, sex was an experience wherein he tried to tap into all his senses, to tap into the power of the universe.

For Bowie, it seemed that constant movement and shifting was tantamount to the experience. Coupled with that, he talked incessantly, gave instructions, and asked questions. Eden was jolted when Bowie placed his hands around his neck and tried to choke him, so he smacked him lightly, and Bowie responded with a groan of encouragement, smacking him back.

"It wasn't a reciprocal slap, motherfucker."

"Huh?"

"Don't hit me, fool."

"What?"

Eden had discovered that Bowie's primary method of comprehending speech was through reading lips, so it was very hard to communicate when the lights were out. Another reason Eden found it ludicrous that the man attempted sexually explicit talk during the act. He'd practically have to scream to be understood, and would, thus, spoil the entire mood.

Perhaps frustration was a better description for what Eden felt. If the television was on, Bowie would moan to turn it off. If the lights were off, he'd want them on mid-stroke, or if they were on, then he'd want them off. Then, if candles were lit, he'd want to blow them out, or he'd ask Eden to hand him the lube, until Eden would demand, "Are we sexing, or are you hosting a talk show? Can you shut up for a few minutes so I can concentrate?"

And there was that: Bowie was always ready. He was always able to get aroused. But his arousal was sort of like an ebb and flow. He would stroke himself in between bouts of going down on Eden, for thirty minutes, forty-five minutes, sometimes hard, then soft, then hard again, but never able to reach climax. Eden would estimate what length of time was considerate, and then he'd climb on top of him, straddle his head and push his dick into Bowie's waiting mouth so that he could cum and then tersely order Bowie to go to sleep.

It wasn't a big deal to him; he figured Bowie couldn't cum because of the psych meds. Eden thought it must be pretty frustrating not being able to cum, but Bowie didn't seem to be bothered by it. Hell, Eden was amazed that Bowie's dick was taut as an arrow, given the cocktail of chemicals he had been prescribed for his entire adult life.

Eden was frustrated that he had spent over a year of

sexual involvement with Bowie and there had been no penetration for either party. Bowie would entice him on the phone with promises that never seemed to come to fruition.

Every morning when he rushed to take Bowie home before the sun rose fully in the sky, so that he could get back home before his father awakened and needed to be bathed and fed, he swore it would be the last time he wasted time on him.

But he always found that after a few days passed he'd miss his company, want to see him, hear his slightly tone deaf voice, his too loud laughter, his off-key singing to YouTube choir clips. He also missed how he felt holding Bowie in his arms. Clutched in the crook of Eden's long arms, their legs and feet intertwined among the tangle of sheets and pillows, Bowie seemed to fit him perfectly. His lean body was like a magnet. Eden's hands moved to touch him of their own volition. He just felt right.

This night, like other nights, he listened to Bowie's refracted snoring: an uneven inhalation of air. He rumbled like a contented cat. Eden held him, feeling the meds twitch through his synapses, making him percolate like a generator. It helped to lull him to sleep, but Eden would usually awaken periodically, as Bowie's limbs would suddenly convulse and jerk. Eden would press the flat of his hands on the hollow of his chest, feel his heart pumping rapidly, transferring the heat through his hands into Bowie's body until the movements stopped, and they'd continue to sleep until the next convulsion.

As he drifted, Bowie's phone began to pulse on the table by the bed. Eden moved over, sitting up on the pillows and looked at the screen.

What are you doing?

Eden watched the screen. It vibrated and lit up again.

What are you doing

What are you doing

What are you doing

What are you doing

Eden shook his head. He'd dated some mama's boys before, but nothing quite like this. He picked up the phone, jabbed at the keys.

Bowie is sleeping. I'll tell him you called.

You don't know who I am

Eden frowned. *Isn't this his mother?*

It is not

My bad.

It sure is. Who is this

who is this who is this who is this

Damn. Chill. You don't need to know who I am. Who the fuck is this?

Eden swore and nervously put the phone back on the table. It was probably Bowie's boyfriend, who Eden had thought was a figment of Bowie's imagination. Now he had fucked up the entire situation.

B owie felt it as soon as he entered the house. It smelled different than before. It lurked behind the smell of old cooking oil and stagnant cigarette smoke, something like soured milk. Nothing so powerful as to be overwhelming. It was only noticeable when he first walked in, then it seemed to dissipate. But the air felt heavier. Walking through the rooms took extra effort. By the time he walked past the basement door to the hallway leading upstairs, he was winded, breathing audibly.

He saw the thing at the top of the stairway landing. It shimmered there, like a cloud of bees or gnats riding on a cusp of air. He blinked his eyes, rubbed the keloid scar above his left brow. He looked again, and the shimmer was gone, then it reappeared, flickering black and purple, pearlescent. He walked to the living room and turned off the constantly droning television, then went back to look up at the landing. He wanted to hear if the thing had a sound.

Hearing nothing, he heaved a sigh of relief, and walked up the stairs.

Magdelene's room was empty. She had already left the

house. He knew, from years of routine, she must have headed out before work to catch a quick card game at one of the houses on the West End. He thought about going out to look for her, of getting her to front him the money to play, too, but instead entered his room and flung himself tiredly on the unmade bed.

Looking up at the ceiling, he saw the shimmer pulsing above him, nearly blending into the wan light refracting through the blind. He sat up, reached onto the nightstand and tapped out tablets from the amber-colored vials into his palm. He sniffed the slight cotton candy smell emanating from the Depakote. Its sweet, luring aroma masked the sickly odor of the other pills.

He lay back on the pillows, his mind racing. He thought of Magdelene, wondered which house she had gone to. He thought of Eden. He thought about food. He wondered what food was in the refrigerator. He knew, from the lingering odor that had greeted him downstairs, that Magdelene had fried some eggs for him. He imagined them sitting on a floral plate in the oven.

He absently reached into his waistband, pulled out his flaccid member and began to stroke it. He thought about his food stamp card. He wondered if Magdelene had left any money on it. He thought about who he could get to pay him money for the use of the card, so he could go play bingo. Maybe Miss Norma Jean. She usually bought food stamps at fifty-five percent instead of the fifty percent most people offered.

He felt the drugs unfurl into his mind like billowing clouds. He drifted off for a little bit, then woke up, his hand still stroking himself. His erection began to subside, but he continued stroking, feeling some satisfaction when his member began to become sore. He looked up at the shimmer. It seemed to curve upward at both sides, dipping down in the center.

Suddenly, the bedroom door flung open and Magdelene's head bobbed in. "What are you doing, you fucking pervert. Something told me to come back here and check up on your ass. Get up from there right now."

He sat up, jumped from the bed and tried to close the door. "Leave me be and close my door." She pushed against the door.

"You don't have no doors in this house. You know the rules. There are no closed doors in this house." Bowie pulled up his pants, brushed past her to the bathroom and slammed the door.

He sat on the edge of the tub, pulling his member from his pants and began stroking himself again. The door opened.

"That goes for bathroom doors, too. What are you doing?"

She watched him, her face a mask of revulsion. "Are you getting sick again? Is that what it is. Do you need me to call the hospital?"

He ignored her, focused his eyes on the shower rod above him, watched the shimmer of gnats hovering there.

She pulled her phone from her pocket. "I'm calling

your case manager."

Bowie jumped up, knocking past her. "Call them. I don't care."

She followed him downstairs, her voice hoarse and strident. "I would think you wouldn't need to be pulling your pecker after you just spent all night fucking around. What's the matter, you didn't get enough out there on them streets?"

At the bottom of the steps, he turned, pushed her on the shoulder. She fell back against the stairs with a gasp. "If you can't let me alone for two seconds, I'll just leave."

"Don't you go nowhere. You stay right in this house so I can see whether you're getting sick or not. You going to cause me to lose my job, missing all this time to look after you."

"You don't miss time for me, Mom. You miss time for those casinos. I don't need you watching over me like you my woman."

She stood up, glared at him with her hands on her hips. "Woman. What do you know about a woman?"

She reached out, tapped the bulge of his still aroused member. "A woman wants more than what you got going on here. What's going on, here, anyway?"

A loud bang sounded from the kitchen wall. They looked at it as Lilith's muffled voice screamed from the other side, "Y'all stop all that goddamn racket or I'm calling the cops!"

Magdelene brushed past him, hammered on the wall. "Go on and call them, bitch, so they can take you and your crackhead ass to jail. Call them!"

Bowie walked behind her and kicked the wall. "And they can take that Mexican motherfucker over there back where he came from, too!"

They both laughed, leaning against one another as the wall began to shake and curses boomed from the other side. They both turned and looked toward the pantry in expectation as Lilith came storming in.

Magdelene said, "I know you didn't just walk your ass in my house like you pay the bills here."

Lilith said, "Bitch, you ain't paying the bills here neither. When's the last time you paid Mom any rent?"

Magdelene grew so furious she could see red clouding her vision, "Don't you worry about what I do over here, Sister. That is between me and my mother."

Bowie shouted, jumping up and down in agitation and glee, "And you don't pay Grandmom nothing but some food stamps. And all you got to pay is the electric bill."

Lilith yelled, "You stay in a child's place. This don't got none of your business on it."

Magdelene said, "Don't talk to my child like that. You crazy?"

"I'll talk to my nephew any damn way I like. I helped raise him, too."

"You WHAT? Lilith, now I know you been through some hard times, but bitch, you must be smoking rat poison if your mind is telling you that you helped raise my child. You been high for the past forty years! Only thing you been raising is your fucking skirt."

"And you was out there in them streets right along with me, don't you forget it. I helped raise Bowie, just like I did Hendrix."

Magdelene leaned on the table, closed her eyes and looked down at her feet.

"Get out. Get out my house before I throw you out."

Lilith stood quietly, watching her. "Sorry, Sister."

Bowie no longer heard what either of them were saying. He watched the shimmer, hanging in the threshold between the rooms. It seemed to grow brighter, to grow larger.

Bowie had been sitting in the tiny lobby for what felt like hours. Many people swarmed through, talking to others, or talking to themselves, waving at friends and cursing at enemies. Each time someone entered from outside, cold air blasted through. He walked over to the receptionist sitting behind a panel of dirty plexiglass. She looked at him while deliberately picking up the ringing phone and directing her attention away from him. He stood there, staring at her intently, feeling this anger as if it were mercury in an old thermometer, rising, rising.

He placed his hands on the counter, gripping tightly, watching the woman not watching him. He counted slowly from one to one hundred. Then, he banged his hand on the window and yelled.

"I know you see me standing here, don't you?"

The woman rolled her eyes, slowly placed the phone back in its receiver and stared at him. "Please don't bang on the glass, or we'll have to ask the police to escort you out of here."

"Call them. I had a ten o'clock appointment to see my

doctor and it's twelve o'clock."

"You just have to be patient. The doctor is in with another patient. She'll get to you as soon as she can."

Bowie hammered a fist on the counter before walking back to his seat, digging into his pocket for his phone.

Magdelene answered on the second ring. "I'm at work."

"I'm about to leave here. I shouldn't have to sit around here all day waiting on these white bitches."

She shouted at him, "You just sit your ass down there and wait. You hear? You need to get new scripts, so you just wait until you get them. I'm not playing with you, you hear?"

He hung up. Then he called Eden. The phone rang five times before going to voicemail. Bowie listened to his voice on the outgoing message. He liked the way Eden spoke, so low and even. He imagined a lion sitting amidst a pride of lionesses. He left a message.

"Pick up the phone, boo. I'm trying to call you."

He sent a text.

pick up u phone boo. where u at

He called again. Two times, before Eden picked up, sounding exasperated but still somehow serene.

"What did I tell you about calling me back-to-back like that?"

He smiled. "Sorry, boo."

Eden sighed. "Come on with that boo shit. How can I help you? What's going on?"

"I'm about to go to jail."

"Again? Aren't you tired of jails and hospitals?" Eden's

laughter, short and staccato, let Bowie know his comment was a joke, so he laughed, too.

"No, I'm serious. I've been waiting to see this doctor for two hours. I'm ready to throw a chair through this window."

"Okay. Do you think that strategy would get you in to see the doctor any sooner?"

"Actually, yeah. These white folks treat you like you invisible until you act like a park ape. Then, they see you. Then they jump around and give you attention. If I start acting crazy then they'll get to me real quick so they can get me out of their nice new building, scaring the women and children."

"Why don't you just ask to speak to the office manager? That's a better way for you to get your needs met. It's crazy to have people sitting around in there like that."

"That shit don't work for us. They don't give a shit about us."

"Let me talk to somebody."

"What?"

"Put the manager on the phone. Let me talk to somebody in charge. And put the phone on speaker mode, so you can hear me code switch like a motherfucker."

"Huh?"

"I'm about to use my white voice. You have to meet these white folks where they're most comfortable. Haven't you heard you get more flies with honey than with shit?"

Bowie took the phone over to the receptionist's window, hit the speaker button and listened. He watched the receptionist's face shift from disdain to respect. He watched her jump up and search for the office manager.

He was in the doctor's office five minutes later.

She settled into her seat behind her desk, her notepad open before her. "My apologies for the delay. We have been very busy today. So. Have you had any feelings of hopelessness in the last thirty days?"

"No."

"Have you had any thoughts of harming yourself or others?"

He sighed and shook his head no.

"Could you answer the question, please."

"No. I don't want to kill myself. Look, Doc, I want to talk about some problems I'm having."

"Okay." She looked at him expectantly.

Bowie searched for the proper words. He struggled to find a way to describe the changes he had experienced since the shimmer.

"I don't have no privacy. My mom keeps coming in my room. She comes in the bathroom when I'm in there."

"Why is she doing that?"

He shrugged. "I don't know. She keeps saying I'm a pervert. It's like she's looking to catch me masturbating."

"Have you been masturbating?"

"Yeah. But every time I do it, she comes in the room. I don't have no privacy wherever I go. I feel like I'm trapped. And all I can think about is masturbating. These meds. It's like . . . it feels like my mind is in a cloud. I can't get through the cloud to my real thoughts."

The doctor shifted the papers on her desk, reading briefly. "Your evaluation from your most recent discharge states part of the reason you required hospitalization was that you were not med compliant for a while."

"What?"

"You were not taking your meds. You have to give yourself some time to become adjusted to the medications. There will be some undesirable effects, but we have to weigh those with the effects that might be beneficial to you."

"Huh? I don't know what you're saying, Doc. Can you repeat that?"

"If you don't remain med compliant you will likely suffer a readmission to the hospital."

"I need you to talk English to me. I'm trying to tell you about these thoughts about masturbating. There's something going on I don't understand. Whenever I'm home by myself, I think about masturbating. And then I hear her voice, or I think about her barging in and I get scared she's going to call me a pervert."

The doctor closed her binder, placed her hands on the desk. "I think you should discuss these issues with your therapist. She will be able to help you work through these things and come up with a strategy to address your identified issues. And then, at that time, we can consult to discuss whether your medications should be adjusted. We can perhaps increase your Abilify now, but you need to meet with a therapist as soon as possible."

"Ain't you my therapist?"

"I'm your psychiatrist."

"What's the difference?"

"I manage your medications and write scripts for you. I make sure that you aren't having any adverse reactions to your medications, but for therapy, we have other professionals here in the outpatient program who develop treatment plans for our members."

"But are those people psychiatrists?"

She smiled at him, patronizingly. "No. They are experts in their fields. They are trained to address psychiatric issues."

He looked at her dazedly as she stood. She handed him a clutch of handwritten prescriptions.

"Here are your new prescriptions for the month. I've read in your history that you have not engaged with group therapy sessions. That would be a good forum where you can work on the issues that you've discussed here this afternoon."

He stood as she approached, she moved him toward the door.

"I don't want to talk about this with a bunch of other people. I know you. I feel better talking to you."

"If you would be more compliant with the treatment modality of individual and group therapy, rather than what you've done thus far, which is only participating in the med management portion, you will find, after you invest in the program, that you'll be able to remain at your baseline for longer periods of time."

"Huh?"

"Bowie, you have not been what we would call committed to recovery because you refuse to do individual and group therapy. That is where the bulk of recovery takes place. Meds are only a portion of what you have to do to stay well."

"I don't even know what the fuck you're saying."

Her lips tightened in disapproval. "Okay, that kind of talk is unacceptable."

"I been coming here, every month, year after year, Doc. And I've been waiting in that lobby for hours past my scheduled time, every month. And you talk to me about—what did you call it—compliance? How about you being compliant with me? You're full of shit."

She closed the door in his face. Bowie banged on the door in frustration, then, when he noticed counselors looking out of their offices, he ran down the hallway back to the lobby.

He called Magdelene. She answered on the second ring. "These motherfuckers. I'm going to stop going to this shithole."

"No the fuck you're not! I'm not doing this shit with you. You need medication. Do you want to get sick again?"

"I'm not going to be treated like shit. These people act like they're doing me a favor. Every time I come to this place they make me feel like I'm small. Like I'm nothing at all."

"Did you get your scripts?"

"Do you think I'm stupid! Of course I got my scripts. You ask some dumb questions sometimes."

"Take them to the drug store right now so you can get them filled."

"No shit, Mom. Like I don't know that."

"Read them to me so I can make sure you got everything."

He yelled into the phone, "Bye, Mom."

Bowie turned down the wing and ran up the flight of stairs to the wing where the counselors' offices were located. He entered the first door he saw that was open.

A squat white man sat tapping at a keyboard. The man looked up and smiled. "Do you need help with something?"

He nodded. "Yeah. I need to talk to somebody, fast. Something's been telling me to do things I don't want to do."

The man waved him into a chair. "Are you hearing voices?"

"Not really voices, no."

"Do you want to harm yourself?"

He shook his head.

"Do you want to harm others?"

"No."

"Do you have people you can go to if you are feeling unsafe? Are you homeless?"

Bowie sucked his teeth. "No. Why whenever you people see people like me you think we bums? I got a house to live in."

"Okay, well if you aren't in immediate danger, we can certainly help set you up with whatever you need. But first we need to conduct an assessment to determine your level of need. Do you have insurance?"

"What if I don't? Then what?"

"We can help determine what you are able to pay on a sliding scale. But first we need to make an appointment for you. So if you could please speak with the receptionist downstairs, she can get you in for an evaluation."

"Can I talk to somebody today?"

He smiled somewhat sadly. "I'm sorry, we couldn't accommodate you for today, unless you are experiencing a crisis. There are many people that we help here. We have to schedule appointments so that we can make sure that everyone that needs help is able to get it."

"Bullshit." Bowie jumped up and stormed out of the room.

The man followed. "Excuse me, sir. Sir? Let me walk you down, get your name and address and insurance information. We don't want you to feel as though you can't get the support you need."

"Don't bother, man. I'm good." Bowie stormed down the stairs and out the door to the street.

The shimmer seemed to follow him wherever he went. Before, he only saw it when he was "sick," coiled in the corner of his bedroom, or standing tall and murky in a dark corner of the house, or watching him from a window when he approached. It no longer seemed to be tied to the house. It now hovered in the periphery of his sight, visible only when he cocked his head a certain way. But he could feel it there, even when he didn't see it, sometimes gold, sometimes purple, always black.

It watched him when he roamed the casinos. It watched him wander anxiously from card game to card game, mocking him when he lost, undulating when he won. It stood behind Magdelene's head when she scolded him. It watched as he and Eden sat in darkened movie houses, when they laughed at restaurants. It mocked him when he lay spent but unfulfilled, unable to ejaculate after untold time spent in a state of arousal, Eden sweating dimly beside him.

"You know, you would get more pleasure from sex if you didn't do it so much."

Bowie sat up in the bed, crooked a sturdy thigh over

Eden's. "What did you say?"

Eden laughed. "You spend all day jacking off, and you never cum. You can't cum because you play with yourself all the time. Your dick is confused."

Bowie grabbed Eden's hand and placed it on his damp crotch. "Does this feel confused to you?"

He yanked his hand back. "Yeah, very."

Eden turned over and lay across Bowie's thin chest, feeling his heart thumping rapidly. "It could be your meds, I guess. They might make it hard for you to cum."

"What do meds got to do with cumming? I cum all the time."

"Okay, sure. I ain't seen you nut, ever. But I will say, you been able to get hard all the time lately. You not on the Prozac anymore?"

"Man, that shit was making me crazy. I couldn't keep still. My mom had me come off that shit."

"You're not able to keep still now! But you weren't able to stay hard when you were on that, either."

"Bullshit."

"What you so defensive about? It doesn't matter to me if you get hard or not. It's not the getting hard, or even the cumming that's important for me. It's the whole experience. I just wonder if it would be more satisfying to you if you were able to cum."

Eden had learned, through his thirties, that his dick would not always be responsive, even in situations where he wanted it to. He read about sexual satisfaction through tantric sex, which emphasized concentration on the entire bodily experience rather than the sex organs. Once he started practicing some of those techniques, his experience of sex changed. He began processing the act through all of his senses.

Bowie said, "So you're saying you don't care if I cum, but this whole discussion is about me not cumming. You know you wouldn't even waste your time with me if my dick wasn't working."

Eden kissed him, smelled the sweet smell the chemicals in his body formulated in his breath, allowed himself to be enveloped in the warmth of their comingled skin. "You still have an ass, even if your dick doesn't work."

Bowie pushed him off, turned on his belly. "So you want this ass. Come get it." Bowie arched up onto his knees, offering himself to him.

Eden felt himself stiffen to the point where it caused pain. The early morning light fell through the window onto Bowie's gleaming body, so dark it seemed to absorb instead of reflect light, making the curves of his ass appear murky, almost a shadow. Eden touched him, his hand warming on the smooth flesh. It reminded him of devil's food cake.

Eden didn't consider this, the first time Bowie allowed him inside of himself, as intercourse. None of the mechanics of sex seemed to occur. Eden could tell Bowie's meds were beginning to take effect. Bowie's usually hyper movements and reconfigurations were slowing down. Where he would normally give instructions or grab a hand and place it somewhere, he was now sluggish.

Eden entered him slowly, tentatively. He felt the all-enveloping warmth surround the head of his dick. He didn't push or move his hips, but just rested there, concentrating all of his thoughts on the feeling in that one location of his body. He pushed down with his chest and thighs, easing Bowie down fully onto the bed, nuzzling his neck and licking his ears.

Bowie responded drowsily, "That feels good, baby. You like it?"

Then, Eden heard the low gurgle of his snoring. He just lay there, content in the warmth of his body, feeling the comfort of his feet nesting above Bowie's feet. He kissed him, moved his arms so that his hands wrapped around Bowie's chest, felt his heart thrumming in his palms. He felt the entirety of his shaft slowly enveloped inside, surrounded in warmth and viscosity. Eden didn't move at all. He didn't need to. The medications in Bowie's bloodstream caused a firing of synapses and twitches that provided an experience Eden had never felt before. He held onto him, feeling his dick gripped firmly, smelling Bowie's scent, feeling every contour of his body as it jerked and rumbled like a cat resting on a car hood with a warm motor, content.

He wasn't sure how long they lay like that. Whether it was minutes or hours, time seemed to stand still. At some point, he felt the familiar surge tighten his dick, and pulled drowsily, unwillingly away from Bowie, and ejaculated onto the contours of his back, his fist stroking dreamily. As he came, he heard a thousand voices surging through him, shouting something he could not decipher.

When he finished, he lay back across him, feeling the stickiness of his semen hold them together as a thousand murmuring voices lulled them to sleep.

Unlike most times, Eden didn't wake him in a rush, anxious to get him home before he had to get his father out of bed. This time, when Bowie rose from the haze of drug-induced sleep, when he groggily opened his eyes, he saw Eden sitting beside him, staring at him. He leaped up, rubbing his eyes.

"What's wrong?"

"Who said something's wrong?"

"Well, why you staring at me, then?"

Eden rolled his eyes. "Because I like your face. You have beautiful skin, so dark and matte. Your beautiful, big nose."

Bowie yanked the blankets from his torso, began to massage his groin. "You want some more, huh?"

Eden thumped him on the chest, yanked the blankets the rest of the way off. "You ruin everything. Your head seems to only be able to comprehend two specific body parts. Get up, dickhead."

Bowie jumped onto his knees, threw his body across Eden, knocking them both back to the bed. "I'm sorry, honey!"

Eden yelped, struggled beneath him, reached beneath the hollow of his armpit and began to tickle him. They tussled in the bed, laughing, scrambling for dominance. Bowie playfully bit Eden's nipple. "That's cheating!"

Bowie placed a knee in Eden's chest. "You can't beat me, man. I told you I used to be on the wrestling squad in school."

Eden was now huffing tiredly. "Can you stop taking me back down memory lane about how you used to wrestle. That was how long ago? I go to the gym regularly."

"That gym don't mean nothing. You a old head. Look at you, you tired already."

Eden wouldn't admit it, but Bowie was right. His breath was far more labored than he expected it to be with this small exertion. He smacked Bowie's ass, hopped out of bed. "Get dressed, shit talker, I need to get you home."

Bowie sat up, kissed Eden's neck as he climbed from the bed. Eden grabbed him, hugged him close, kissing the back of his head. "Hey. You're not bothered about last night, are you?"

"Bothered about what?" he asked absentmindedly. He leaned into Eden's kiss, like a love starved puppy.

"Sex. You sort of fell asleep."

"Why would I be bothered about sex?" Bowie laughed. "Ain't that what we always do?" He moved Eden's hand down to the warmth of his groin.

Eden pushed him from the bed. "Hurry up. I want to be able to get my dad dressed before the nurse gets here."

"Why have a nurse if you do all the work before she gets here?"

"I don't want her running back telling people I'm neglectful. Plus, she's white. I don't want that white woman thinking we're disgusting or that my dad's dirty."

Bowie let himself in through the front door, his chest heavy with trepidation. He quietly closed the door, listening. Through the quiet cacophony, he heard gospel music playing tinnily through a cell phone speaker. He knew that meant Magdelene was doing laundry in the back pantry. She always played gospel on Pandora while she did laundry.

He swiftly walked toward the stairs, looking into the kitchen where an ironing board held a steaming iron. The pantry door leaned open, blasting the scent of fabric softener and scalded cotton. He walked up the stairs with the weight of his feet applied to the treads closest to the walls. He knew from experience that these locations would be less likely to creak as he ascended to the upper level.

In his room, he buried himself beneath bed linens that slightly reeked of sleep-induced drool. He yanked off his pants, kicked his shoes to the floor and began to stroke himself. He heard the far-off droning of gospel, mixed with gibberish from the news program blaring from one of the televisions, and the constant whispers that came from some-place else. All the sounds seemed to wisp up into one long, expectant inhalation, stopped there, and then crested along with the wave of his passion as he stroked himself.

He saw shadows descending upon him. It reminded him of when he sat on that cold, hard bed at the state hospital, in a Benadryl-induced haze as orderlies held him down and inserted needles into his arm. The blanket was pulled off, and Magdelene glared at him.

"I knew I heard some commotion up here. Look at you. Disgusting. Get up from there." She stared at his eyes. The pupils rolled up into his head as if he hadn't heard her. She watched his hands moving angrily, jerkily. She swatted at his hands, they kept moving.

"Get up from there before I throw water on you like the nasty dog you are. Didn't you get enough of that out all night?"

Bowie sat up, put his head down into his hands. "Get out of my room, Mom. Just let me alone, would you."

She pulled the sheets from beneath him. "I'm going to wash these blankets, clean this filth out of here. You go get in that tub and clean the filth from your body. You're disgusting."

He pulled on his pants, pulled on his shoes, brushed past her. Magdelene fell against the wall with a gasp. "You just hit me."

Ignoring her, he bounded down the stairs.

"Where do you think you're going? I told you to take a bath. You need to calm your nerves."

He ran through the shimmer, it roared as he split through, then collected itself after him, rising toward the ceiling.

The last word Eden heard from Bowie was a text, shortly after dropping him off at home.

you coming to get me tonight, young head?

He texted back: *didn't i just drop you off at home? no I'm not.*

way not?

Eden thought his misspellings were cute. If you thought about it, they were really an honest extension of who Bowie was. Eden didn't know how much he couldn't hear, but he knew that he mostly read lips, and that he heard virtually nothing in the dark, and so Bowie's understanding of language came visually and his spelling of words was primarily based on his phonetic phrasing of words he could not hear properly.

As he got caught up in the monotony of his day-to-day obligations, he didn't notice that Bowie hadn't called all day long, hadn't texted him nonstop nonsensical or sexually explicit content.

But as the mind-numbing tedium of day one moved to day two, then to three, he felt the void of Bowie's non-presence like a weight driving down on his shoulders, making it harder to move, harder to breathe.

Bowie's silence made the mundane nature of what his life had become shout at him. Each morning he bathed his father, fed him, easing the stroke stiffened limbs into clothing, adjusting the body from bed, to chair, from car to specialist appointments, back home, and into chair again. Waited for the nurse to arrive so that he could spend time alone in the den with his laptop opened to the university website, where he took classes more to distract himself from what his life had dwindled down to than any sort of academic inclination.

Saturday night, his sister would come to spend her predetermined twenty-four hours ignoring the shimmer lurking in the darkened corner on the ceiling of their father's room. Eden would pack a bag, spend time at his boyfriend's house, where they would watch a carefully curated selection of British television shows. Shows Eden's boyfriend had determined to be intellectually stimulating. He would tolerate the TV shows, just as he tolerated the boyfriend. Just as he tolerated the perfunctory and obligatory blow job and coitus, mostly initiated by the boyfriend, usually at approximately midnight. Mostly all this benevolent toleration took place because Eden was a coward and found this toleration to be a less stressful option than all of the conflama that he expected would result if he could only formulate the words that would allow him to be finally free of a fifteen-year union that he no longer wished to be in.

He had thought that a split would gradually and organically evolve seven years ago, when he had moved out of their shared apartment and moved back home to his childhood home to take care of his senile father. But his partner's abhorrence to becoming newly single had proven to be even more resolute than Eden's long dormant filial rage.

Bowie was the only thing in his life that was not an obligation. He was the only unexpected thing. The only spontaneity in a life heavy with the expectations of other people.

He sat in the room with the body that was little more than a husk. Although it still breathed, still ate, still pissed and shit, it was dead. The spirit of that body was gone. Now, it shimmered just slightly above Eden's peripheral sight in the same room as the body it had once inhabited. It was something he could sense more than he could see, really, off there in the outermost corner of the room. He marveled that he was able to sit with it so calmly.

But it was far less a disruption in this form than it had ever been when it was inside that body.

In that body, it had raged and fumed, struck out at people, pushed children down stairs, physically assaulted spouses. It had stashed liquor bottles in every room, ignored bills, snuck local harlots into back rooms late at night, demanded good grades, withheld love, mislabeled love, confused love with the business end of a belt, disowned love, sneered at same sex love.

After the third day of not hearing from Bowie, Eden felt a dread he could not describe. It jettisoned him back three decades to a child sitting with his sister in an empty house wondering where their father had disappeared to, and when he would return, or if he would return. Whether his return would be in the company of the state police, his father nude and ranting obscenities. It brought him back to that day when his father never came back and the woman he no longer called his mother said that she was going out to find him, but the dead look in her eyes and the suitcase in her hand told him she, too would not be coming back.

Eden called his phone. He wasn't able to leave a voicemail. Bowie didn't have voicemail.

where u at?

Nothing in return.

hit me back

More days passed. Eden's heart grew heavy. He grew leery of what the silence implied.

hope u ok

if u busy, that's fine, just send me msg u ok

hope u not in hospital

After day seven, against his better judgement, he drove to the house on Maple Leaf Street. He drove up the hill, past the people sitting on stoops all watching his car. He parked and climbed the stairs with trepidation. He rapped on the door. He felt like he heard a gasp in the wake of his knocking, but there was only silence.

When he knocked again, he heard that gasp that was not a gasp again. He stood there, felt the eyes watching him, pretending not to watch him. As he turned to walk down the stairs, the door moved quietly back. He peered through the screen, saw a thin figure, squinted eyes. She was clearly a woman, but there was a certain masculinity in her stance, in her appraisal of him. She inhaled on a cigarette, said nothing.

"Hello. Is Bowie here?"

She blew a plume of smoke through the mesh, out into his face. He turned his head through the smoke, squinting. She recognized his voice from when they had spoken briefly on the phone. She assessed the smooth depth of his voice as a good match with his appearance, tall and sleekly muscular, broad shouldered and slim hipped, angular cheekbones with a voluminous clutch of dark hair at his jawline, dark brows and large, intelligent eyes. Her acknowledgement of his comeliness was grudging. He was accustomed to this reaction from women who knew him to be gay.

"Bowie," she said his name.

He smiled, briefly, not too effusive. He didn't want to give her the impression that he was friendly. He had found that giving straight women the impression of friendliness sometimes led to them not taking him as seriously as he expected to be.

"Yes. I haven't talked to him for a few days, and I just wanted to make sure he's okay." He almost added, I worry about him so, but had caught himself. That comment might have caused consternation for this woman. Although he had just met her, he knew her type.

Magdelene took another puff on her cigarette, deliberately letting him see her cast her eyes from his head down to his feet, blew out a tuft of smoke, then spoke. "My son is fine, thank you for asking. I take care of him just fine, but I thank you for your concern."

He watched her. He moved to stand with his feet spread, more of a defensive stance than before. His voice dropped a bit deeper.

"If he's home, I'd like to just talk to him for a second. Say hello." Eden couldn't tell if she was shaking her head no or moving her head away from the smoke she blew.

"I don't know if Bowie's told you, but I don't allow men to come around here looking for him at my house. But if you give me your name I will surely let him know that you were worried, and thank you kindly."

Eden smiled, the corners of his lips curled cruelly. He nodded, crossed his arms across his chest. "That won't be necessary. You have a good day now."

She watched him walking to a tiny, black BMW, watched the muscles in his back flex as he moved. She weighed her anger against her more urgent need. She banged out the door and followed behind him.

"Wait. Excuse me . . ."

Eden turned, his face a dark cloud.

She smoked furiously; her head seemed to be immersed in a cloud of its own. "Listen, I didn't mean to be rude. You were nice to me on the phone before. Maybe you can help. Bowie got arrested. He's in jail."

BEHAVIORAL HEALTH COURT
PSYCHIATRIC EVALUATION

PATIENT: Bowie Long
EVALUATOR: L. Dopinger

This assessment has been compiled at the request of County Mental Health Services and the County Correctional Facility of behalf of Bowie Long.

This evaluation is completed to determine suitability for diversion of the individual from incarceration to Behavioral Health Court, where he would be released to the community and required to report before the judge on a weekly basis to ensure the individual is meeting requirements of probation, paying fines, remaining medication compliant and adherent to treatment. Assessment also determines level of threat to general community such release would present.

Current incarceration is resultant of a report of indecent exposure at County Library. Individual was discovered by security staff in men's room in a state of undress. Individual has prior involvement with court for charges of robbery at a local casino. Review of related records indicate probability of incidents of a sexual nature also took place at that time. Prison reports individual to be in constant state of sexual preoccupation. He is, at present, in isolation for safety of self and general population.

INITIAL IMPRESSION: Unkempt and sloppily dressed. Minimally cooperative. Individual is not acknowledging awareness or responsibility for the incident that led to present incarceration. Respondent is verbally combative and suspicious of authority figures. Grandiose demeanor, at odds with what should be displayed by current circumstance. Self-report of five prior inpatient hospitalizations over course of lifetime. Self-report of current outpatient treatment program from age eighteen to present. First psychiatric episode reported to have occurred at age eighteen.

As most recent inpatient crisis occurred less than thirty days prior, Mr. Long is in severe category of psychiatric distress. As such, he requires immediate and comprehensive triage. Catalyzing event of the most recent acute crisis was violence of homicidal nature toward maternal parent. Individual appeared at parent's place of employment brandishing a kitchen knife and threatening bodily harm. Also threatened emergency responders, requiring mechanical restraint to circumvent destruction of county property.

It is clear to this reviewer that maternal parent is extremely fearful of family member and fears for personal safety should family member be discharged without full array of psychiatric services in place. Individual benefits from having a very involved and loving parent, who has advocated on his behalf.

To ensure medication compliance it is recommended that individual receive monthly intramuscular injection of psychotropic medication as a baseline in addition to daily oral medications as a requirement for acceptance to Behavioral Health Court and the Mockingbird Program.

Failure to appear for daily programming and/or medication noncompliance will result in immediate violation and remanding to correctional facility.

DIAGNOSIS (TENTATIVE):

Sexual preoccupation secondary to reported history of Bipolar Disorder

Conduct Disorder

Childhood Onset Severe Intermittent Explosive Disorder

History of childhood sexual abuse

History of Childhood Reactive Attachment Disorder

Rule out Post Traumatic Disorder

SIGNED: Lola Dopinger, Intake Manager, Mockingbird Partial Program for Men with Sexual Health Issues

He didn't really remember what becoming a convict felt like. It seemed pretty much the same experience as when he had gone crazy. Just like when he went crazy, the police came, spoke to him with kind words and a hand resting on their batons. Each time, he tried to control his rapidly escalating passion, tried to express himself in a calm manner, but he was able to read the derision behind their eyes as they tried to placate him. He saw laughter twitching at the corners of grim mouths as they minimized or exaggerated his words. The more he tried to express himself, the more it seemed the words he used weren't the ones he wanted. He tried to remember what Eden had told him when he had been unable to get people to slow down and listen to him that time he went to the psychiatrist, to code switch, he had called it. But it didn't seem to be working.

Just like when he went crazy, his voice merged with their voices and then he couldn't be certain whether the voices were from without or within.

Just like the hospitals, this place had cold cement walls and echoing voices shouting threats and pleas. They made him strip and they said, "What's in your wallet," and somehow he knew what they wanted. He had to bend over and cough while the laughing men in uniforms searched him. His clothes were taken from him and replaced with scratchy blues, just like at the hospital.

Shadows unfurled toward him in the dank cell reeking of stagnant urine and vomit. The good thing about this place was that you had a cellie, and the cellie helped to keep the shadows at bay, kept the voices silent.

Once he had been processed, he was released to general population. It was a terrifying place. He understood the looks that were thrown his way. He was accustomed to the way that men who were larger than him assessed him. They shouted out as he passed, offers of comfort, threats of debasement, laughing jeers and evaluations of his body parts. His heart thrummed against his ribcage so loudly it caused blood to surge in his ears, muting the surrounding cacophonous riot to a dull murmur.

He didn't know how many hours had passed. He tried to sleep, but he imagined hands touching him, whispers wetting his ears. He sat up in his bunk, his back against the wall. This was not just like the hospital. In the hospital you got warm, comforting, chemically induced sleep. Here, he just sat thrumming with anxiety, his stomach constantly purring with hunger, even after he ate.

What he did know was, just like the time when he went to the hospital, Magdelene was the reason he was in this place. If she would just let him have a moment's peace.

But she wouldn't. She was constantly on him, bursting into his room, calling his phone whenever he left the house, asking him what he was doing, accusing him of things.

When she had come into his room calling him vile names, he ran out of the house in such a hurry that he left his phone. He wanted to call Eden, but he didn't want to go back in that house and listen to her yelling. He went to the library. At least he knew he would have quiet there.

He didn't like to read so much, but he got on the internet and looked for apartments. He had to find a place of his own, to get away from her constantly hovering over him. She didn't allow internet at home, afraid he would log onto "those filthy sites." She had been burned by a thousand-dollar phone bill when he was sixteen and curious about the M2M 800 numbers.

He thought it would really fix her ass if he found an apartment and moved out. Then, when she spent all her money at the slots she couldn't run to him as a backup, telling him they would be out on the street if he didn't sell his food stamps so they could pay the electric bill. Then they would depend on his grandmother to bring them food to eat for the rest of the month as they waited for the next pay period.

His apartment search was cut short when he noticed someone at another computer watching him with knowing eyes. They completed the ritual of lingering looks that gradually led to the men's room. Sound bounced from the tiles, disbursing in his ear canals so that he couldn't separate his moans from the sound of footsteps. Then there was hammering on the stall door and a confrontation with the security guard. And now he was in this place, where time didn't move.

He knew it was night when the metal doors clanged shut and were locked. His cellie's presence was no longer a salve against the voices. Now, it was a constant, low drone demanding him to do things he did not want to do. He heard clothing rustle, heard the man shifting on his bunk, rising. He felt warm, broad hands reach for him, touching his body.

He got a brief flash of Magdelene, tapping his crotch, asking, "What's going on here?" He got a flash of his Aunt Lilith's hand rubbing his ass, complimenting him, saying an ass like that was a waste on a man, bemoaning that it would have been of far better use to her.

As the hands pulled at his pants, Bowie pushed him off, sat up against the wall, pulled his dick from his pants and began to masturbate. Jerkily. Furiously. He stared at his cellie, who drew back in surprise. He leered at him, licking his lips, tugging at himself maniacally.

The cellmate shook his head and climbed back in his bunk. "Never mind man. You better put that shit away. I ain't with that faggot shit."

Bowie moved from his bunk, stood in front of the other bunk, glaring at the man, yanking on his dick and moaning. He knew how to keep people like this away from him. He knew passivity was a target and aggression was a protection. He moved forward, his dick stiff in his hand. The discomfort on the man's face was satisfying, gave him an erotic charge. He felt strong and powerful. He felt like he was in control.

He grinned at the man's discomfort, his eyes wide and unfocused.

The man jumped from the bed, ran to the door and began to yell.

"Yo guard! Come get this crazy motherfucker out of here! Guard! Yo, I'm about to kill this nigger!"

Bowie followed, stood behind him, stroking himself. The man turned, swung a fist, connected with Bowie's temple.

COUNTY CORRECTIONAL FACILITY

INMATE NAME: Bowie Long
IDENTIFYING INFORMATION: African-American male, 32 years of age. 5 foot 4 inches height. 155 pounds.

CHARGES: Indecent Exposure, Open Lewdness, Obscene Lang/Gest, Disorderly Conduct, Hazardous Physical Offense, Resisting Arrest

STATUS: Awaiting sentencing

NOTES: Inmate # 04632-90113 has been moved from General Population to the Isolation Unit, where he has been remanded for 37 days resultant from exhibition of behaviors of a sexual nature toward a fellow prisoner.

Upon release from the Isolation Unit, 04632-90113 will be remanded to the Medical Unit based upon reported history of mental health diagnosis (bipolar d/o per self-report and parent report).

Inmate's mother contacted Social Work Unit to provide list of psychiatric medications.

The Correctional Facility will provide baseline medications of Depakote and Tegretol to support against further decompensation.

They called it the hole, which was pretty accurate. Solitary confinement. Cells for inmates who did not or could not follow the rules were smaller than the other cells. They didn't have beds or windows. The only light emanated from the fluorescents in the outer hallways, where guards sporadically roamed, banging a black stick along the walls.

But Bowie felt safe here. He sat clutched in a far corner, as much for warmth as for solace. Even though he heard voices telling him things, he knew he was safer here than he had been in general population. Here, the only hands that might cause him harm were his own, compelled by frustration or sensory deprivation. The guards would haul him out from the hole for an hour each day, where he was allowed to shower and exercise under close supervision and strict instruction of no talking or eye contact.

It was much harder to determine the time of day in the hole, since the doors were always locked, and sunlight was never present. Prisoners in the hole gauged the time of day based upon estimates related to their hourly walk when the guard told them the time.

Bowie's food was brought to him three times each day. Most days he ate ravenously, since there was little else to do except think about his life. He thought about how surprised Magdelene would be seeing him eat so much food. At home, he was usually so amped that he had little time to sit through a meal. He preferred to grab a piece of fruit, grab a bunch of grapes and head back out to one of the card games held throughout town. Or Magdelene would demand that they sit together and eat something she prepared, using the promise of them going together to the casino afterward as a lure.

He missed his mother's cooking. She made great gumbo. They had seafood, crab, shrimp, sometimes even lobster each week. On special occasions she'd even work all day cleaning chitlins and making pig's feet. He still blamed her for everything, but he wished to be home.

"Long!"

Bowie looked up as the door clanged open and a guard banged a stick on the doorjamb.

"Let's go, Long. You been discharged."

At first Eden was more concerned about Bowie and what he had done that landed him in jail. That came before his amazement, his disbelief in the woman's gall to treat him so rudely only to turn in the next breath and ask for his help.

Of course she would think to ask him for money. A man so much older than her son. Of course she had placed him in a preconceived role: It scathed him to think of himself that way. He was no sugar daddy. First off, his gross net did not warrant that he could be anyone's sugar daddy, but more importantly, while he was certainly much older than Bowie, Eden knew that he was still physically alluring, still had the glow of youth, for whatever that was worth. The only reason that he felt confident enough to court a man so many years younger than himself was that he made sure to keep his physicality on par with those that nevertheless looked at him as the old head.

Eden was insulted by the implication of Magdelene's request.

"What is he in jail for?" he asked, then watched as her eyes darted around to the people sitting out on their stoops, as she clutched her cardigan close to her throat and asked him to come inside for a moment.

She turned, and he followed her up the steps to the door. He noticed the sparse hair in random tufts on the back of her head. When he entered the living room, before his eyes adjusted to assess his surroundings, sounds, like a million whispered thoughts, rushed at him, clouded his head like a swarm of bees. It descended on him so fast, so quick, he dropped a foot behind her to catch his balance, then, the sounds receded, moving back to a light hiss he could barely hear.

"What's wrong?" Magdelene asked. "You okay?"

He nodded, peered around at the tidy room. There was not an item out of place.

Furniture stood stoically against walls, like sentries guarding a treasure. Tabletops gleamed with polish. He tried to listen to the sounds that had assaulted him, but now it sounded more like the gas hissing through a stove pilot.

He had expected the room to be more scattershot, based upon his limited knowledge and the presumptions he developed. He was unsettled. Both by the voices that had come at him when he first entered, and also by the fact that there were no pictures or books lining the shelves of the console that stood along the longest wall in the room.

"He got picked up for indecent exposure."

Eden shook his head. "He. What?"

Magdelene agitatedly grabbed a pack of cigarettes from the table, along with a lighter. She offered the pack to

Eden, who shook his head.

"You know he's bipolar?"

Eden nodded. "He told me."

"He's been sick his whole life. So he does things that get him in trouble. That's why I keep him home. He was at the library and apparently someone said he was seen in the elevators or the bathrooms or something."

Eden thought back to the men's room at the library. The haunted eyes of lonely white men. The stalking pseudo security guard.

"Well, was it the elevator, or was it the bathroom. Those are two different scenarios."

"Does it matter? So he was home and the police came here, told me they had a warrant for his arrest. I asked them if they could let me drive him to the jail. I promised I would. I didn't want them taking him out of here in handcuffs, putting him in a squad car with all these prying eyes watching, laughing at him. Thank God they let me have that one grace."

"It matters because the bathroom there has long been a meeting place for men. So if he was seen there it's a different thing than if he was in the elevator."

Magdelene looked at him quizzically, laughed. "They're both against the law. This is why I try to keep him from running around with strange men."

Eden bristled, "Just because you don't know them doesn't mean that he 'runs around with strange men.'"

"Listen. You don't know my son. I do. And I know what he does during manic phases. He has no discretion. He's not aware of half the shit he does when he's like that."

"I wouldn't deny that you know your son, but if he's gay then it might be confusing to you when . . ."

"He's not gay. He's confused."

Eden laughed. "Confused about what?"

Magdelene ignored the question. She didn't want to get into a debate with this man who might be able to help her get Bowie out of jail.

"I told the police about his mental health diagnosis. I was hoping they'd let him go."

Eden nodded, looked around. "I would think you get a fine for that sort of thing, not jail time. Unless there were minors involved."

Magdelene blew out a tuft of smoke, motioned for Eden to sit, he declined.

"No. Nobody else was mentioned. But there's a bail of twenty thousand dollars to get him out. And I don't have that kind of money. I'm a working parent with lots of bills . . . ." She looked at him.

Eden thought it odd that this woman called herself a working parent when her child was over thirty years old. "I don't have that kind of money!"

"We only need ten percent, so that's two thousand. I've asked around, my mother, she owns this house, she has plenty of money, but she's never liked Bowie, she refuses to help. I asked around to all our friends, the people we play cards with. They've taken up a collection. So I got one hundred dollars."

During the course of the conversation, Eden's vision had grown dim. He slowly closed his eyes and refocused them. He had been subconsciously ignoring it, the thing standing in the corner, growing from a pinprick to the size of a grapefruit, but now he could see it there, up in the corner, close to the ceiling, shimmering with a dark pearlescence.

He looked at Magdelene with new knowledge. He looked from her to the shimmer, trying to make her see that he saw it there, but she continued talking, oblivious. He backed toward the door, feeling behind him for the knob. "Sorry, I don't have it. I can't help." He opened the door and swiftly turned to the outside, closing the door as the voices once more surged.

Bowie stood waiting for the rest of his belongings, practically vibrating with the urge to move. He could feel it in his feet, like pinpricks stabbing at his undersoles. His desire bounced off the concrete walls, pinging from concrete to human. Even the guards were able to feel it.

Magdelene's desire was as palpable as her son's. She stood amongst the lockers in the narrow entryway, smoking like her life depended on it, pacing in a tight oblong pattern, her ballet flats smacking the floor in a tense staccato. The uniformed people stood behind the glass bubble, staring amusedly at the woman talking to herself in a low, graveled voice, gesticulating between tufts of expelled smoke.

Eden sat in his red jeep, or rather his father's red jeep, looking for the hundredth time at the judicial paperwork in his hands. He hadn't wanted to come, but Magdelene insisted that he needed to be present as the signatory that was accepting responsibility for Bowie's release. He hadn't really thought about the ramifications of posting bail.

He read the documents in his trembling hands. If the individual did not show for the appointed court date, if the individual absconded the jurisdiction, or in any other way failed to adhere to the rules stipulated by the court, including Behavioral Health Court and pending mental health treatment, Eden would lose his money, and, at least according to these documents, would be held responsible.

Magdelene had swished his misgivings away, waving away the smoke she blew into his face with it. "Don't pay no mind to that bullshit. Just legal mumbo jumbo to try to scare you. Besides, you can best believe we going to make sure to get Bowie to that partial program. It will keep him off the streets while I'm at work, and he will be in a safe place. And that's a goddamn good thing."

"Why does he need to be off the streets?" Eden asked. "If that's the case, he might as well stay where he is."

"Hush your mouth. He don't need to be in that place, with all those criminals and degenerates, treated like an animal. I'm just trying to keep him safe."

Eden folded the papers and put them back in the envelope, along with the receipt for two thousand dollars that had been provided by the screw-faced clerk at the county courthouse.

He watched Bowie and Magdelene walk out from the low, ugly building. Bowie was hop-skipping, practically bouncing along the tarmac, clutching a brown shopping bag to his chest. Magdelene held onto the back of his shirt collar holding him back from a full sprint.

Eden tried to mute the big smile he felt pulling the muscles in his face as he saw him approach, saw the joy spring to his eyes as soon as he spotted Eden's car. He wanted to keep things subdued in front of Magdelene, but he couldn't hide how joyous he felt just seeing Bowie's face.

Eden got out of the car and opened the hatch for Bowie's belongings. Bowie rushed into him, wrapping his sinewy arms around his waist. "Hey young head, what you doing here?"

Eden hugged him back, briefly, before gently pushing him back, sizing him up. "Hi, pumpkin. We gotta stop meeting like this."

"Huh?"

Magdelene placed a hand on Bowie's shoulder, guided him toward the back door. "Stop putting on a show out here, y'all can talk in the car."

Bowie hopped in the back, then leaned excitedly forward, his elbows on the headrest in front, jabbing at the back of Magdelene's head as she climbed in.

Eden couldn't stop looking at him. It was like he was some sort of diamond that he had freshly mined. Even while he steered the car out of the parking lot, his eyes were drawn to the rearview mirror, watching Bowie bounce around in the seat. "What you come here, for, though, for real? I didn't expect to see you."

"I came to bring you home—"

Magdelene cut him off. "I asked him to drive me up, to help me out. You know I don't like talking to these educated motherfuckers, acting like they know everything. I like having somebody else do all the talking."

"I look stupid to you, huh. Eden paid the bail, didn't you?"

Eden nodded, drove through the gates out onto the road.

"Why didn't you use my money? I know you cashed my check."

Magdelene's voice grew strident. "Don't start cutting up already, hear? We can turn right around and head back to the jail if you think I'm going to put up with any nonsense."

Bowie spoke quietly, sat back against the seat with a huff. "It's okay. I know you had to pay the bills while I was up here, right? I'm not mad about it."

Magdelene cranked down the window and reached into her bag for her cigarettes. "Do you know how stressful all this has been? Worrying about you up in that place, you not calling. I didn't know if you were dead or alive."

Bowie reached out and squeezed Eden's shoulder. "I'm going to pay you back soon as I get my next check. I promise you, buddy. Thank you for thinking about me."

Eden patted his hand. "I know you will."

Magdelene said, "No thanks to me? If it wasn't for me asking, and going around collecting money from our friends, we never would have been able to get you out."

Bowie glared at the back of her head. Said nothing. He sat back, closed his eyes, wrapped his arms around himself.

"Drop me off at the church."

Eden said, "What?"

"I need to go to church. Take me to New Hope."

Magdelene said, "You need to go home and rest."

"You heard what I said. I'll come home after."

"You promise? Don't make me go around looking for you. My nerves ..."

Eden had expected, needed Bowie to come home with him. He hadn't known how he was going to pose the question in front of Magdelene. His heart sagged. "Where's New Hope?"

A dark finger jabbed out past Eden's head. "Turn here!"

Bowie seemed to jump out of the car before it even came to a full stop. There were people standing outside of a low-slung brick building, milling about.

"Look who's here. It's Shouting John."

People laughed. Some clapped his back as he moved past. Eden watched them, saw Magdelene wave knowingly at a few people. While some of the laughter seemed to be in goodwill, the laughter seemed too strident. The smiles too earnest. Bowie raced into the inner sanctum barely acknowledging anyone.

"He's okay here?"

Magdelene nodded. "You can take me home, around the corner. This is the only place I know Bowie's safe. When he goes to church, he can stay there all day. Or to bingo. He's not going to get into no trouble when he's at those places. Ever since he was five years old, he would go running off to church all by himself."

"A little boy all by himself on the streets?"

"It was just around the corner from our house. He was

fine."

"But now he's not?"

"He wasn't sick then. You might think of me as an overbearing parent. But you try losing a child. When Bowie's brother died, it was like we all just fell apart. I just wanted to keep him safe."

"Sorry to hear that. What did he die from?"

"Oh, it's not important." Magdelene reached out and turned up the volume of the radio.

Just then, "Golden Years" began to play.

"I guess you like this song."

"Why you say that?"

"I take it you're a fan. You named Bowie after him, right?"

Magdelene heaved out a tuft of smoke. "I named him after the pain. He ripped out my uterus like a fucking bowie knife when he was born."

She watched the impact her words had on him: His posture straightened, and his eyes peered at the road ahead. "And he's been causing me pain ever since."

Eden drove up the hill toward Maple Leaf Street.

"About the bail money . . ."

"What about it? Bowie said he'd pay you back. He's very honest when it comes to stuff like that. He will definite-ly pay you."

"Oh, I believe him. But you said you had collected money from some of your friends."

"Those motherfuckers are no friends of mine. People

we played cards with, is all. They been laughing behind our back for years. Making fun of my kid. Yeah, it's a big joke."

"Well if you could give me what you collected, I can use that as the first repayment to my credit card."

"Oh you want that money? Well, it's only a hundred dollars. But you can have it, if you really think you need it. I just have to go in and get it. It's mostly nickels and quarters. I couldn't haul that around. It's in my drawer."

He stared at her. "Nickels . . . and . . ."

"Unless somebody came in and took it from my stash." She opened the door in front of the house. "Sit tight."

"Uhm, you know what? Let's just forget about it."

"You sure? It's no problem."

"No, I'm good. When Bowie gets home can you ask him to give me a call? Just so I know he's safe."

She smiled at him as she slammed the door. "You know I surely will. Later."

Bowie did not hear much of what the pastor preached. The booming voice bounced off the cavernous concrete walls with echoes that troubled his senses. Bowie ignored the collection plate each of the three times it was circulated through the pews. He ignored the calculated eyes watching to discern whether he added to the piles of cash crumpled tumultuously in the carved teak bowl and the eyes making sure that he did not remove any.

But when the organist primed her instrument in preparation, when the choir rose from their seats, Bowie's hands were a thunderclap heard above the jubilation. His off-key voice rode alongside the baritones, the altos and sopranos. His feet stomped the frayed carpet louder than the other foot stomps. His tongue spoke a language both unintelligible and known from a time before man spoke in words. With his head thrust back and his throat open wide, he yelled to his God and exhibited his gratefulness with such rapture that he could feel the approval of every congregant wash over him like a wave.

Wrists agitated wooden, handheld fans that dried the

sweat that burst from his pores. White-gloved hands guided and caressed him, keeping him safe when he flung himself to the floor.

Women patted his shoulders and soothed his brow. The pastor praised his fealty, admonished those that were less demonstrative, scolded the timid and the shy, demanded the righteous show themselves; come forward and be known. The congregation shouted loud and strong. The church said God is good. The church said Amen.

After a weekend of nonstop church worship, line dancing, card games and sex, Bowie arrived for his first day of partial inpatient hospitalization. The Mockingbird Partial Program sat on the dilapidated grounds of the once grand state hospital. In the nineteenth century, the sprawling campus had been known as the state-of-the-art solution for those suffering mental maladies. It had also been an invaluable resource of revenue for the state, as patients had, at that time, been expected to earn their keep with the contribution of labor in exchange for housing and treatment.

The hospital had boasted a profitable slaughterhouse, pig and dairy farms, and garment factories. Those who were unable to work in those facilities (read: colored people), were hired out to work on maintaining the railroad tracks and bridges.

When America desired to become more humane, following the mirror held up to their faces by the atrocities of eugenics and the Holocaust, the state began to shutter many of the buildings, focusing more exclusively on a talk therapy treatment model rather than compulsory labor and segregation. All but the most severely chronic and the criminally insane were moved out, farmed out into community living arrangements. The once glorious buildings faded to rot.

The state, always cognizant of opportunities to replenish its coffers, rented out the vacant buildings to nonprofit social organizations.

Mockingbird was the only facility in the county that treated men with sexual compulsions of a criminal nature. It also provided residential services for those whose challenges were so severe that they were no longer permitted in the general population. It would have been preferable to some that those men languish in the prisons so that decent tax paying citizens would remain safe, but alas, even the most criminal among them eventually served out the time of their respective sentences.

Mockingbird was a set of two hulking, interconnected bi-level buildings that sat behind a fence that was locked by the grounds keeper each day at five p.m. promptly. One of the brick buildings sat more to the front, with an elegant gray canopy boasting a logo of a burgundy bird in flight, flapping above a flat, gray metal door. That building housed the partial program. The other building housed the residential program, for those forbidden community tenancy by legal decree. That building sat behind a matte green dumpster and a high wooden fence. The only part of the residential building visible from the road was its steeped, burgundy roof.

Access to both facilities was permitted solely through the door beneath the gray/burgundy canopy. Two black, chipped speaker boxes sat beside the door. Written in black marker next to two white buttons, one beneath the other, was "Mockingbird One" and "Mockingbird Two." Not knowing which one to push, Bowie pushed both buttons. He waited in the cold.

Looking out over the hilly campus, he could see the large, red-bricked square of the inpatient facility. He glared at it, cursing, grabbed the cigarette from Magdelene's hand through the car window where she sat, inhaling. Magdelene grabbed it back, cursing.

"Why the fuck they take so long to answer. I got to be to work."

A voice squawked on the box, "Mockingbird."

Bowie put his lips to the box. "It's me, Bowie Long. Reporting for programming."

"Stop being a smart ass," Magdelene rasped, "and get your mouth off that filthy box, for you get AIDS or lice or something."

After much waiting, the box squawked again. He recognized the voice, clipped and clearly enunciative. It was Lola Dopinger, the woman who had come to the prison to ask him a whole lot of questions he didn't want to answer.

"This program starts at eight a.m. It is now ten. You have been marked as absent without leave, which will be reported to your probation officer."

"Huh?"

Magdelene climbed from the car, mashed the button. She cursed during the lull before someone answered. "He was scheduled to get his Abilify shot at the outpatient program today. So he had to wait for that."

"He is late. That is an excuse." The voice was smooth, like a tumbler of cognac with no ice.

Magdelene struggled to control her temper. Bowie watched her lips, determined what was going on by her facial expression. "How is it an excuse when this program stipulated that he had to get this shot as part of treatment? *And* that he was not to show up for programming *unless* he received the shot, and that he had proof that he got the shot? What you expect us to do, get the shot when the place ain't open? I took him to get his shot, and we had to wait around for the nurse to order the shit and give it to him, and as soon as we got done I brought him here. Now I got to go to work, and I don't have time for this bullshit, so what y'all going to do?"

There was silence. Magdelene stood staring at the box. Bowie stood staring at Magdelene.

"What she talking about?" he asked.

"That bitch talking about you late and she's calling the PO. How the fuck you late when you had to get your meds, and they said you can't even come to this place unless you showed evidence that you got this shot?"

Bowie rubbed his ass. "That shit hurt, too."

"Don't be a pussy." Magdelene flicked her cigarette butt across the lot to a thatch of brown grass.

They both looked as the door opened. Lola was tall and copper colored. She had straight, black hair loping over broad shoulders. Her features were strong: broad angular cheekbones and a square jawline. Magdelene gauged Native American ancestry. She reminded her of that old seventies antilittering commercial where the wizened, old Indian in feathered headdress cries a solitary tear at the oblivious white family tossing trash out of their station wagon.

Lola, too, sized her up. She was lean, like beef jerky, and just as stringy, with eyes that glittered like volcanic rock, and a grim line of a lip. The texture of her wig at odds with her complexion. She also noticed Bowie watching the woman intensely.

"Hello, I'm going to be Bowie's principal therapist, Lola Dopinger."

Magdelene looked at the woman's extended hand as if a rat had just crawled from a hole. "Yeah. Well. Bowie, show them the slip that nurse from Northwest gave you. You people expect miracles, you know. How is he even supposed to get here that early every day when the bus don't come out here."

Lola took the paper Bowie held out to her, spoke slowly while reading the slip. "That is a dilemma that Bowie needs to figure out. All I know is that it is stipulated by Behavioral Health Court that he get here by that time each day, and if he fails to do that I am required to report that."

"Y'all sound crazier than Bowie."

Lola looked at Bowie. "I will also need to have a copy of all other medications that have been prescribed. Do you have that?"

Bowie nodded, reached into his back pocket and retrieved the folded papers. "I can walk here. No problem."

Lola nodded. "I will let you in this time, but you need to keep in mind that your outside obligations have no bearing on the requirements of this program."

Magdelene said, "Look, can we talk inside, rather than standing out here for all the world to see and hear?"

"That sounds like a good idea. I'd like to get some historical information from you so that I can add that to Bowie's paperwork."

"Oh no. I don't have time for that. I have to get to work. Can you call me for that some other time?"

Lola looked from mother to son, then back. Magdelene was already walking back to her car.

"She needs you to give her some information!" Bowie shouted.

Magdelene waved him off. "I'm not the one in the hospital, you are. You give her the information."

"You come back here! I don't know anything."

"Don't worry about it," Lola said. "Whatever you don't know, I can get from her later by phone."

As the car pulled past, Bowie shouted, "Get your bald-head ass back here!"

"Hey! That talk is unacceptable! You don't disrespect your mother like that."

"Well, when she starts acting respectable, I'll show her respect."

Bowie saw the shift in her features. Identified the move from layperson to therapist. It made his stomach churn with disgust.

"Why do you feel your mother is undeserving of respect?"

He put his hands on his hips, glared at her. "Did you see the way she just treated you? You think that's okay for her, right? Because she's a regular person. Or because she gets a pass for having a crazy kid, right, so she's under a lot of stress? But what about the stress that she puts me under? I don't get to show that because when I do, it gets a category from the DSM, right?"

"That's not it at all, Bowie. Our parents deserve our respect."

"No? So you not thinking I'm 'labile,' or maybe intermittently 'explosive?'" Bowie laughed at her.

"Don't be a smart ass. You know where smart asses end up? They end up back in jail." Lola grabbed the lanyard around her throat, unlocked the door and waved him toward the dark interior.

"Yeah. I know they do. No opinions outside what gets put in the treatment plan allowed, right?"

"Listen. You can either make this a hard stay or you can make it an easy one. That is entirely on you. Your probation officer will be given a summary of your level of cooperation each and every week. So you decide how you want this to go." She grabbed his shoulder and directed (read: pushed) him inside. "Welcome to your first day at Mockingbird."

Bowie followed Lola Dopinger up the dark staircase to a large, metal door that had to be opened with a key. The door opened to a cafeteria, where heavy wooden chairs surrounded about eight round wooden tables. The smell of fried food lured him in.

"Smells good in here," he said.

Lola kept walking, her voice floating above her shoulders. "The meals here are for residents only. You need to bring your own lunch from home."

"What you say?"

Lola unlocked another door, which opened onto a large cement-blocked room that echoed many voices. "This is our dayroom. Most of the time between group sessions will be spent here, where you can socialize with the other members. We have morning group from ten to eleven thirty, then lunch until one, and then afternoon group until two thirty. You will meet with me on Fridays for individual therapy. We will work on creating your treatment plan at that time and discuss your progress with meeting your treatment plan objectives."

There was a smaller room set off in a corner, where

women stood leaning on the wall looking at their cell phone screens. Lola walked him over to the room. There was a handful of men watching a television screen playing *Back to the Future.*

Lola pointed to an empty chair. "Since you arrived too late for this morning's group, you can watch a movie."

A short, plump girl with cherry red hair and ebony skin put her hands on her hips, gnashing Hubba Bubba between her teeth.

"Hey, Bowie. What you doing here?"

Bowie grinned and gave the girl an effusive hug, before Lola's hand grabbed his shoulder, pulling him back.

"There is no bodily contact here. Ever. With either participants or employees. Sheena, you know this."

Bowie said, "You work here, Sheena?"

The girl rolled her eyes at Lola. "What you think, fool? I sure ain't here for treatment. This a men's only facility."

Lola said, "Well, I see you know someone here, so I'll leave you to get oriented by the floor staff. I will see you on Friday."

"How long you worked here?" Bowie asked.

"About a year."

"They pay good?"

The girl sucked her teeth so hard her very large breasts shook in their cloth containment. "Shit. What you think?"

"Guess you get enough for them casinos and Miss Pitty's card game, though, huh?" He laughed and clapped, loud and thunderous. The male staff shouted out in protest, told him to keep it down.

Sheena whispered, "Shit, I don't do those card games no more. You sit around all motherfucking day waiting for a seat at the table. By the time you get to play, you ready to go home. Fuck that."

"When you going to the casino? I can go with you."

"Listen, you can't have any contact with people that work at Mockingbird outside of the program. Immediate termination. Now, get in there and watch that movie. We'll talk afterwards."

"You do therapy sessions?"

Sheena shook her head. "Do I look like a therapist to you? I'm floor staff. We make sure everybody stays out of trouble. Goes where they supposed to go. Hell, I don't really work up here in partial. I work residential in the evenings, but they always need extra staff up here during the day, so I do it for the overtime."

He nodded. "You making that big OT money. I see you."

Sheena brushed a stray strand of hair from her face, looked around furtively, then whispered, "I don't know why you even here. You know what kind of people they take care of in here?"

Though Mockingbird's marketing materials described the facility as "providing services for adults with disabilities who do not fit into existing forensic or behavioral health care services for improved community function," locals knew it was a place to keep the child molesters, serial rapists, and pedophiles where they would not be seen. Improved community function sounded great to the few family members that continued to have minimal involvement, but the reality was that the men that were in treatment were not taken into the community except with one-on-one staff supervision for medical appointments. Most of the men here, particularly the men that had been remanded to residential treatment, were only permitted to leave the grounds for funerals, preferably their own.

Treatment modalities were created with a focus on modifying challenging behaviors of a sexual nature. But the reality was that modification was not elimination. Therefore community functioning was not a likely outcome for most.

Bowie's entry into a room of pedophiles, paraphilics, and predators was like the detonation of a bomb. Bowie felt those eyes watch him in the dark. He felt the heat of their stares. The room grew entropic with their unspoken desires.

The staff monitoring the room felt it, too, though they were not consciously aware of what exactly had shifted in the room.

"Eyes on the movie," someone shouted.

Bowie sat in the dark, deliberately ignoring the hooded attention, struggling to hear the sounds that came from the TV. He heard nothing but deverbalized sound.

As he sat there, his phone vibrated in his pocket. He looked at the screen, ended the call. Seconds later, the phone shook again. He sent it to voicemail.

He sat in the darkness. The shadows and light moving

around him reminded him of sitting at home watching TV when he was a kid, unable to hear what the actors were saying, being forced to watch anyway. Looking at the screen in the darkness, paying close attention to the white faces with their happy expressions. Ignoring the adult hands creeping along his legs, loosening his pajamas, cupping his genitals.

The phone in his pocket shook briefly. A text.

okay. play your games if you want to. I got something for your ass. you think you're too good to pick up the phone now then don't call me when you need me to come pick your black ass up.

He blackened the screen, put the phone back in his pocket. It shook again.

You don't have to answer the phone. Just send me a text that you're okay so I know that you're still at the program and you're not in trouble so I can rest my nerves.

Bowie tried to ignore the phone. Just like he tried to ignore the man sitting beside him, staring intently, rubbing his groin and making a low growl in his throat. The man stretched his legs out in front of him, looked down at Bowie's feet swinging above the floor, saw his bare ankle flash above the rim of his shoe. The glow of light on Bowie's ankle sent an erotic charge through the man's brain.

Bowie saw the lump of arousal rise in the man's tan chinos. He felt a sense of power. He was the reason the man's dick had gotten hard. He had created that. He also felt a bump to his memory: his younger self sitting in the darkened room, watching but not watching the TV, the hand taking his hand and placing it inside an unzipped fly, onto heat and flesh.

Bowie reached inside his pants and began to touch himself. He leaned his head back, his eyes unfocused. The man next to him quickly sat up. "Hey! What you doing!"

Sheena walked through the line of chairs, saw Bowie shuffling in his chair. She tapped his shoulder. "Come take a walk with me."

He followed her swaying hips out of the darkness into the disparate sounds of the dayroom. "Where we going?"

"Let me show you around," she said.

They walked into a hallway of aged, tiled walls, past wooden doors with glass panels that reminded him of classrooms at the old elementary school. He sniffed at the damp smell.

"This place smells old and musty. Just like the crazy house."

Sheena opened a door, walked him inside. This room was painted a forest green. The windows were high along the wall. There was an old, leather sofa at the far end, above which sat a landscape painting that looked exactly like the paintings that lined the walls at the psychiatric hospital.

"That painting looks just like the ones at the crazy house, too. Did Dr. Herrera paint that?"

Sheena turned to him, hands on her hips. "You keep mentioning the crazy house. Sounds like you miss it."

He frowned. "Why would I miss that place? It's terrible there. Stinking. Unwashed bums."

"Well if you keep doing the dumb shit like you was

about to do in that movie room, you can best believe that's where these white folks will be taking you. What the hell's wrong with you?"

Bowie sulked, crossed his arms defensively. "He started up with me."

"Why you think he here? He's in treatment. And he ain't never getting out. Do you want that to be your life? While you here, you got to toe the line, do what they tell you. Number one: Don't ever do anything of a sexual nature here. If you do, you'll be in this place forever. Now, you see this here room? This the green room."

He looked around, at the green walls. "No shit."

She punched him in the arm. "Stop being a smart ass and listen." Sheena walked out into the hall and showed him the therapy rooms that lined the hallway. "The green room is a smaller room you can go to when too much is going on in the dayroom. You can go there if somebody is triggering you."

"Trigger? I'm a gun, now?"

"See, that's why you in here now. You got all that mouth and you don't want to listen to nobody. Sometimes, when we bump heads with somebody, or we see something that makes us do something and we don't know why, other people's behavior reminds us of some shit that we went through before. That's a trigger."

Bowie thought back to the movie room. He nodded. "I don't like sitting in the dark. Especially with a bunch of people I don't know."

Sheena huffed exaggeratedly. "You sit in them card games in the dark all damn night and you ain't one bit bothered by it, so how's this any different?"

"Card games ain't dark. If they dark, how you going to see your hand? Plus, they mostly women."

They walked back out to the dayroom. By this time, people were drifting out from the movie room. Staff were grouped together talking while the patients drifted out individually.

Sheena said, "So you don't like sitting in a room full of men?"

Bowie laughed. "I don't have no problems with a man. What I want with these raggedy motherfuckers? I got me a real man, a whole man on the outside waiting for me."

"Hold up. You go that way?"

"Huh? What way? Where you want me to go now?"

She huffed, annoyed. "No. You …" she whispered, "gay?"

He laughed. "What you whispering for?"

Another voice chimed in, "That was hardly a whisper. And if you gay, you need to sit down right over here and let me give you the REAL tour."

They both looked over at the pudgy Black man sitting with his legs crossed at a table. He was holding an empty cigarette holder in one hand, and flinging a scarf over his shoulder with his other. A large staff person leaned causally against the wall a few steps away, watching him between scrolls on his phone.

Sheena said, "What I tell you about eavesdropping on

other folks' convo, Jose?" She looked to the staff person manning his phone. "Raheem, get your client."

Raheem smiled briefly then went back to his phone.

Jose stood from the chair. He was taller than Bowie had expected him to be. He wore a wool cap rolled low on his forehead, despite the oppressive, institutional heat blasting through the decaying vents. Mascara faded down from drooped eyelids. He reached out a hand toward Bowie, who tentatively reached to take it. In a flash, Raheem strode over and stood in between the outstretched hands.

"You know the rules. No touching."

The man sucked his teeth. "Come on with the theatrics, Raheem. What you think? I'm a just start in sucking his dick right out the gate?"

Sheena gently pushed his hand down to his side. "Knowing you, you might."

"Honey, ain't no secrets up in this place, and you know it. Fuck what you heard about HIPAA and privacy rights. My name is Jose Bueno. But they call me NoBueno around here."

Raheem laughed. "Cause you ain't no good."

NoBueno laughed. "Keep fucking with me. You know how many one on ones I done ran through up in here? You can be the next."

"What they call you?" He asked, looking at Bowie. "You so cute, you like a little doll, so petite and tiny."

"I'm Bowie."

NoBueno flung an arm out toward the round table

where no one was sitting but him. "Well you just sit right down, Bowie, and let me tell you all you need to know about Miss Mockingbird."

By this time, Sheena had gravitated toward two staff members that stood laughing at some tweet on their phone, and Raheem had gone back to leaning against the wall with his phone.

"You Puerto Rican?" Bowie asked.

"No, darling. I'm full-blown nigger, just like you. Sit. Sit."

NoBueno watched him, his eyes glittering like stars. "What you here for?"

"Taking my dick out at the library."

NoBueno reared back, a hand to his chest. "Oh my! How dramatic! Why would you do that?"

"Huh?" Bowie shrugged. "Somebody wanted to see it."

"Oh? Is it that simple? It's available for viewing simply by request?"

"What?"

NoBueno breathed exaggeratedly. "Darling, if you're going to just let any old body see it, you should at least monetize the endeavor."

"What?"

"Charge a few coin. Get pizzaid."

Bowie laughed. "I ain't no prostitute."

"But you are, darling. We are all prostitutes. Anyway, what do you do? What do you like?"

"I just told you, I'm gay. I like men. Don't you like men?"

NoBueno shook his head frustratedly. "No, no. I don't mean that. And by the way, yes, I'm gay all day. I mean what do you like to do. I mean when you are not flinging your private regions out into the ether for all and sundry to behold."

Bowie shrugged. "Nothing."

"What do you mean?"

"I don't like to do nothing. Oh, I like to play cards. And go to the casino. And I like bingo. Do you play bingo?"

"Jesus no. I like to sing." Just then, NoBueno broke into a powerhouse refrain of "Free Yourself" by Fantasia. What he lacked in melody, he made up for in volume.

Raheem didn't even look up from his screen. "All right, kill all that noise, man."

NoBueno piped down. "As you can see, the staff here are not just intent on stifling our physical empowerment, but our creative ones as well. So I have to be satisfied with listening to music on the radio."

He pulled out a transistor radio from his pocket and turned on the volume. Bowie jumped up. "Hey! That's my song!" Bowie began to gyrate his hips to "Red Nose," singing along just as off key as NoBueno had a moment before.

Bowie spun in a circle, tucked his fingers into his waistband and thrust his hips. NoBueno laughed gleefully, clapping his hands, extending them toward Bowie in encouragement.

Other patients, curious about the commotion, began to drift over, some laughing, a few pointing and clapping. Bowie noticed the attention, began to dance more animatedly. After spinning, he flung himself to the floor and did a push up, grinding his hips toward the linoleum before leaping back up and bending backward, stretching his lean arms toward the fluorescents above.

He arched his back and bucked his knees in a marching motion, closing his eyes in private glee. He clapped loud and thunderous, the sound reverberating off the far walls. People pointed. Men nodded their heads in appreciation. They began to chant, "Fancy Feet, Fancy Feet."

Older men remembered their younger selves, their lives before Mockingbird, when they danced in bars, on street corners, at house parties in dank basements and dimly lit cabarets. Remembered blue lights in tight spaces, the perfumed smell of a soft neck, the laugher of a special woman, the curve of a breast, the caress of soft hands. Bowie's rapidly moving feet also brought to mind storefront houses of worship, where they had gone faithfully on the mornings after cabaret. Where their shouts to God, their dances of praise were just as loud, just as fervorous as their nighttime revelry. The dancing boy tugged something deep in them, reminding them of a time when they had been free, when they had been in charge of the direction of their lives.

"Look at Fancy Feet go!"

"I used to dance just like that."

"Man, when you ever move like that?"

Bowie arched back to the floor, flung himself there, swayed his hips until the music suddenly stopped.

Lola Dopinger stood in front of him fuming, her arms

crossed tightly across her chest. "Get up from there right now."

Bowie sat up, the swift shift from effusion to disapproval leaving him dazed. He looked at her, not understanding her look of displeasure.

"You come with me. The rest of you get back to your areas."

B owie followed Lola down the dark corridor to the last
door on the end. He followed her pointing finger toward
the chair positioned opposite a desk, jumping slightly as she
slammed the door behind him. Her heels clicked sternly
on the tiled floor as she crossed to sit at the chair behind
the desk. He watched her, slouching down in his seat as she
peered at him.

She steepled her fingers in front of her, waiting a beat
before speaking.

"This is a very serious program, you know. And you are
remanded to this program for a very serious problem."

"What?"

She huffed. "I'm sure you know what the problem is.
We discussed this when you were incarcerated."

Bowie tilted his ear toward her, watching her mouth
to better understand her words. "You came to see me when
I was in jail?"

Lola tapped the desk with a pen, agitated. "You know
full well that I conducted an assessment of you at the prison, Bowie. You playing these games will not lead to a good

outcome for you here. Do you understand that? This is a program for men who have gotten into serious trouble from displays of sexually inappropriate behavior. And yet, here you are dancing in a sexually provocative manner. On the first day, you are already troubling the waters here . . . ."

"What's prov—what did you say I was dancing?"

"This is not a game, Bowie. You know full well what you were doing. That behavior will not be tolerated here."

"I didn't do nothing."

"Okay. Just like you didn't do anything at the public library. You took your dick out in a public place and you were caught masturbating there."

Bowie lunged from his chair, thrusting his face toward her, his hands splayed on the desk. "That's a fucking lie! I wasn't masturbating."

Lola swept her hair back, stood up and thrust her head back at him, speaking in a loud voice. "Sit your ass down. Now."

Bowie continued to stand, but moved back a bit, surprised that she did not back down.

"I wasn't masturbating. That's a lie."

Lola crossed her arms over her chest. "One of the first requirements for consideration of discharge here is that you need to acknowledge the crime for which you've been charged. Until you do that, you are considered unwilling to face up to your problem. So you go on and continue to deny things. All it means is that you will be with us for a long, long time."

"I took my dick out. I said that. I didn't masturbate."

"I told you to sit down."

He smirked at her. "What if I don't?"

She picked up the phone, shrugged. "No problem. I can always call your PO. Maybe you need to spend a little more time in jail. Is that it?"

He watched her, his jaw thrust out angrily, then slowly sat in the chair.

She grinned victoriously, sitting as well. "Let me get something straight with you, I'm not scared of you, and I am not impressed with your little bullshit games of intimidation. I have been in this game for a long time, and I know every stunt before you can even think of it. So you can either go along to get along or you can sit your black ass in jail like those white folks want you to. The choice is yours."

Lola stood and walked around the desk, sitting on the edge in front of him. "Provocative dancing is not acceptable behavior here."

"What's provocative?"

Lola didn't understand that he was asking for an explanation of the word. She thought Bowie was asking for an explanation of what sorts of dancing were considered provocative. "What you were doing."

He shrugged. "Okay. You going to tell my PO?"

"I have an obligation to report your progress or lack thereof to the courts. That is part of the agreement for your participation in this program and Behavioral Health Court. All information will be reported to the courts so the judge can determine if your course of treatment is helping."

"So I'm going back to jail for dancing."

"I don't make those determinations. Your PO does."

"I'm doing what I'm supposed to. I'm taking my meds. I get that shot even though I don't like it. Even though I told the doctor how it makes me feel."

"How does it make you feel?"

He hesitated, struggling to find the words. "I . . . I don't know how to say it."

"Just say that shit. You don't have to be eloquent."

"Huh?"

She looked at him, waiting.

"After I get the shot, all I think about is my dick. Beating my dick. And I can't get no privacy at home unless my mom is out at the casinos spending all my money."

Lola shook her head. "You have it backward, Bowie. The medication is what helps you to *stop* with compulsions to masturbate. It's going to help you with your urges."

"Come? What?"

"Compulsions. Urges. The medication helps so that you won't want to think of sexual things so much."

He shook his head. "No. That's not how it's working."

She stood, tapped his shoulder consolingly, walked to the door and opened it.

"Trust me. You just have to give it time to do what it's supposed to do. You'll see, in time. Now, I need you to go back to the milieu so that I can write up your treatment plan for the judge."

"Who's Millie?"

"The dayroom. You can go back to the dayroom. But that dancing shit—there'd better not be any more of that behavior, if you expect to ever get out of here. Got me?"

He stood and walked past her mumbling, "Got it."

Eden liked going to Movie Tavern because you could order food and cocktails at your seat and be served during the movie. He listened to Bowie's low, steady snoring in the seat beside him, finding comfort there, the same sort of comfort he felt from the steady hum of a fan blowing on him at bedtime. The heat of Bowie's head on his shoulder was also a comfort, hot and heavy. When his snoring began to grow louder, Eden nudged him with his elbow.

Bowie sat up with a snort, whispering apologies, then began to laugh loudly at the screen in places where Eden found no comedy. Eden looked quizzically at him, as he continued laughing, clapping his hands in derision.

"Will you hush," he whispered. "What the hell are you laughing at?"

"Sorry, baby."

As the lights came up, Eden swiftly grabbed at his jacket, rushing Bowie to exit before the full lights came on and people could see who had been laughing so loudly. As he walked toward the doors, Bowie reached for his hand. Eden returned a squeeze as they moved through the crowds.

Outside, Bowie lowered his hand and touched Eden's ass. Eden pushed his hand away. "Are you crazy? Don't touch me like that out here. You want to get us killed?"

"What's the problem? These niggahs know what's up. What's the problem with two gay niggahs holding hands?"

Eden smirked. "Uh. That's not my hand."

Eden couldn't help being overwhelmed with self-consciousness when Bowie displayed affection in public, but he also knew it was part of what he liked about him. Bowie did not seem to care what other people thought, or he was confident enough in his abilities to handle any possible flack they might get if confronted with animosity. "I grew up in a different time. Everybody wasn't as accepting of two men showing affection in public when I was coming up."

"Fuck these niggahs. I'm me."

"But even still, you touching my ass makes me feel like you want these people to think I'm your bitch."

Bowie's brow crinkled, then he grinned. "You are my bitch, bitch. And I'm your bitch, too. Ain't that right?"

Bowie grabbed him at the waist and pulled him close. Eden lost his balance. He held onto Bowie's broad shoulders to keep from falling and leaned into him. He noticed the conflation of self-consciousness and discomfort and fear, but he asked himself what he was fearful of. Being perceived as gay or being a target for violence?

"No, that's not right. Now let me go."

Despite his protestation, Eden felt heat bloom in his groin as Bowie laughed and grabbed him tighter.

"That was a good movie, though. What was it called again?"

Eden laughed. "How would you know when you slept through most of it?"

"Sorry about that, baby. I don't know why I can't stay awake at the movies."

"Probably your meds. What do you take?"

"A whole bunch of shit. Abilify, naltrexone, Depakote . . ."

"It's a wonder you are able to stay awake at all." Eden stopped talking as Bowie's phone began to ring. Bowie grabbed it, sent it to voicemail. "That phone was blowing up all through the movie. Is it your man calling you? You can answer it. I don't have no problems with that . . . ."

"Fuck him. I'm ready to kick his ass to the curb anyway. I got me a new boo." Bowie once more reached out to grab him, but Eden skipped out of his grasp, pushing against his bony chest. Bowie backed up a few paces, laughing.

"I am not your boo."

"What you call it, then?"

"I'm your friend."

"What's the difference?"

"What do you mean what's the difference? You know the difference between a friend and a boyfriend. You got a man, and so do I."

"Ever since I was twelve years old, niggahs been telling me they my friend. And guess what? That always came with them sucking my dick. Not one time did any of my 'friends' not still want to fuck."

Eden shrugged. "I know what you mean. I'm not talking about the pseudonym, though, for fuck buddy."

Bowie laughed loud and long. Eden looked around to see if anyone was staring.

"I love to hear you curse. It sounds funny. Say *fuck* again."

"Uh, no . . ."

"Say *pussy*." Bowie laughed uproariously.

"Get in the car, will you. You're making a spectacle of yourself."

"What? I'm making a what?"

"Will you get your black ass in the car?" Eden smiled despite himself.

Bowie saw him smiling, ran around to his side of the parked car and began to dance, thrusting his hips violently, banging his pelvis against Eden's thigh.

"Come on, baby, shake it like a red nose."

"What are you doing, man? This ain't the club."

"I bring the club wherever I go. Come on, baby."

Eden laughed, grabbed his head. He liked the feel of smoothness and the slight bump at the nape. He kissed the top his head furtively, hugging him, feeling his heat. "Yes, you do, pumpkin. Come on, let's go home."

Bowie understood the words Eden did not say. He looked into his eyes and then ran around to the other side and hopped into the jeep. "Let's do it, then."

Bowie's phone rang. He took it from his pocket, frowning at the face.

"Why this bald-head bitch calling me all night. Fuck. She knows where I'm at."

"Why don't you just answer it, then? Then she can stop calling."

"No, she won't. That won't stop her. She's trying to fuck up my night. She'll call me all night no matter if I answer or not. She knows I got money, so now I'm on her radar."

His text messages began to blink.

okay play your games then see what happens when you come back here i wonder what the p.o. will think when i tell him about you staying out all night running around with men

Bowie sighed, leaned back in his seat. He reached for Eden's hand, squeezed it.

Eden squeezed back. "I still think if you answer it, it would be better than ignoring it. She's worried about you."

"That bitch ain't worried about nothing."

"You always call your mother out like that?"

"What? Bitch? If she don't want to be called bitch, then don't be a bitch, then, BITCH."

Eden tried to hold onto his stern expression but couldn't stop the laughter that erupted in spite of his best efforts. Bowie watched him, began to laugh, too. "I like to see you laugh, baby. It makes me happy."

okay well then fuck you too. and dont be surprised when you come home and see i threw out all your shit on the curb you keep thinking im a joke and we will see who the joke is in the end next time your ass gets thrown in jail you can just rot in there...nobody

*else gives a shit if you stay in jail the rest of your life...all you got
is me and you think you can keep disrespecting me but this is the
last time youre going to get away with it*

"You said you take naltrexone? Isn't that for opiate addiction? They give that to addicts to help them stay clean. You have a drug problem?"

Bowie gave him a crazed look. "I look like a crackhead to you? Fuck no, I don't got no drug problem. Besides, what you know about naltrexone anyway? Are *you* a drug addict?"

Eden laughed. "My Pops used to be. Heroin. Man, he was a beast. He was out there, I'm telling you. When he finally went into treatment they gave him that stuff. Said it does something to the chemical impulse in the brain that gets triggered by the drug and so if you take drugs while you are on it, you get violently sick. Throw up and everything."

"My new therapist put me on it. The psychiatrist at Mockingbird, he's real cool, Dr. Alcatraz, he said that they use it for people with sexual urges, too. Lola says it will help keep me out of trouble."

"I thought your psychiatrist was at Northwest, not at Mockingbird?"

"No. I just go to Northwest for the Abilify. You have to have a nurse give you a shot of Abilify, and Mockingbird don't have no nurses. So I gotta go there for that, and the doctor at Northwest writes the script for that."

"Sounds a little bit confusing to me."

Eden was concentrating on the dark highway, and so he wasn't aware of what Bowie was doing until he heard the telltale sound of a fly being unzipped. He looked over.

"What the hell are you doing?"

Bowie grabbed his hand and pulled it to his exposed crotch. Eden moved his hand back, laid it on his flat belly.

"Put that shit away."

"What's the problem? You don't like me now?"

"We're in public. Wait till we get home."

"This ain't public. This your car." Bowie began to massage himself.

Eden punched at his crotch. "You heard what I said. Are you fucking crazy? With all the shit you're going through I would think you'd give more thought to how you behave out in these streets."

Bowie shrugged, leaned back and pulled his pants down more.

Eden swerved onto the shoulder and slammed on the brakes, tires skidding along the gravel.

"I'm serious, Bowie. These cops out here are just looking for the smallest excuse to give us a criminal record, and you already been got, now you want to bring me along into that shit with you? You better pull your pants up or you can walk the fuck home from here. You must be crazy."

"Yup. You know I am." Bowie hesitantly began to pull up his trousers.

"You know that's not what I'm talking about. Crazy don't mean you have to do dumb shit. Doing stupid shit is a choice. So, yeah, we do tearooms, and we do the parks and all that, but it's still illegal, so when you make the choice to engage in sex in public you know you're taking a chance, and so you have to be extra vigilant. I don't do the baths anymore because I don't have to, and because I don't want to risk my reputation by getting caught. You guys have phone lines and apps now, so you don't even have to do it. Now, these 'experts' got you taking a pill because you got caught in flagrante delicto."

"What are you talking about? I take a bath every day."

"Don't you know about tearooms and bathhouses? Do you know anything about how things used to be?"

"You know I'm clean, baby. Smell me." Bowie pulled Eden's hand toward his crotch. Eden punched him in the chest.

"Cut it the fuck out. I'm driving, here!" Bowie flinched, rubbed his chest. "You ain't have to hit me so hard, babe. I'm sorry you got upset. Let's go home so I can love you."

Eden watched him warily, watched his eyes, which seemed to be bulging from the sockets. He started the car and eased back onto the highway.

They rode in silence for a few minutes, then Bowie switched on the radio, hopping in his seat and turning up the volume. Eden recognized Jill Scott singing "A Long Walk."

"What you know about this song?"

"Huh? Oh, my therapist plays this song during group. It's not a bad old head song. She says this girl's from Philly. Is that true?"

Eden nodded. Then, remembering Bowie's hearing problems, said, "Yes. She's from Philly."

"Lola played this song, and she played some song about loving our hair and our brown skin. She asked me if you and me ever go for walks in the park or go out on a date. She's kinda cool. Even though my mom said she's a bitch."

"Why would she be asking questions about me? How do I factor into therapy sessions?"

"Well she didn't say you, really. This was in group, and we were talking about the ways that people take advantage of other people. And she was asking each of us about how we take advantage of other people."

"Do you take advantage of other people?"

Bowie shook his head. "You should hear those motherfuckers talk. Some of them had sex with kids and all kinds of sick shit. And they say that the kid lied on them. How would a kid lie about something like that? How do kids even know about it unless a grown-up showed them. One of my mom's boyfriends used to try that shit with me. Every time my mom would go to work, he would get me alone in a room, turn off all the lights and tell me to come watch a movie with him. Then he would say to my mom, 'watch out for that boy, he going to turn into a faggot.' And look"—Bowie snorted in derision—"he was right."

"But why are you in a place like that for getting caught with a consenting adult? Is it because of the location? I mean, a library usually has children, so is it sort of the same thing as getting caught selling drugs near a schoolyard—guilty by proximity? This shit sounds so weird to me . . . ."

"Prox, what? I don't know what you talking about. But

you know they always looking for a way to put a Black man in jail."

"Well. If *you* think like that, then isn't it stupid for you to do things that you know will get you put there? I mean, don't you have to take some of the blame for that?"

Bowie reached over and turned the volume even louder as India Arie came onto the radio. "Hey! This that other song Lola always plays. She needs to start playing some rump shaker shit. But she don't like me dancing in there. She called it provocative." He snorted.

Eden turned the volume back down. "Isn't dancing in and of itself provocative? What did you do, get on the pole or something?"

"They like it," he shrugged.

As the jeep veered from the highway onto the circular exit ramp, Eden looked over at Bowie's sharp profile, watched the streetlamps cast shadows upon his blue-tinted skin.

"What's it like? I mean jail. How's it feel in there?"

He shrugged again. "It feels like jail. What you mean how's it feel?"

"Were you scared? That place has people that have done terrible things, right? People that have killed other people. I watched *Oz*, I know about all the raping that happens. Did you have to fight anybody, or did you just give it up?"

Bowie laughed. "Oh you want to know about the get down? I was in the medical unit, so I wasn't really scared like that. And anyway, I grew up with half them niggahs in there, so it was sort of just like being out here. Except you can't leave, and plus they put me in the hole, so then I didn't get to see nobody."

"Hole? Is that solitary confinement?"

"Sol—what?"

"How long were you in there?"

"I was set to be in for twenty-seven days, but then I got discharged."

"Like, you have to get strip searched when you first go in, don't you? So how's that feel? Treating you like an animal. Standing naked in front of some man you don't know. Him looking up your ass . . ."

"Like I said, no different from out here. You get treated the same way out here. Your mom's boyfriend touching you in the dark or the pastor of the church taking you to the back room for private Bible study after church."

"Those things have never happened to me."

Bowie laughed loudly. "You bullshitting, man. It happens to everybody."

They sat in silence for a while, the drone of the radio the only sound. Eden's heart ached.

That night, while they were in bed, he couldn't focus on the constantly shifting demands made by Bowie. He was too immersed in his own thoughts. He couldn't stop thinking about Bowie, sitting in a darkened cell, sitting in the tight confines of solitary confinement, a confused little boy sitting in a blackened living room.

Bowie's phone began to vibrate on the nightstand, its

face glowing indigo in the gray shadows of Eden's bedroom.

While advertising brochures detailed ancillary services such as physical and occupational therapies, job training, resume building, equine therapy, behavioral modification, and a host of other options for treatment, budget cuts had reduced Mockingbird's offerings to individual and group therapies and oversight of medication by a psychiatrist who was only on site two times per week, as he had the obligation of a full-time private practice of his own. Dr. Alcatraz prescribed medications for the residential patients, but only supervised the therapeutic effects of medications prescribed to outpatients. This consisted of sitting with the individual to determine drug efficacy.

Bowie looked at Dr. Alcatraz, who did not look at him, immersed as he was in the documents on the desk in front of him.

"Have you been med compliant?"

Bowie couldn't see the doctor's face. He frowned. "Huh?"

Dr. Alcatraz sighed, exasperated. He had been seeing patients all day and he was tired. "Are you taking your meds?"

"No. Yeah. What you want to know? If I'm taking my meds?" Bowie looked at the doctor, surmising what he meant: "No, I'm not suicidal. No I don't have trouble sleeping. Anything else?"

Dr. Alcatraz made a note: *obstinate.*

"How have you been managing your compulsions? Any problems?"

Bowie stared at him.

A woman with neatly clipped, short hair sat behind him. She looked at the documents in her lap. "There has been a report of possible exposure on day one of treatment and displays of provocative behavior, attention seeking."

Bowie turned his head in the direction of the disjointed words coming from the woman's mouth. He was better able to hear her than Dr. Alcatraz. He had more trouble ascertaining voices in the lower register.

"I don't want her here," he snapped.

"Nafissa is here to help you. She is only reporting clinical information that you might not have yourself."

He snorted. "She's a secretary. How she reporting clinical shit? She ain't no therapist."

"Nafissa is able to relay notes in the absence of your therapist."

"What? I don't know what the fuck you're talking about. Don't I have rights to privacy? I don't know that lady."

Dr. Alcatraz made another note. *Explosive, easily agitated.* "Of course you have rights. As you know. Every patient at Mockingbird has the right to humane treatment."

"So I'm a patient now?"

Dr. Alcatraz continued as though Bowie had not spoken. "Of course, due to your legal status and your obligations to Behavioral Health Court, should you decide you do not wish to comply with our treatment modalities, that can be reported to the judge. We don't force anyone to be here that would prefer to be . . . elsewhere."

The doctor then looked up, held Bowie's attention, waited for Bowie to lower his eyes in acquiescence.

MASTER TREATMENT PLAN

PATIENT: Bowie Long
DOB: 12/25/84

CONDITION FOR DISCHARGE: Absence of sexual inappropriateness

BARRIERS TO DISCHARGE: Sexual acting out

DIAGNOSIS:

Axis I: Impulse Control D/O
Axis II: Sexual Compulsion
Challenge 1: Assaultive to family and masturbating in public
Goal: Free of violence to others and free of public masturbation
Intervention: Individual Counseling
Frequency: Daily
Staff: Psychiatry
Challenge 2: Public masturbation
Goal: Will not masturbate in inappropriate places
Objective: Will comply with prescribed medication
Intervention: Will educate regarding benefits of medication compliance

Staff: Psychiatry (nursing will monitor for side effects)
Intervention: Encourage Bowie to attend groups
daily to work on coping skills regarding inappropriate urges

PATIENT TRAUMA ASSESSMENT
This assessment is resultant of answers from respondent.

1. Did a parent or other adult in the household often or very often swear at you, insult you, put you down, or humiliate you? Or act in a way that made you afraid you might be physically hurt? **NO**

2. Did a parent or other adult in the household often or very often push, grab, slap, or throw something at you? Or ever hit you so hard that you had marks or were injured? **NO**

3. Did an adult or person at least 5 years older than you ever touch or fondle you, or have you touch their body in a sexual way? Or attempt or actually have oral, anal, or vaginal intercourse with you? **NO**

4. Did you often or very often feel that no one in your family loved you or thought you were important or special? Or your family didn't look out for each other, feel close to each other, or support each other? **NO**

5. Did you often or very often feel that you didn't

have enough to eat, had to wear dirty clothes, and had no one to protect you? Or your parents were too drunk or high to take care of you or take you to the doctor if you needed it? NO

6. Were your parents ever separated or divorced? **NO**

7. Was your mother or stepmother often or very often pushed, grabbed, slapped, or had something thrown at her? Or sometimes, often or very often kicked, bitten, hit with a fist, or hit with something hard? Or threatened with a gun or knife? **NO**

8. Did you live with anyone who was a problem drinker or alcoholic, or who used street drugs? **NO**

9. Was a household member depressed or mentally ill, or did a household member attempt suicide? **NO**

10. Did a household member go to prison? **NO**

NOTE: Respondent became verbally aggressive during the course of this assessment, questioning what was the purpose of questions asked. Respondent replied at end of assessment, "y'all motherfuckers are trying to get me taken out my house to live in a group home. I got a home. I don't need no group home."

During the lull between morning and afternoon groups, Bowie sat off at a corner table with NoBueno, in the shadow of NoBueno's one-on-one staff standing a few feet away. Although NoBueno's treatment plan stipulated that his one on one must be within arm's length at all times, staff was confident that within eyeshot was sufficient. NoBueno, constantly looking exaggeratedly over his shoulder at his staff, whispered running commentary on every patient that walked by. He regaled Bowie with stories of which men were interested in him, who was really crazy, which person was a true degenerate.

"See that one right there?" NoBueno nudged Bowie with his elbow, nodding at the tall figure shuffling past. "Closet case. Always talking about how much pussy he got on the outside, but always trying to get me to follow him to the bathrooms."

Bowie laughed at NoBueno's girlish giggle, slapped his knee. "Yeah right. How you going to get into the bathroom when your one on one follows everywhere you go?"

NoBueno splayed a hand at his chest, displaying mock horror. "I would never go with that brick! You don't think I can do better than that?"

"Nah. I really don't."

"You just don't know, honey. You just don't know. There

are always ways."

"Like what?"

NoBueno nodded, squinting his eyes at him. "You just stay with me, you'll see. You too new for me to school you now. I got to get to know you first. But I don't fuck with none of these dudes."

"You live here, right? In the residential building. So you don't get to go nowhere, NoBueno! So how you figure you get to do anything? I'm not trying to be mean, man. I feel bad for you guys that have to stay here, but I'm glad I got a house to go to, and a boyfriend, too. A whole niggah."

"I got one, too. See what you know. I been with a guy that lives here, too. We been together ever since I been here."

Bowie grinned at him. "Where he at? Which one is he?"

NoBueno put a finger to his lips, shushing him. "He don't come to day program. He refuses, and they don't fuck with him. They let him stay in the residential unit all day. He got it like that."

"Everybody don't have to come to the program?"

NoBueno shook his head. "I'ma introduce you to him, too. Sooner or later. We got to get you used to the place, so staff ain't eyeballing you all the time, then we can skip off the unit, and you can meet my husband."

Bowie laughed. "How you going to have a husband? Can't no man marry no other man."

NoBueno huffed. "Whatever child. Figure of speech."

They watched as the congregates began to mill about

the door to the therapy rooms. Standing, they walked slowly toward the throng, the one on one absently shadowing. As the men walked down to the rooms on the lower level they began to split off into the various rooms, assigned, as they were, to designated therapy groups: Anger Management, Medication Education, Accountability, Arts & Crafts and Entertainment, which consisted of watching a movie. Bowie was glad that NoBueno was assigned to Accountability. He didn't want to be alone in a room full of strangers.

The group consisted of eight men, sitting in a circle, manned by a thin, red-haired woman that appeared to Bowie to be in her late twenties. As everyone got situated, the woman clapped her hands to silence the room.

"Hi everyone. Why don't we start with a mindfulness exercise. Can everyone bow your heads? Who would like to lead?"

Dead silence.

"I'll remind everyone that willingness to participate is also compliance with treatment . . . ."

Bowie peeked to his side and saw NoBueno crossing his eyes and sticking out his tongue in derision. He muffled a laugh.

Blessed is he who has regard for the weak
the Lord delivers him in times of trouble.
The Lord will protect him and preserve his life.
He will bless him to the land
and not surrender him to the desire of his foes.

The Lord will sustain him on his sick bed
and restore him from his bed of illness.
I said O' Lord have mercy on me
heal me, for I have sinned against you.
My enemies say of me in malice
when will he die and his name perish.
Whenever one comes to see me
he sneaks falsely, while his heart gathers slander
then he goes out and spreads it unafraid.

"Okay great. As we have a new member to today's group, let me welcome you, and introduce myself. I'm Kylie, your therapist for today's session on accountability. Would you like to introduce yourself?"

Bowie was looking down into his lap. He noticed the silence and peeked up to find all eyes on him. "Huh?"

"Would you like to introduce yourself?"

"No."

The room erupted into laughter. Kylie frowned, crossed her arms over her chest. Someone shouted, "That's Fancy Feet, man."

"Yeah, man." Laughter. "Fancy Feet."

Grudgingly, "My name's Bowie."

"Hi Bowie. Will the room welcome Bowie, please?"

There were derisive welcomes all around, more murmurs of "Fancy Feet" with comments about how fast he moved his feet. "It was like the Tasmanian Devil and shit."

They had all already met the new guy, so this was a

waste of time.

"So Bowie, would you like to tell the room the reason that you are here?"

He thought he misunderstood her. "What?"

"What is the behavior that resulted in you attending Mockingbird?"

"The judge told me I have to."

Some men laughed, others nodded in agreement.

"Okay, right. Part of the road to recovery is that we must acknowledge that we are aware of actions and the consequence of those actions. We cannot heal until we face the impact of the thing we have done. So. Bowie. Why don't you tell the group what you did that brought you to us. This is a safe space. Everyone here is here because of behaviors that are not acceptable in our society." She smiled compassionately. "So, do you want to tell us, your new friends, why you're here?"

"Fuck no."

NoBueno stood up, huffing. "I'll go."

Kylie exhaled with relief. "That's fine. As long as Bowie understands that he is expected to share with the group."

An older man with a raspy baritone said, "How you expect him to just blurt that out when he just got here and don't know nobody yet? I don't think that's right."

A few mumbled in agreement. Others, wary about repercussions, reports to probation officers, stayed silent.

NoBueno put a hand on his hip, flounced briefly. "Anyway, so, yeah. You already know me, Bowie. You know I been living here since ... well let's say it's been a minute."

"How you like it?" Bowie asked.

"It is what it is. You know? I've seen worse. Seen better, too."

Kylie interrupted, "Will you tell the group the reason you are here?"

"Yeeeup. My sister put me here."

"Your sister did not put you here, Jose. Nobody has that power but you. What did *you* do that got you here?"

Bowie said, "The judge got the power. The po-po got that power. What you mean nobody got the power?"

NoBueno jumped in before Kylie could spout anymore recovery 101 mumbo jumbo. "You want me to say that I did something I didn't. My sister reported to the cops that I touched my nephew. And she's a fucking liar."

Kylie said, "Why did you offer to speak if you're continuing to deny the behavior that got you here?"

"Okay, how 'bout this? I'm here because there was a charge of child molestation, and the courts determined me to be guilty. But it's still because of my sister. If you really want to know what got me in here, I'll tell you. She found out ... she caught me sucking her husband's dick in the basement. That's why she made up this shit about me. She couldn't stand the fact that her man, when he finished with her each night, he was up in my guts so he could really get off."

The room groaned. "Don't nobody want to hear that faggot shit, man."

NoBueno gathered himself up, spun to glare at the person who had spoken, then grandly sat in his seat, crossing his legs. "Yeah, I can understand nobody wanting to hear the faggot shit. It's a perversion, right? In a room full of child rapers and peeping Toms. *That's* where you draw the line." NoBueno laughed.

Someone said, "Didn't you admit you did it? Fucked with your sister's kid when you went to court? That's what you said before."

Another person chimed in, "So you admitted you did it, man. So why you keep backpedaling now. You must not ever want to get out of here."

NoBueno stood again, his arms tensed at his sides, fists balled tightly. "What court? Poor people don't go to court. They make deals. I took a plea. The district attorney. And my public defender. Who *works* for the county, just like the district attorney does, said if I agreed to molestation, it was a lesser charge than rape. I could've got twenty years in jail for that. I wasn't going to go to no jail for twenty years. I took the plea, applied to Behavioral Health Court, they remanded me here. So that's how you all got the pleasure of my acquaintance." NoBueno curtsied, resulting in shouts of derision, calls of "sissy" and "twinkle toes."

Kylie clapped her hands. "Hey! Out of line. That word is not welcome in here."

Bowie said, "That's what they did to me, too. Told me if I didn't say I exposed myself, I could get a whole lot of time upstate. They would charge me with indecent exposure to minors. So I took it. Ain't nobody trying to go upstate.

Wasn't even no minors around. They said there *could've* been. Some kid *could've* walked in on us."

Kylie frowned. "That is a smokescreen, guys. You're still finding a way to place the blame for your actions onto someone else. It's the police, it's the judge, it's everybody, anybody but yourself."

"That's how it is, though," said Bowie. "You get tricked into saying something you didn't do because you want to go the fuck home. And then you find out you still ain't going home."

"The courts have found you guilty of the crime. In the eyes of the law, you are guilty. Those are the facts, guys. You did this to yourselves. We are here—that's the purpose of this group session. That we take accountability for our actions."

NoBueno sat down with a heavy sigh. "Yup. This is where I found out that 'facts' don't always mean truth."

"Turn right in point eight miles onto Poplar Street," the disembodied GPS instructed in an impressive British accent. Kaitlyn Dodges, gripping the steering wheel with one hand and a mascara wand with the other, wondered how the fuck she was supposed to know what amount of driving equaled point eight miles. The car slowed at the traffic signal, and she quickly dabbed a third coat of pigment to her eyelashes, blinking rapidly at her reflection in the rearview mirror.

Kaitlyn was unfamiliar with the narrow streets that meandered along the hill leading to the border of town. She noted how different this section of town was from the more suburban feeling West End. Brown people stood around on corners, warily eyeing the county coat of arms on the side of the car. She felt a degree of safety behind that coat of arms. It informed people that even though her white skin marked her as an outsider, she was here on official business. She was an emissary of power.

Of course she had driven through this area before, as had most people during the course of running errands, or people employed in the downtown area as they drove out of town to the nearby shopping districts to pick up a quick lunch or on a coffee run. It had always struck her, the marked difference, the subliminal change in feeling when houses directly abutted the sidewalk, with nothing but a few cement steps dividing private space from public. The houses here felt closed in, the narrow streets lined with parked cars leaving a single lane of blacktop for two lanes of traffic. Comparing these houses to the larger, more ornate structures on the other side of town, Kaitlyn marveled that something as simple as a stretch of walkway, a picket fence, a patch of trimmed grass or a porch with a shaded swing set could convey such a different feeling.

She pulled off as the light turned green, making the turn as instructed by the device on the dash, moving around the trash truck slowly going down the street, its huge, gaping maw emitting an unpleasant stench that Kaitlyn subconsciously affiliated with this location. She watched the Black men, their clothing caked with filth, shouting to one another as they dragged large containers from the curb and dumped the contents into the truck. Their laughter, loud and deep, struck her. She wondered what there was to laugh about when your job demanded that you smell garbage all day long.

She felt their eyes on her as she passed, saw one grab his crotch and make an unheard remark, his mouth undulating, his eyes flashing wickedly. She sped up and silently cursed Brittany, who had previously held jurisdiction of this territory, now promoted to Administrator of Probation Services, unceremoniously dumping her caseload at her lap.

She pulled the car up to the assigned destination and yanked the gears into park. The house was larger than the others. There was a colorful spray of flowers on the door. As she had been trained, she surveyed the scene, making note of any persons standing nearby, observing alleyways and side entrances. She looked for places of cover.

The folder of pertinent information sat on the passenger seat. She briefly eyeballed the contents, making sure she had the specifics down. It was sometimes hard to keep all this disparate information clear. Which person had done which crime. What crime had been committed. Misdemeanor 1, misdemeanor 2, petty crime, felony, summary offense. She looked at the black and white photo. Dark skin, bullet-shaped head. Ears small and close to the head. Eyes slitted and angry, glaring back in defiance. Just like those of the men sitting silently, watching her from low cement stoops.

Indecent exposure. At a public library. Pickpocketing. Petty robbery. She wondered how robbery could be considered petty. Oh sure, she knew the textbook definition, had been tested numerous times during her pursuit of a criminal justice degree on the minute differences between one charge and another, but in her opinion, robbery was robbery. You either intended to steal something that didn't belong to you or you didn't. Disturbing the peace. Threatening destruction of public property. Assault. Lewd and lascivious behavior. Under jurisdiction of Behavioral Health Court.

She again cursed Brittany. Kaitlyn had minimal knowledge about how Behavioral Health Court worked. She knew it was a diversion process, but that was all she knew. She was more familiar with Drug Court, another diversionary process, where people with addiction issues who had been arrested for certain non-felony crimes could be given less prison time if they agreed to take part in social service programs, such as rehab or detoxification treatment, medication management, Alcoholics Anonymous or Narcotics Anonymous, or whatever ancillary services the presiding judge, working in collaboration with a group of case workers, determined to be the best course of treatment.

In her experience, the people she had worked with in Drug Treatment Court were looking for a way to avoid serving time for their crimes. They cycled in and out of the program, relapsing and returning to jail, and reapplied for Drug Treatment Court numerous times until a frustrated judge determined the program was not effective and forced the person to finish out their original prison sentence.

Huffing in exasperation, Kaitlyn flipped down the mirrored visor, smoothed down her bangs, pulled strands of blond hair behind one ear. She blinked her blue eyes, satisfied with the thickness of her mascara and exited the car.

The bedroom was stiflingly hot, even stripped down to his flimsy white boxers. Bowie shifted around on the bed, trying to find a cool spot on the rumpled sheets. Wiping the sweat from his neck, he hopped up and walked to the window, tugging to open it, but met resistance.

Cursing, he remembered Magdelene nailing them shut, to make sure he didn't try to sneak out in the night while she slept. He roamed downstairs, disrupting the cloud of shimmer at the landing as he passed through.

The sofa was just as uncomfortable as the bed had been. He punched at the cushions, lay back onto the mounds of upholstery, and lowered his shorts to his knees, tensely flexing his quadriceps, absently stroking himself. He looked over as his cell phone began to vibrate on the glass tabletop. He picked it up.

"Yeah?"

"Where are you at?"

He huffed. "Mom. Where do you think I'm at?"

"I don't know where you're at. That's why I asked."

"Where you at?"

"I'm at work, where the hell I'm supposed to be. You stayed at the program until the time you were allowed to leave didn't you?"

"How'm I doing to get out before then, Mom? The place is locked up just like a jail. Can't nobody go nowhere."

"Where are you now?"

"I'm home, Mom!"

"You didn't stop off nowhere before you went home, did you?"

"You was supposed to pick me up, you said."

"I got other things to do, Bowie, then running you back and forth every day."

"Yeah? What? Chester Casino or you at Parx?"

"Don't ask me no fucking questions. I'm your parent, you aren't mine. And you better stay in the house and wait for that white bitch to come."

"What white bitch?"

Magdelene screamed, "Your PO is scheduled to come see you today!"

Bowie sat up, pulled up his shorts, dropped his phone.

"Hello! Hello!"

He picked up his phone. "Yeah, I'm here."

"And when she's finished don't you go no fucking where. You understand? I'll be there shortly."

"Yeah, I'll bet. Why don't I come down there? You kicking they ass today?"

"I'm fucking them up."

"How much you win?"

"Don't you fucking worry about how much I won! I got fifteen hundred."

Bowie whistled, then clapped his hands loudly, once again dropping the phone.

"Hello! What the fuck is going on out there?"

Bowie picked up the phone. "Sorry. Dropped the phone. I won fifty dollars on the scratch off."

"So you didn't go straight home. You took your ass around to that bodega to buy scratch offs. You going to give me half?"

Bowie calculated. If Magdelene admitted to winning fifteen hundred, he surmised that she probably had made at least twice that amount. "You must be kidding me. You going to give me half your fifteen hundred?"

"Don't I always give you something?"

He barked a laugh. "I ain't say something. I said half. I'm coming down. You at Chester, ain't you? You always hit there. That's your lucky place. I can't win shit at Chester."

"Don't you bring your ass down here! You wait there for that white bitch like you got some sense. How you going to come here, anyhow? You got banned for that shit you pulled in the bathroom last time. Which is why you now got visits with a probation officer, so you sit your ass there and wait for her to get there before they haul your ass back to jail. Listen, and don't let that white bitch walk her nosy ass anywhere else in my house but the front room. You hear? I don't need her nosing around through my shit like she with welfare and shit."

"I wish that bitch would try it."

Bowie heard the sudden ringing of a jackpot, heard Magdelene scream, then curse. "I gotta go, now. Later."

The phone went dead before he could respond, but he said it anyway: "Later."

Then, he looked down at his phone, began to punch the letters.

hey young head what you doing
minding my own business. what are you doing?
thinking about you and betting my dick
so that's nothing new. how was program?
fucked up. no it was ok
did you remember what we talked about?

about you getting some of this ass boo

no, Bowie. your meds. remember that article i showed you, the one that talks about one of your meds having side effects of compulsive behaviors. makes you have an increased need to gamble, and increased sexual urges?

I got sexual urges when I think about you boo

come on Bowie, stay focused will you? act like an adult for two seconds.

am sorry honey

you need to talk about this with your doctor. ask him to take you off that shit so you can see if that is the reason you are preoccupied by sexual thoughts. why you spend all your money on gambling.

them white people don't listen to me

did you try? remember what i told you about code switching? you can't go up in there throwing chairs and acting like a park ape and expect to get anywhere. it's your treatment. you have the right to decide what you will or will not take. just talk to them, and remember to stay calm. if you shout nobody hears what you say, they just hear that youre are shouting.

doctor told me she never hard about my meds making me bett my dick

so what. i'll print out the articles for you so you can take them in to her, okay? there's going to be a lawsuit about this shit somewhere down the line. white people always got class actions going on to throw money at their fuck ups.

so you say I can sue them and get me a lot of money

i'm not saying anything. i'm just saying.

send me a pecture of you dick boo and I send one of me
bye Bowie
what tim you coming to get me tonight boo

come on eden tex me back

okay I call you later

I be waiting at are spot

Kaitlyn was taken aback when Bowie flung open the door, but no more than he was. He hadn't heard her repeated knockings on the door and had opened it to let some cool air into the house, and there she stood, blond and officious. He began to vibrate a manic sort of energy, his eyes darting beyond her to the street, then back, a hyperkinetic sort of energy coming from his eyes as he glanced at the identification badge she proffered.

It was primarily the white boxers, which seemed to glow off the contrast of his dark, hairless body that caught her off guard.

He leaned forward and opened the screen door for her. "Sorry, man. I didn't hear you knocking. Was you here long?"

She smelled a slightly dark scent, cocoa butter and perspiration, mixed with something she could not identify specifically, but something familiar to her from visits to other, similar households. She wrinkled her nose to lose the memory.

Remembering her training, she spoke in a firm, direct tone, stepping over the threshold and looking around at the room rather than at him. "Kaitlyn Dodges. You are Bowie Long, right? I've taken over your supervision from Miss Pope."

Bowie put a hand to his mouth. "Oh shit. I hope she didn't get fired. Brittany was cool."

"She did not."

Kaitlyn looked around. The dark interior, the drawn blinds. "Would you mind opening the blinds? Or turning on a light?"

"Sure, sure. No prob." Bowie darted toward the window, drew up the blinds. Sunlight danced through dust motes whirling on the air of stagnant cigarette smoke and long deadened incense.

It seemed that Bowie's self-awareness ignited when the light entered the room. He realized he was wearing only his boxers. "Oh, shit!" he yelped. "I'll be right back." He darted up the stairs, taking them two at a time.

Kaitlyn heard a door slam and then muffled cursing.

She looked around. Observed the fading paint on the walls, the stacks of unopened mail on the table. Stepping closer, she saw the word DELINQUENT stamped in red, read return addresses for the electric company, the water revenue service, cable TV. There was an ashtray piled with a mound of ashes and burned-out butts, a bit of ash sprayed out upon the table, a crushed, empty cigarette package on the floor beside a worn pair of woman's slippers, the heels mashed down from use.

Bowie hopped back down the stairs, clasping a belt and zipping up a pair of faded denim pants, his feet and chest still bare, sweat dampening his torso. "Sorry about that, man. I didn't even know you was at the door. My bad . . . uh, what did you say your name was, Kayla?"

She watched him with officious eyes. "Miss Dodges. But you can call me Kaitlyn."

He nodded. "Cool. Cool. My niece is named Kayla, too."

She gave him a card, so that he could see her name. His brow furrowed as he glanced at it before throwing it on the mound of papers on the table.

"Brittany was just here like two days ago."

Kaitlyn folded her arms across her chest. Standing awkwardly, expecting him to offer her a seat so that she could refuse it.

"Well, we will be visiting you regularly, initially. Perhaps even daily, if we see fit. Until it has been determined that visits can be faded back in frequency."

"Huh? You said y'all will come regular?"

She nodded. "Correct."

"You need my initials, though? No problem. Where do you need me to sign?"

"Excuse me?"

"What?"

"We will also be visiting your program at Mockingbird and collecting reports on compliance with treatment. Have you been going there every day?"

He looked at her, widened his eyes. "I'm sorry, buddy, what did you say? I didn't hear you."

"Have you been going to Mockingbird every day? On time?"

He nodded. "Oh yeah. I been there. Every day."

"You're not working, are you?"

"Working? I want to get a job."

"Oh no. Working is not an option for people receiving services at Mockingbird."

Bowie nodded. "I need a fucking job, bad."

"You don't live alone, right? Where is the supervising parent?" Kaitlyn looked around as though she expected someone to pop up from behind the furniture.

"You mean my mom? She's not here. She'll be back soon, I guess. Soon's her winnings run out."

"Pardon?"

"Nothing, man."

"How have things been going since you've been home? Not gotten into any trouble, I take it? Are there any guns in the house?"

Bowie did not know which question she wanted him to answer, so he just nodded at her, his hands at his sides.

"How are you spending your downtime? Are you staying indoors?"

Bowie smiled. "I ain't been doing much, really. I spent the night with a friend last night. We didn't do much, just chilling really."

Her eyes widened. "You what! You spent the night somewhere besides here?"

He looked at her, confused. Nodded. "My friends . . ."

Kaitlyn turned to the door. "I'm going to my car for a moment. I need to make a call."

Bowie heard muffled sounds and the word *call*.

"What you say?" He walked to the screen door, watched her walk rapidly toward the car with the county logo on the side: a man and a woman flanking the scales of justice.

The windows were opened to pull a breeze into the clammy dayroom. Various voices floated on that breeze, wafting across the room and settling in corners like dust motes. NoBueno and Bowie sat in a small room pretending to watch the television that droned from a metal rack bolted to the cement wall. NoBueno's one-on-one staff stood leaning against a wall, lazily watching the girl he towered over, nodding to her suggestively.

"Watch," NoBueno whispered. "He trying to get him some poontang."

Bowie watched, as instructed. "Huh, what you say? How you know?"

"See him licking his crusty lips? What more do you need?"

Bowie watched for a second, then tapped him back, barked a laugh. "Look look look. See him putting his hand on his dick?"

NoBueno nodded. "What I tell you. That's all that be happening around here. These staff do more fucking than working. They going to go off to one of the lavatories in a minute. Then, we can go over to residential while nobody looking, and I can introduce you to my husband."

"Husband." Bowie smirked. "Gay ass shit."

He crossed his legs, blinked languidly. "You better know it. Gay all day. You want to meet my man, or what, you too scared to go off unit?"

They watched as the two staff looked around, then walked over toward them. Raheem nodded at them, "We 'bout to go do rounds. Don't you leave the room, hear?"

"Where I'm going?" NoBueno huffed, crossed his arms across his chest.

After the two walked around the wall of the media room, Bowie said, "I ain't scared of shit."

Jose watched him. Sized him up. "Yeah. Why don't you show me your dick?"

"What?"

"You said you in here because you flashed your pecker. What's so special about your pecker that makes you think everybody wants to see it?"

Bowie laughed. "I didn't say everybody wants to see it. But you do. Faggot ass."

"And what are you, then? Didn't you flash your shit to another man?"

"I'm a gay ass Black man. I ain't no faggot, though."

NoBueno shook his head pitifully. "Potatoes, potahtos. What do you think is the difference?"

"Show me your dick, then."

Jose gasped. "I think not!"

Bowie smirked. "Right. That's the difference." Then, without further fanfare, Bowie loosened the drawstring of his pants and pulled his member from the fly of his boxers, recognizing that familiar glint blaze from NoBueno's eyes, that same look that he had seen flash across adult faces as far back as he could remember. The look that made him think of Christmas mornings and moments after church services spent with elders, praise dances and speaking in tongues.

Jose loudly popped his lips. "Easy, honey. You're too easy."

Bowie pulled up his pants, drew the drawstring tight. "What?"

"Where's the thrill in getting it when you offer it so freely? You need to learn about the value of withholding, if you ask me."

Bowie felt a little ridiculous, like the brunt of a joke. "I ain't ask you shit."

Jose looked around melodramatically, clutched a splayed palm to his clavicle and whispered, "Quick, follow me."

He thought about refusing, just staying put. But the lure of the unknown outweighed the fear of repercussion, so he followed Jose's undulating, bulky form off down a darkened hallway on the opposite side of the building from the administrative wing.

He could smell the dust caked in the old vents, the tinge of rust and stagnant water in the old pipes as they descended an old stairwell, shadows casting them into darkness as they went lower. He wanted to tell NoBueno how disgusted he was with the surroundings but feared that his hearing deficiency would not properly regulate the volume of his voice and that they would then be found out. He kept his opinion to himself, quickened his pace as NoBueno began to walk faster, keeping his body close to the crumbling, moldy walls, turning corners, going deeper and deeper, where windows cast no shadows.

They stopped short at a wide metal door with a narrow window at the center. Jose rose on his toes, attempting to see through the murky glass, then jumped so that he could peer through. He reached out, grabbing Bowie's shoulder and pushing off.

"Give me a boost. Want to make sure the coast is clear."

Bowie waved his hands, dispersing cobwebs, then bent low. Cupping his hands, he thrust Jose high enough to see through the window, gasping at the weight. Jose fell against the door with a muffled curse, pushing himself away from the filthy metal, making a quick, high-pitched noise at the spiders cascading down his broad torso. Bowie giggled.

The door moved, opening slightly. Jose climbed down from Bowie's hands and pushed the door further, enough to allow his girth to pass through. Bowie followed effortlessly. They both looked around.

There was a narrow vestibule and another door at the end of it.

Closing the door, Jose put a finger to his lips. "That's the door to residential. These old buildings all have underground passageways that lead to all the other buildings. They don't use them no more, but back when the crazies fully populated all the buildings and they didn't want nobody trying to escape, they would escort them underground from one appointment to another. This way, if somebody got out of line or tried to get out, staff could fuck them up without any bleeding hearts trying to interfere or make some claim about respect for humanity or some other bullshit."

"What? This shit is creepy. Dirty ass shit. Smells like piss."

They both approached the other door. This one was in better repair than the other. Jose turned again. "This door won't have nobody on the other side. For real, there's probably two staff at the most on residential during the day shift. One stays back to keep an eye on anybody that's sick and didn't go to program. The other one is housekeeping. They got some Mexican broad to clean up the shit and vomit. She's scared to death to be in here with all the perverts. She runs a dirty mop across the floor and is out of dodge quick fast and in a hurry. As long as the supervisors smell bleach, they think everything's clean as a virgin's twat."

Bowie laughed. "Twat."

Jose rolled his eyes in exasperation.

They walked casually through the vestibule, passing a timeclock and a small reception area. There was an open closet lined with cleaning products, shampoos, rows of toilet paper, toothpaste, neatly folded towels and washcloths.

Bowie noticed the padlock swinging on the door. "They

lock up the toilet paper and shit?"

"Of course," Jose said. "This is a building full of society's unwanted. You know, the pederasts and all, they might try to strangle a bitch with a ream of ass wipe, or gag you with an unsecured tube of toothpaste. Safety first."

As they approached the end of a hallway, Jose slowed at the last door on the left. He put his hand on the knob, then turned to Bowie. "Don't try any shit, now. He startles easy. We're just going to say hello. No funny business."

Bowie scoffed. "You scared I'm going to take your man. I got a whole man at home, baby. Don't you worry."

"So you keep telling me. And yet, here you are."

The room was small and tidy, emanating the smell of pine oil. A small radio played low volume yacht rock on the windowsill. The room was sparsely furnished: a narrow bed on one wall and a wooden This End Up dresser on the opposite.

In the center, his back facing the door, sat a large, dark form. He wasn't obese, but his size seemed to engulf the room—almost absorbed all light. He was hunched forward, rocking slightly back and forth, the long mat of dreadlocked hair swaying with his movement. As they approached, Bowie's nose burned, his olfactory memory flashed a scent familiar to him: beeswax, rising off the man's hair and releasing into the air.

Jose walked around to face the man, smiling warmly. "Hey, I came down to see you, just like I promised."

The man said nothing. His broad shoulders shifted,

spreading wide as he sat up. He looked at Jose. His eyes were golden but rheumy.

"Oh look. Those assholes left a mess on your shirt. Did you just get done your lunch? Let me clean you up."

Jose went to the drawer, took out a T-shirt and approached, wiping the particles of food from the man's shirt. He grunted in response, lifted up his own hand to take flecks of egg and bacon bits from his chest and handed them to Jose.

Jose smiled as he took the bits of food from him, then stretched out a hand toward Bowie. "I brought a friend with me. To say hello."

Jose flicked his fingers, beckoning to him.

But Bowie did not see him. He stood back near the doorway, mesmerized by the shimmer, bigger than any he had seen before, revolving in a rapid elliptical, an eye of radiant vermillion dancing in the center of violet and indigo.

When his phone buzzed at dinnertime, Eden knew it was him because he had not heard from him all day. Bowie was already talking when he picked up, speaking rapidly, agitatedly.

"They said they taking me back to jail!"

Eden turned the water off, dried his hands, turning to lean against the sink where he had been washing dishes.

"Whoa, whoa. Slow down. What are you talking about? What did you do?"

Bowie was talking very fast. His words tumbling into one another. "That white bitch came up to the program today, and she's talking with that other bitch, and Lola calls me in her office. They both looking at me like I smell like dog shit."

Eden heard Magdelene's voice rumbling in the background. "I told you you can't trust that Black bitch. She ain't nothing but the white man's puppet."

"Mom! Please!" Bowie yelled.

"Called you in her office for what, then?"

"They asked me if I told the PO that I spent the night

with you. Then she wanted to know your name, and she asked how old you are. I always dated men older than me, I told them. That ain't no big deal."

Eden felt a fist squeeze his heart. "My na . . . ? Why are they asking about me?"

"She said she wanted to make sure that I wasn't with no kids."

Magdelene shouted, "They trying to make you out to be something you're not. They think you're a child molester; you're going to have to be on the sex offender registry. You watch."

"Kids?" Eden walked into the dining room to sit down. He gripped his forehead with one hand.

"I don't fuck around with no fucking kids. I told them that. She said they just have to make sure that I'm not in no danger. I shouldn't have been staying out all night. That they have to keep me safe."

"Keep you safe. Is that the exact words they said? Why would you need to be kept safe?" Eden tried to think back to all the times he had been with Bowie. Tried to remember if he had ever seen his photo ID. He had read stories about people going to jail for statutory rape. Men saying that they had thought the kid they were caught having sex with was an adult. Was it possible that Bowie was underage?

He said, "Wait a fucking minute. You said you were twenty-seven. Aren't . . ."

"I am fucking twenty-seven! What the fuck are you cussing at me for? Did I cuss at you?"

"I don't give a shit if you cursed at me! What the hell is going on here?"

Bowie yelled, strident, but with tears in his voice. "You're mad at me and I didn't do shit. You're trying to break up with me."

"Break? We aren't . . . what? What does that have to do with what you're telling me?" Eden heard Bowie's voice far-away, then muffled sounds: "You talk to him. I can't do this."

Magdelene yelped, "You talk, Bowie. No. Yeah we're in the car outside Mockingbird now. He's too upset to go home. I think I should take him up to the psych unit to be evaluated. I think he's getting sick. You hear him shouting?"

Eden could hear Bowie screaming about going to jail, about not being sick, accusing Magdelene of interfering in his relationships. "This is why I can't ever keep a boyfriend. You always get in the way with your shit!"

Eden tried to calm himself. "He's upset. I don't think being upset means that he needs to go to a psychiatric uni—"

"You don't know him. I can't deal with no crazy shit. This shit is stressful."

Bowie shouted, "How is this stressful to you? It's my life. It's me they talking about going back to jail."

"Well they said you exposed yourself in there today. What you think was going to happen if you taking your pecker out."

Bowie snorted in derision. "So what. That wasn't nothing."

Eden said, "Listen. I don't understand how my name

has been pulled into this. Was he not supposed to leave the house or something? Was that a stipulation of his probation?"

He heard her blow out smoke. "Nobody said anything about that one way or the other. But I told him to stay in the house. The cops know him now. Anytime they see him, they fuck with him. He's the town lunatic. He damn sure don't need to be laying up with some man all night."

"But why is that important to them? What does it mean that they need to make sure he's safe? They're talking like he's an infant."

"How the hell should I know what them white people mean. They make shit up as they go along."

"So he's going to jail because he spent the night out?"

There was more shuffling, then Bowie was back on the phone. "I didn't tell them nothing. I said you and me are friends. We been friends for a long time, now, haven't we?"

"I don't understand what's going on here? Do they think I took advantage of you or something? Did they ask how long we've known each other?"

"Yeah. She asked if I had known you when I was a kid. If you were my teacher or my Sunday school teacher." Bowie laughed. "I told them fuck no."

Eden heard a loud, white noise in his head. It muffled Bowie's voice, clouded his vision. "I'm going to have to call you back."

Bowie shouted, "You're not going to call me back! Please talk to me."

"I need to think for a minute. I'll call you back."

"You promise?"

Eden ended the call.

Shit. What was this? Was he now on some list of degenerates? Would police be descending on his house, hauling him away in handcuffs for all the neighbors to see. He recalled newspaper reports of men caught in sting operations—where police acted as decoys in the well-known gay pickup spots, like the gay acres in Philly, the men's room at John Wanamaker in King of Prussia, the ramble at Valley Forge Park. The newspaper gleefully printing the names of the men picked up soliciting other men, listing their towns of origin. Would his name be emblazoned across the local newspaper for the world to see?

But that sort of thing had happened in his youth. In the 1970s, when he was too young to have engaged in acts of solicitation. But he had always been aware of these happenings due to his voracious reading, his consumption of all sorts of written word. He wasn't sure that sort of thing even happened anymore. And, he asked himself, would it matter if it did happen? While he didn't live his life as out loud as did Bowie, announcing to all who would listen that he was gay, he also didn't hide it.

It had always been one of the things he admired about Bowie, the way he announced his sexuality as if it were an afterthought, like announcing his eyes were brown or that he liked gospel music. He had always admired the honesty of how Bowie lived his life. But now he wondered if that honesty was true bravery or if it was the aftereffects of mental illness. Was Bowie living his life the way he did because he had made a conscious effort to do so or was it because he had grown up in a small town where everyone knew everyone else, where the police knew its citizens by name, and therefore everyone already knew about him anyway?

Eden decided it would be better, easier to just no longer communicate with him. He did not need, or want any complications in his life. The primary lure of Bowie, for him, had always been what he represented—simplicity instead of confusion, easy, casual sex instead of the minefield of past transgressions represented by his current partner, joyousness and spontaneity. He had not expected the spontaneity to include jail, and institutionalization, and bail, and most importantly, his own name being brought to the attention of the police state apparatus.

Eden had lived his life making sure to stay under the radar. To stay out of trouble, abide by the law. He knew, from years of having his parent drum it into his head, that the best way to stay out of the clutches of the prison system and the judicial system that feeds Black men into that system was to make sure that you were not individualized to them. You had to remain invisible. Keep your nose to the grindstone, mind your own business, buy property, pay your taxes. Be a good citizen. And now, Bowie, in one fell swoop, was about to destroy all the work Eden had done over the years to stay anonymous.

When his phone began to vibrate, not ten minutes after he had ended the call, Eden knew it was him. He ignored it, sent the call directly to voicemail.

But he called again. And again.

way aren't you answering my call Eden

are you mad now

please call me back

okay, I'll call you back later

Then, the phone rang again. Sighing, Eden put the number on block.

NORTHWEST OUTPATIENT TREATMENT CENTER PSYCHIATRIC EVALUATION

PATIENT: Bowie Long
REPORT CONDUCTED BY: Dr. Janet Hildebrand PhD.

CHIEF COMPLAINT/REASON FOR ENCOUNTER: Presently a patient receiving medication management by Dr. Hildebrand of Northwest OP Services and court-mandated partial hospitalization through Mockingbird Services for men with criminal charges of sexual nature.

This evaluation was requested in response to recent revocation of Behavioral Health Court privileges due to reports by therapist at Mockingbird of incidents of indecent exposure at the program. Patient was remanded to correctional facility as report of possible sexual offenses by Office of Probation wherein offender self-reports acts of sexual nature during period of home release.

Patient had originally been represented by the Public Defender's Office, but has obtained private representation. This evaluation is in response to request by

John Phillips Esq.

Original offenses according to attached docket are incidents of public solicitation, indecent exposure, public masturbation, robbery, attempted assault of officer of the law, assault of parent, property destruction.

Patient does not take ownership for charged offenses. States he was urinating at local casino when apprehended. He is unsure of the benefit of the partial program and Behavioral Health Court. He may have some difficulties with sexual boundaries as a result of trauma (reports having been raped at age 9/10 by stepfather). Reports behavior episodes of masturbation, about twice per week. Reports increasingly isolating behaviors, but has difficulty expressing frequency. "I have, like, no friends I can talk to."

Denies SI/HI history, but also alleges to have a boyfriend that mother reports to be untrue.

As patient has been under medication management by this Doctor for many years, consideration of change to medication regimen will be recommended. Monthly intramuscular dosage of Abilify should continue in support of baseline support/remediation of mental health symptoms in response to parent report of medication noncompliance as the explanation for behaviors that resulted in contact with law enforcement.

Luvox will be added to current regimen to address racing thoughts and episodes of mania. Trazodone will be added to address reports by parent of inability to sleep. As patient no longer receives outpatient services, Northwest will no longer provide administration of intramuscular shot. Medication management will need to be provided by Mockingbird Partial.

Patient has agreed and acknowledged that copies of this report will be submitted to Behavioral Health Court, Mockingbird Partial Program, and John Phillips Esq.

Eden had only been able to put Bowie's number on block for about an hour. After that, while he spooned mashed potatoes into the old man's mouth, he worried. He worried that Bowie might run into a problem and call him to talk him through it, or that he would be picked up by the police while Magdelene was otherwise occupied by flashing lights and echoing sounds, and Bowie would have no one else to call.

So he unblocked the phone. Placed it on vibrate mode as he drove into the city to spend the night with the boyfriend. While watching home renovation programs, he was hyperaware of the weight in his jeans' pocket, imagined he felt a vibration against his thigh. Pulled the phone from his pocket under the boyfriend's side eye, felt foolish when he saw the black screen. Put the phone back in his pocket, removed his clothes, reached out a hand to caress the boyfriend, substituting one warmth, one desire, with another, less satisfying one.

The next morning, as the rising sun illuminated the grime on low-slung, newly gentrified edifices, as he carried his overnight bag to his car, he pretended to ignore the quiet of his phone. He reached to move the phone from vibrate to sound, tweaked the remote entry fob, reached for the door handle, drove along the clotted expressway, noted the continuing silence amid the roar of engines, the blaring of horns, the drone of morning drive radio.

He parked the car in the dark cool of the garage, entered the house through the side door, bathed his still-sleeping father, awakened him to void into the commode, sighed in relief as the wizened man released, like clockwork, wiped him, returned him to the bed, raised the bed to a supine position, clicked on the television and sat himself in the dining room, stared absently into a container of Greek yogurt topped with blackberries, watched his reflection staring back at him from the dark face of his cell phone sitting on the table in front of him.

Days of repetition stacked upon themselves, the only difference marked by which nameless television program blared canned laughter into the empty, meticulously polished, dusted and vacuumed rooms.

By day five, he had grown accustomed to the quiet. So when his phone gently pulsed, he assumed it was the boyfriend. He absently picked up. He felt a surge of blood coursing through his veins at the familiar voice.

"Hey baby, what time you want to see me?"

"Where the fuck you been?" He sat heavily on his bed,

leaned back against the pillows.

"What you mean, where I been? You know I got locked up."

"For spending the night with me. You got out that soon?"

"I'm on house arrest."

He sounded preoccupied. Eden recognized the familiar sound of water in the background. Pictured the dark body in cloudy water.

"House arrest? For how long?"

"They didn't say. My mom went up there, got my doctor from Northwest to write me a letter, told them all this stuff so I could get out. So I'm wearing this ankle thing on my leg. Gotta call in every morning and charge it up at night when I go to bed."

"What did your mother tell them? Was it about me?"

"Just about me being in the hospital. How I had a nervous breakdown and all that. She didn't know about me and my stepdad, him messing around with me when I was a kid. She said I should have told her, but I didn't."

Eden felt a fist curl in his stomach. "Your dad did something to you?"

"He wasn't my real dad. Stepdad."

"Where's your real father? Is he alive?"

Bowie barked a laugh. "That motherfucker ain't dead. I don't know where he is. Last time I went to his house, I was trying to get some child support. When I was in high school. His wife told me never come round there again, so fuck him and the horse he rode in on."

"But what did your dad say? Did he tell you not to come around there?"

Eden heard more splashing. "I don't want to talk about that bullshit. I want to *see* you."

The emphasis on the word *see* made Eden's dick thicken against his underwear. "Well, you're on house arrest, you said. So how do you plan to work around that?"

"Come over here," Bowie screamed. "Don't ask dumbass questions, baby."

"You want me to come over there, to that woman's house, and fool around with you? She won't be putting no root on me."

"Fuck that bald-head bitch. Anyway, she's not here. She out at Delaware Park. She won't be home till tomorrow morning, more than likely."

"Are you sure about that?"

"You coming now? I'm just getting out the tub. Come on!"

He wanted to say no. Tell Bowie that it was probably better for both of them if they didn't see one another anymore. He didn't know, really, if it was better for Bowie, but it would surely leave things less convoluted for himself. But he was astonished to realize he missed him.

When Eden knocked on the door, Bowie flung it open, bare chested and barefoot, a pair of jeans slung low on his hips, snapping his fingers. He greeted Eden with a beaming, off-kilter smile, pulled him into the house and stood on his toes to kiss him.

He was wearing a large pair of headphones, attached to the cell phone in his pocket, from which Eden could hear the muffled noise of "Pon de Replay." He slammed the door, causing Eden to jump, and reached out a hand to grab his hand, gyrating furiously.

"Come on baby, get it." He bumped his pelvis at Eden, singing loudly off-key, words not even close to the words Rihanna was singing. Eden laughed and grabbed at his thick neck, pulled him close, kissed the top of his head while rocking slowly against him. He smelled the heat of him, tropical, like pineapple, making him feel comfortable, familiar.

Bowie let him go, made a flourish, and then spun around, sticking out his ass and moving himself along Eden's groin. Eden laughed, felt a little self-conscious as he noticed the blinds at the front window were wide open. He moved over to sit on the sectional. Bowie raised a leg, put his foot on Eden's lap and shook himself, obliviously loud, immersed in music.

Eden touched his foot, felt the bulk of the ankle monitor and pulled up Bowie's pantleg to look at it. His ankle was bound with a band of rubber, about an inch thick. There was a dark oblong device hanging from the band, winking a red light at him. He mouthed words to him. Bowie removed the headphones.

"When's the last time you cut your toenails? These bitches are about to rip a hole in my pants."

Laughing, Bowie fell onto him, grasping him in a bear hug. "Oh you funny, huh? You know how much toenail clippers and shit cost in jail? Those motherfuckers kept asking 'haircut, haircut?' I said, 'nah, motherfucker, you won't be jacking up my head. My baby gonna cut my hair soon's I get out of here.'"

"How'd you know you were going to get out so soon?"

Bowie took the phone from his pocket, turned off Pandora. "My mom told me, go in there and act a fool. Then they try to get you out of there and over to the state hospital. But since I'm going to Mockingbird, I probably wouldn't have to go to state."

"So that's your strategy when you run into trouble with the law? You just act a fool?"

Bowie pushed himself up from Eden and sat close enough that their thighs touched, then shrugged. "It worked."

"You want me to cut your hair?"

Bowie grinned, leaning against him. "You want to cut your man's hair? You like your man looking good, don't you, baby?"

"Why didn't you say something on the phone?" Eden stood up, straightening out his pants, shifting the fabric so that his erection was less noticeable, and walked toward the door. "You're lucky I keep a just in case bag in the trunk of my car."

"What you say?" Bowie followed him, watched him from the screen. "Where you going?"

Eden waved him back and unlocked his car. He removed a leather grooming case. Bowie, ignoring his signal, walked down the steps, and Eden walked back toward him and pushed him toward the house.

"Are you crazy? You know you aren't supposed to leave the house."

"I thought you were leaving me already because of my ankle monitor."

Eden closed the door behind them. "Now does that even make sense?"

Eden enjoyed cutting his hair. He ran his large palms over the smooth surface of his head. He loved touching him, was turned on by the jutting ledge of bone at the base of his skull, like some elemental, prehistoric thing. Bowie was like metal, attracting his touch like a magnet. While cutting his hair, Eden cupped the curled tufts in his hand, feeling their heft, letting them collect until he had a fistful to hold. He then moved the clippers to the angular planes of Bowie's cheek, running the steel blades up through the sparse growth, the sound of the clippers soothing them both, encouraging silence.

Eden could feel Bowie watching him. As he drew close to see better, he felt his gaze and then felt his heat as Bowie reached out to touch him. Bowie mashed his lips together when the clippers neared his mouth. Eden shook his head no and clipped so that the curve of his upper lip was emphasized. Bowie began to twitch in the chair. His hands, resting along Eden's waist, jerked against him. Bowie pulled his hands back, tucked them at his side, sat on them.

When he finished cutting his hair, they moved to the sofa and Eden took one of his feet onto his lap. He took the toenail clippers from the bag on the coffee table and ran his hands along Bowie's feet, feeling the tips of his nails to ascertain appropriate length. Bowie leaned back against the cushions, watching him calculatingly.

Looking at his feet, Bowie's darkness sent a charge through him. He caressed his arch, held the width of his foot in his hand. Bowie's foot twitched, and he yanked it away. Eden reached out, motioning for the other foot.

"Why are you shaking like that?" he murmured, looking down, softly massaging his foot. Bowie shrugged, took his foot back. Eden reached for it, placed it back on his lap. "What are you doing that for? I like it. You know? It's like your some kind of generator. A battery."

Bowie slowly grinned. "You know what? I love you, man."

He moved forward and they fell back. Just lying there, Eden's hands moved to cup his head. Driven by some compulsion, he was unable to stop his hands from roaming Bowie's body: the bone at the center of his chest, the muscle in his bicep. "My dad, back when I was a kid, used to take Haldol to help him with his schizophrenia. And that medicine had side effects that made him twitch like you are. Do you take Haldol, maybe?"

Bowie shrugged. "What? I know I'm taking Depakote. I don't remember all that other shit."

"You mean you put stuff in your body and you don't know what for? You mind if I look at what you take? You know you can ask your doctor to give you something so that you don't shake as much."

Bowie sat up, rested his elbows on his knees. "I'm already all fucked up. I don't want any more of that shit."

Eden rubbed his back. "I'm sure. I wouldn't even be able to think straight. I used to take an antidepressant, back when I was working corporate, dealing with those white people and their bullshit. And that shit worked so good. People were just . . . like taking credit for shit I had developed, leaving sales events with all our equipment still not broken down, telling the coordinators 'oh Eden will take care of it,' you know? Like I was the goddamn mule. And I'd be all like, 'that's okay, it's not a problem . . . .'

"I couldn't even get mad. And then I realized I like my anger. My fury at white people is an elemental part of who I am. I'm not going to go around letting motherfuckers cut me off on the highway and white bitches cut in front of me at Starbucks like I'm invisible, without cussing them the fuck out. So I threw the rest of that shit in the trash."

Bowie nodded, reached for Eden's leg, stroked him. "Yeah, fuck that. Taking this shit, sometimes it's like I'm at the bottom of the ocean and I'm trying to swim up to get some air, but I never get there."

"Well, all I'm saying is, it's your choice. If you're uncomfortable with the shaking then you can do something about it. I think it's sexy, though."

Bowie jumped up and raced to the kitchen, returning with an armful of papers and amber vials filled with pills in his fists. He dropped all of it in Eden's lap and sat beside him, putting his headphones back on.

"You keep talking like I can just go tell these doctors what to do. You think that's how things really work?"

Eden laughed. He looked through the papers in front of him. "That *is* how it works. They work for you!"

"Huh?"

Eden looked up so Bowie could see his mouth. "They work for you."

"No they don't. They work for Northwest. And if I start telling them what to do, you best believe my black ass will be back up in county."

"Abilify. So you didn't tell them about the studies related to gambling and compulsive behavior?"

"What's that? Compulse. I think that's what Lola was saying to me."

"When you can't control the things your mind tells you to do."

"What? Oh no. I don't hallucinate. I did that before. I don't even think I did. My mom tells me I did when I got sick, but I don't remember."

Eden stood up and hugged him close. "If you want to stay on it, stay on it. I would think you get tired of not being able to cum. You talked about thinking about sex all the time. All that might be related."

At the mention of sex, Bowie reached low, touched

Eden, and Eden let him, but he looked at the wide-open blinds apprehensively. "Don't you want to close the blinds?"

"What for?"

"I don't do free shows."

Bowie laughed. "You stupid. Thank you for helping me out, though. I love you." Bowie pulled him up the stairs to his room.

Eden looked around, aghast. There were mounds of clothes, furniture stacked haphazardly along the huge expanse of space. At the back end, near a window, he could see a bed with unmade sheets and rumpled, stained pillows. "What the hell happened in here? You sleep in this mess?"

"This my mom's shit. She put all her shit in here. I told her to get rid of it."

"This is your room, right? Why don't *you* get rid of it."

Bowie barked, "You crazy? She would flip her wig if I touched her stuff."

"Well, look, we got to do something. I can't even think straight in all this confusion. You know, your living space can have a direct impact on your mental state."

"What?"

"Let's clean some of this shit up, man. Get some fresh bedding, open up that window and move this stale air around. My dick can't even get hard in all this conflama."

Bowie leered and reached for his fly. "I bet you wrong."

Eden smacked his hands away. "Cut it out."

He shrugged. "Okay, where you want to start. I can throw her shit in the basement. She gonna blow her top but fuck it. This my room. Thank you for helping me, young head."

"Why do you keep thanking me? I didn't do shit. Can you stop it?"

Bowie hugged him tight. "But I love you! I want you to know that."

Repugnant isn't a description. It's more of a feeling. But Eden could think of no other way to describe it, the thing that made itself known to him. It gleefully whispered obscenities into his ear. A pus-colored drool oozed from its mouth as it forewarned him of things he could never have imagined. He didn't even have words that could adequately describe the abomination its mere presence embodied.

They had vacuumed, rearranged, and disinfected the room into a modicum of acceptability before falling ravenously upon one another, saying things with the heat of their breath, their sighs of satiation taking the place of words. They fell off into sleep like two overfed lynxes.

It was really Bowie that fell off into a contented, chemically predisposed slumber, emitting that familiar rumbling snore that Eden found so comforting. Eden lay thinking about the documents Bowie had thrown on his lap. Psychiatric histories, criminal dockets, medication regimens.

In his mind, he tried to line up the dates for certain events, certain criminal acts, with the timeline of when he had sex with Bowie. He asked himself if having sex with him re-traumatized him, if it brought him back to the episode of rape by his stepfather.

His thoughts all merged together like whispering voices in his head. He wondered if having hallucinations or hearing voices felt like this. He remembered his father's erratic behavior when he was younger, how he responded to internal stimuli and his mother responded to phone calls telling her where to pick up her husband: unclothed at the car dealership or washing at the restroom sink or carrying a briefcase full of newspapers, insisting that he was the owner of one million dollars in cash and would be bestowing riches on a few lucky people at the local bank. And the calls from police, always the police, or calls to the police, requesting intervention, remediation they had not been trained to provide.

These thoughts rushed around until they became a low whisper, lulling him into a light sleep. (Eden had never been able to go into a deep sleep when in someone else's bed.) His heart rate and body temperature dropped as he descended into astral sleep—a state wherein he was aware of his sleeping body and his environment, but waking required a concentrated effort. It was from here that he could recall minute details from dreams, such as color or smell.

He could sense himself lying in the bed, sense Bowie beside him, but he also felt light, as though his soul had floated above his earthly body, and that soul could feel the weight, the pull of that body below.

While he lay there, he casually noted its presence. Above him, coiled in a corner near the ceiling, it began to slowly spin, moving from a pinprick to the size of a golf ball, then larger, then a baseball, then larger, then a volleyball, then larger.

As it grew in size, the black expanded to include violet, indigo. The original black pinprick remained coiled at the center, up there by the ceiling, spinning, growing larger and morphing to an eye of vermillion. The largest outer ring of space fragmented into shimmering colors around the eye at the center, which slowly opened, pried wide by what looked like the searching legs of a black widow. The legs moved slowly, exposing themselves to be the curled tips of talons. They slowly grasped the edges of color, pulling them apart. Out stepped a cloven hoof, with a matted hide of dark brown, as if some animal had crawled through the blood of a dead animal.

Eden told himself it was a dream. He was used to this dream state, had experienced it many times before. His subconscious screamed that it was a dream, struggled mightily to waken the body. His astral body floated back, arms flailing as it was pulled to the earthly shell by panic and fear. But even returned to his body, Eden could not fully awaken himself.

He looked over, carefully not moving his head, and tried to roust Bowie. He saw him lying there immobile beside him, his eyes glimmering, wide with fright, drool sliding from his slack mouth.

Two rows of yellowed teeth, gums bleeding pus, filled the room with the reek of spoiled eggs. It grinned, pushing its sleek, dark head forth from the shimmer, lowering, descending slowly toward him with a long, low piercing peal, moving lower, lower, like lava from some vulgar volcano.

Eden could feel its heat, radiant like lust, pulsing toward him, drawing sweat from his frozen brow. His mouth stretched wide, pantomiming a scream that would not come. And the thing saw that panic. Like a flash, it darted out its filthy talons into his open mouth, forcing it wider, wider. He felt the dried hide on his palate, clumped and brittle, mashing down his tongue, pressing it against his teeth, pushing a weight that made him feel as though his jaw would snap.

Then, the head leaned close. He smelled its breath, like shit, as it whispered things in his ear, filled it with vile, unspeakable, unimaginable things. A wet, unctuous feeling clotted his auricle. Saliva spooled from Eden's immobile, slack mouth, ran down his neck, soaking the pillow beneath his head.

Then he heard Bowie's phone, charging on the dresser, buzz, and the thing angrily snapped its neck around, searching for the sound. It turned its back to him, arched its back, then, abruptly, it withdrew, retreating from Eden's body.

Eden, stiff with horror, watched the bulbous-shaped head, the wide shoulders and narrow, horned ass as it reached up into the shimmer and again stretched and pulled the vermillion center open. It created a space to let itself in and then pulled itself up, higher, higher, until it rested on the ledge of the dazzling pinpricks of light. Pulling in its feet and dropping back, it closed the shimmer into the nothingness from where it had come.

Waking was like climbing out of a sewer. He rose from the prone position of his encounter, an invisible weight pressing down on his shoulders. Eden sat up, placing his feet on the floor, and rested his head in his hands, elbows on his knees, trying to make sense of what had just happened. Just like a dream, he struggled to grasp the specifics, tried to keep everything in chronological order: the opening of space, the split in the universe, the first appearance of those tentacles and the mouth, that gaping maw rimmed with blade-like teeth.

He jumped, yelped, when Bowie touched his back. Turned quickly around, then relaxed when he realized the touch came from something familiar. Bowie wrapped his legs around him, hugged him close.

"You had a dream, baby? I scared you?"

Eden wiped sweat from his brow. "What the fuck. Wha? What was that thing? Did you hear it, too?"

Bowie kissed his shoulder blade. "Hear what?"

Eden pushed up from the bed, lifted blankets, waited for his underwear to fall out.

"Don't tell me you didn't see that, Bowie. I watched you. I saw you see it."

Bowie stood up, grabbed Eden's pants from the floor, handed them to him. He laughed. "Baby, you had a dream."

Eden shook his head, refusing to believe this. "That was no dream."

Bowie took his phone off the charger, reached to plug in his headphones. "What did you see, then? What was it?"

He didn't know what he had seen. He couldn't put it into words, didn't know how to describe the revulsion, how to give physical attributes to the feeling of nausea washing over him with just the retrieval of the memory. He stood there baffled, disbelieving, as Bowie put the headphones over his head and turned up the volume, singing loudly, his dick bouncing along his thigh as he clapped like a boom of thunder. "S-s-s-s-s, m-m-m."

Eden searched for his socks, found them balled under the bed. Bowie danced around him, running his hands along his body as Eden tied up the laces on his boots. Bowie began handing him his shirt, then swished it around like a bullfighting lure, yanking it back, then tugging it in front of Eden's face, until Eden finally snatched it and pulled it over his head.

"Look. You can block me out all you want, but you saw it, too. You did."

Bowie's back was to him, he shook his rear, the muscles in his back flexed, his head dipped. "I may be bad but I'm perfectly good at it. Sex in the air I don't know I love the smell of it."

Seeing the folder of court documents on the dresser, Eden lifted it and waved it at Bowie, mouthing words. "You deny things. You think if you say something didn't happen that you can just pretend it didn't."

Bowie made an elaborate motion of turning down the volume and widened his eyes at him. "I didn't hear you."

He turned the volume up again as Eden began talking. Eden walked over and tried to remove his headphones, but Bowie kept dodging his head out of the way as he continued to dance. Finally, Eden grabbed them and tugged.

"Hey! Don't break my shit."

"Look. These cheap ass Five Below headsets. I can get you four more pair."

Bowie laughed. "Don't talk shit on my headphones. They work, don't they?"

"For about three days, then you'll be back up at Miss Five Below for a replacement. Listen, let me ask you a question."

Bowie watched him.

Eden sat back on the bed and motioned for him to come over. Bowie came and let him pull him down onto his lap. Eden tossed the folder onto the bed and pressed his mouth against Bowie's head. "One of these reports. You told them you masturbate two times a week."

"I didn't want to tell them I do it every day. They would think I was really sick."

"Why are they asking you about that? Why are you

answering a question like that? That's a private thing that they don't have a right to ask. Don't they mean if you've masturbated outside?"

He shrugged. "I don't know what they mean. They ask the questions. I answer."

"But you don't have to answer, you know? You have a right to privacy."

He snorted. "You don't answer, you go to jail. So no, really, you don't have a right to shit."

"They're asking this question like jacking off is a pathology. Do you think there's something wrong with jerking off?"

"My mom sure does. Every fucking time I'm in my room, here she come—what you doing in here, don't close these doors—I can't even take a shit in privacy."

"I hope you're joking."

"Do I look like I'm joking?"

"There's a trauma assessment in those papers, right, that asks all these questions. Like did a parent ever insult or swear at you, or has anyone touched you, all that stuff. And you answered no to every single one of those questions."

"She don't insult me. Nobody touches me. That shit was all a long time ago."

"How can you say she doesn't insult you? I've heard some of the things she says."

"That shit don't mean nothing to me."

"It's abuse, though. And those things pile up. My dad had mental health issues all my life, and instead of treating it, he drank, used drugs to keep his demons away. And everybody suffered because of it."

"What's that got to do with me?" Bowie pushed off from him and turned onto the bed, resting his head on Eden's lap. "Let me tell you, them assessments ain't so those people can help. All they do is, some white woman reads them and says, yup, I knew these niggers live like animals, we got to go in there and take the kids to foster home, we got to put them in jail for not taking care of the kids. Don't nobody give a fuck about helping me, or you, or any of us. We feeding their pockets. Insurance payments, bail, lawyers, judges. Everybody is getting their cut and feeding on this."

Eden was quiet. He hadn't expected eloquence. He knew Bowie was smart, but he also knew how he usually cracked a joke or just stayed silent when conversation moved toward spaces he did not want to go to.

"I'm not saying you're wrong. But pretending things didn't happen won't make them go away, either. Like what happened last night. That thing that . . . that came in here . . . that happened. You know it as well as I do."

Bowie reached for his headphones, shouting an offkey song, gospel this time. He scrolled through YouTube until he found the right song.

"You can turn that volume as loud as you want. You know what I'm saying."

Bowie clapped his hands, *boom*.

Shrugging Eden lay back and continued reading the papers from the folder. After a time, he noticed the volume on Bowie's phone lower. Bowie stopped dancing and sat on the floor, scrolling through his phone. He was quiet for a while. As was Eden, fascinated by what he was reading.

Bowie laughed, walked over and flopped down beside Eden, who was lying on his back. Bowie thrust the phone in front of Eden's face. The glare of the screen annoyed him. He pushed the phone back a bit so he could see the screen. There was a picture of a slightly overweight guy that looked to be Puerto Rican. Bowie scrolled the screen so that Eden could see a chain of texts.

What up

What's up with you? I thought you were going to call me?

Am busy way whats up

I just wanted to see you. I really like you?

what u like about me

You seem to be cool peoples

you dont even now me

Bowie laughed. "I met this fat boy down Thirteenth Street back in the summer. He want to get with me so bad."

Eden watched him tap a message. He showed it to Eden with a laugh.

Well, I would like to get to know you better

how you going to now be batter you went to be my man

Maybe after we get to know each other. I want to be able to spend my life with someone.

Bowie laughed. "This guy really likes me."

can we live together boo

Maybe. Some day. That would be nice.

send me a pic of that ass and I will send you mine

They waited, watching, until a picture of a pale ass blinked onto the screen. Bowie threw down the phone, fell back on the bed, kicking his legs and laughing.

"You see that flat ass shit! I think I'm going to throw up!"

I'm waiting on that pic from you

Bowie picked up the phone and held it at a distance, reaching down to pull his dick to a flattering angle. Eden's hand flashed out and covered the eye of the camera lens. "What the fuck are you doing?"

"Don't worry, baby. I'm going to text him that I got a fucking man and stop fucking texting me."

"You were about to send him a dick pic."

"I was showing him what he was missing." He laughed.

Eden pushed up from the bed. "Are you fucking kidding me. You think it's cool to be laying here with me and just send dick pics all willy-nilly? Maybe you do have some kind of problem with compulsion or whatever."

"Huh? What's your problem? I don't want that sissy."

Eden put his hands on his hips, glaring at him through a mask of fury. "That's even worse. And I'm not the one with the problem. I'm not the one in treatment."

"I didn't hear you. Say that again?"

"Look, we don't have any commitment, none of that. And guys send dick pics all the day long, I know. But why would you want to do something mean-spirited like that?"

He laughed weakly. "I was just having some fun."

"That's fun to you?"

Eden flopped back on the bed. "Think about it like this. You talk about all the things that have happened to you when you were a kid. People taking advantage, treating you badly. What about the karma you create when you do mean shit to other people? You can't expect people to treat you any better than you treat other people. That's just simple humanity."

"I didn't hear you, baby."

"I think you're hearing me just fine. And stop calling me baby. That shit doesn't mean anything coming from you. You say the same shit to strangers you've just met." Eden laughed. "I mean, do you. But don't try to run that same shit on me. You're a grown ass man living with his mom, on house arrest because you don't seem to know what acceptable public behavior is. I think you better grow up and get off your mother's tit before you end up in a morgue somewhere."

Bowie smiled, swung a leg over Eden's and kissed his neck. "I'm sorry, baby. You accept my apology?"

Eden shook his head, smiling lazily. He grasped Bowie's narrow hips. "Don't try to bullshit me. No, I don't accept your apology."

"Why not?"

"It's bullshit. You have to put positivity into the world to get it back. Don't you understand that?"

Bowie put his hands around Eden's throat, leaned forward and kissed him. Eden laughed, pushed him back, laughed more as Bowie squeezed. "Okay, stop now. I'm getting up so I can get out of here before your mama gets home for your evening breast feeding."

Bowie pressed down, applying his weight, pressing harder with his thumbs against Eden's jugular. He felt a slight sting, a bit of pressure, but really, it was more the glazed look on Bowie's face, which belied the laugher coming from his mouth, that caused him to panic.

"Get up now, Bowie."

It was as if he didn't hear him.

Eden was fifty pounds heavier, so it was no effort to lift himself to a sitting position with Bowie still pressing at his neck. Bowie wrapped his legs around Eden's waist, squeezing with his muscular thighs. Eden stood, teetering at the added weight, and grasped him by the waist. He picked Bowie up, lifted him off and slammed him onto the top of the dresser.

"No more playing, man. And don't tell me about that wrestling shit, either." He pushed himself off from the dresser. Eden had turned from him and was heading toward the door when he leaped on his back, grabbing again at his throat. Eden fell forward, felt the sharp pain as one of his knees hit the thinly carpeted floor, heard the crack of bone.

Bowie's assault was not physically painful to him, but it was jarring. He was accustomed to violence being episodic. A slap from a drunken father, a push against a wall or the beating of a belt. Over in a flash. But Bowie seemed to have unending energy. Eden looked into his eyes and it was like Bowie wasn't there; he was sitting somewhere behind his eyes, watching to see how this panned out.

Eden was winded and felt his strength ebbing. He

knew he did not have enough energy to continue to hold him at bay much longer, and he didn't want to hurt him. Rather than striking out, he was primarily trying to stave him off. But when he hit the floor, the electric jolt of pain firing through his synapses, he was no longer himself. He was the child hiding under the bed while his father raged. The child jumping in front of his mother, taking the punch intended for her. Eden was not in the room when he grabbed Bowie's naked form and lifted him from the ground. He heard Bowie grunting from someplace far away, and he carried him like a baby to the doorway. As they entered the hall, Bowie continued to grapple. Eden heard nothing but a roar in his head as he lifted him overhead, standing at the head of the stairs.

Bowie looked behind him, saw the stairs in front of him, and grabbed at both sides of the threshold. He emitted a deep, low sound: "Whoa.' It was that sound, that *whoa*, that brought Eden back to the present. He looked at the stairs in front of him, stepped back and lowered Bowie to the floor.

And still, he didn't stop. He lunged up at Eden, slamming them both against the wall, and wrapped himself around his head, making it hard for Eden to breathe.

"Get off." His voice was muffled.

"You going to calm down now?" Bowie huffed.

"Get off," he repeated.

"Not until you calm yourself down."

Bowie's chest was pressed against Eden's face, so Eden reached around his back to hold him close, opened his mouth and bit him.

Bowie howled, spittle flying from his mouth as he dropped from Eden like a burned tick. Eden sat there, breathing heavily, sweat dripping from his forehead. Bowie sat opposite him, blood bubbling from his bruised knees.

Bowie's phone emitted a muffled chime from far off. Panting heavily, Bowie crawled around him into the bedroom.

Eden sat with his head low, trying to breathe, trying to make sense of what had just happened. Tried to remember the conversation, what words, what sentences had led to him sitting on the floor with a torn shirt and a slowly swelling knee.

"I tried to kill Eden!" Bowie wailed. "I don't know. It just happened!"

Eden leaned against the wall, his head thrown back, listening to Bowie cry.

"He said he was leaving. I just—I was trying to get him to calm down but he wouldn't. What? I don't fucking know. Stop asking me questions!"

Eden thought about that. While Bowie had not done that much bodily damage, he wondered if he really meant that he was trying to kill him. Was that his intention? He heard movement, and Bowie crawled out into the hall, laid his head in Eden's lap, crying, wailing, loudly.

"I love you, Eden. I don't know why that happened. I'm sorry."

Eden put his hand on Bowie's damp face, stretched out his legs along the width of the hallway, and closed his eyes.

Eden's phone continuously buzzed the entire drive back to his house. He ignored it. He also ignored the texts that constantly pinged.

He ran a hot bath and immersed himself, staying until the water ran tepid, pruned his skin.

As the day moved from bright to dim, he lay in his bed, and, finally, his phone went quiet. He covered his face with a pillow and dropped off to sleep.

When he woke, his room was dark, except for the light coming from his phone. It was an unknown number.

"Yeah?"

"Bowie asked me to call you."

He could hear Bowie in the background. "What for?"

"What happened between y'all?"

"What did he tell you?"

"Bowie didn't tell me anything. He's all upset, talking about going to the hospital before he kills himself."

"Well then you better take him there if he's pretending he's going to kill himself."

"He never says stuff like that. This is serious."

Eden snorted. "Yeah, okay."

"Listen, I wanted to ask you a favor."

"You want to ask me a favor?"

"It's not money or anything like that."

He said nothing.

"Part of what happened when they put Bowie on house arrest, they still got to have a meeting to figure out if they still want him to be in Behavioral Health Court. They're having this meeting with the PO, the social worker, somebody from the insurance company, his psychiatrist, a whole bunch of people. They sent me a notice of the date, finally. It's going to be at the outpatient offices."

"Uh-huh."

"I would be ever so grateful if you could come. All those people there against just us. If we could have somebody else that can be an advocate . . . ."

"Oh, no. That's not for me. I'm sure those people are going to work to create a plan that's best for Bowie."

"You kidding, right? When's a Black man ever been given a break?"

Eden tried to paint a happy picture, but he remembered his father, sitting for years in mental health facilities, sometimes neglected, sometimes worse, depending on whether his insurance was active or invalid.

He sighed. "Look, I thought I knew Bowie. But I really didn't know about all this."

"All those people throwing around their big degrees and their *expertise,* I just want somebody there that can talk at their level. I get so tongue tied."

"I have never seen you at a loss for words."

"That's different. I don't want my son to be shipped off like some animal. He deserves better than that. He's been through so much. He deserves a break for once in his fucking life."

"Look, I can't promise you anything. I'll think about it."

"That's all I can ask. I thank you so much."

Eden said goodbye, but before the line disconnected he heard Bowie's voice: "What did he say?"

Then, the line went dead.

His shaking hands, gripping the steering wheel, and the burning feeling in his belly communicated to him just how nervous he was. He wasn't sure if it was the thought of walking into a room filled with strangers or because this would be the first time seeing Bowie since the incident. They had spoken on the phone sporadically, but each time he asked Eden if he could see him, Eden had put him off. For the first time, Bowie hadn't barraged him with appeals to change his mind.

Pulling in front of the house on Maple Leaf, he saw a petite, dark brown woman, wearing jeans and a loose T-shirt, leaning against the house smoking a cigarette. Though her features were softer, more youthful, Eden could see the similarity in facial features, in angular bone structure: She looked like Magdelene, but she had Bowie's prominent Aztec nose, his dark brow. He marveled at how the same features could read so differently on a man compared to a woman.

Bowie had asked him to call at seven a.m. to make sure he was awake so that he could get dressed for the meeting at Northwest, but when Eden called his phone there had been no answer. He had tried to call for over an hour, then showered and dressed and decided he would just drive over to the house. He stepped from the car, absently pulling at the creases in his dark pants. He wore dark, slim-cut pants and a thin Armani sweater, along with well-made Italian shoes polished to a buff shine. He figured being well-dressed would impress the social workers at the meeting. It also helped bolster his self-confidence by creating a figurative wall that allowed him to establish and maintain a professional, some might even say standoffish, presence.

As he approached the house, the woman pushed herself off of the wall and smiled dimly at him. He smiled back. "Hello. Do you know if Bowie is home? He was expecting me to take him to a meeting this morning."

Lilith took one last drag and flicked her cigarette into the street, nodding at him. "They sleep like vampires. The door's unlocked. He can't hear too good, so knocking won't do no good. Just go on upstairs. The door on the left at the top of the landing, just go on in."

Eden thanked her and walked up the stairs to the front door, feeling the woman watching him intently. When he looked back, she lowered her head and turned around, walking along the side of the building.

The television blared Gayle King's unctuous celebrity pandering. The room was cast in shadow, the shades drawn and curtains closed. He walked up the stairs to the open door of Bowie's room. He passed a closed door on his right. He approached the bed, rumpled with pillows and bedclothes, saying Bowie's name as he lifted the sheets.

There was no one there.

He looked up at the ceiling and remembered the thing that had not been a dream. He remembered the hissing. The foul thoughts unfurling into his ear. He rushed back out of the room and approached the closed door. He knocked. Knocked again.

"Hello? Anybody there?" He cleared his throat and repeated his greeting, then, with trepidation, he turned the knob. As he turned it, the doorknob turned against his hand, and the door was pulled open.

Eden squinted to see into the dim, past the rot of stale cigarette smoke.

Magdelene pulled the door open. Eden's eyes looked down at her exposed breasts, then looked away, then looked at her face as she pulled the sash to her pink robe together, the color vivid against the sheen of her skin. Eden thought he said, "I came to make sure Bowie was up," but he wasn't sure. He stood there, in the hall, as she turned away from him, showing him the knot on the back of the scarf tied around her head.

Through the roar of sound in his head, he thought he heard her say something, but he did not know what. Then, he saw Bowie jump out of the tumult of blankets on the bed that was pushed against a dark wall at the far corner of the room. He was a flash of paisley boxers as he dashed past, running to his room.

"I'm sorry, man. I didn't hear the phone. I'll be ready in

a second, just let me brush my teeth." Eden smelled him as he passed: morning breath and sweat.

As the sounds of morning activity echoed through the house, Eden descended the stairs and walked out into the burn of the sun. Lilith stood smoking, again leaning against the wall. She surveyed him as he passed. "You find him?' she asked. He wondered if the decay he heard in her voice was real or imagined. He continued to his car.

He sat there, letting the heat lick his face through the windshield, allowed the discomfort of the temperature to comfort him. The rap on the window startled him. Magdelene knocked a knuckle on the glass. He noticed she was wearing the pink robe, barefoot. He cracked the door open.

"We can just meet you there. You know where it is, right?"

He nodded, looking straight ahead.

"Okay, thank you so kindly."

He watched her walk back to the house, watched the other woman mouth something to her, then started the engine and pulled away.

He sat in the parking lot of Northwest Outpatient, vacillating between waiting and pulling off. He could get his number changed. Never hear from Bowie again. He thought about him in the hole, sitting in a dark cell with no clothing, no phone contact, no medication for days, weeks.

He saw them pull into the space next to him. For the first time that he could remember, Bowie didn't break into a huge grin when he saw him. He looked nervous. When Eden got out of his car, Bowie hugged him tightly, pinning his arms to his sides, mumbling into his chest. "Thank you so much for helping me, man. I love you."

Magdelene grasped his shoulder, pulled him back. "We need to get going. There goes that bitch from the program. What's her name? Lolly Dopey Ganger?"

Bowie laughed loudly. "Yup. That's her name. Dopey ass bitch."

"I thought you said you like her," said Eden.

"How you going to like the bitch that's trying get you locked up? Trying to get you to say shit to get you in trouble?" Magdelene interjected.

"I didn't say I like her. She's cool, though. She got me out of jail, not locked up. That's that white bitch. The PO."

"They're all the same. That's what everybody at this meeting is trying to do, so don't you forget that."

Eden said, "You have to advocate for yourself. Don't let these people intimidate you. This is your life. You have to remember that you are just as important as they are. You are the one that knows your life. They only have bits and pieces. Things written down by other people—"

"You go in there," Magdelene cut him off, "and you don't say shit. If you start running your mouth they going to trip you up and you will be right back in jail. You let Eden do the talking."

Eden shook his head. "He has to do the talking. Just be honest with them. If you are having mental health issues, or you have uncontrollable urges related to your meds, or even because you forget to take your meds, this is the time to get it all out in the open so you can get whatever it is you need."

Magdelene pushed Bowie away from Eden, toward the door. "He don't need no help other than me. We can figure it out together. Without all these nosy people thinking he's some freak."

Eden was startled by the number of people that appeared for the meeting. There were three probation officers: Brittany, who was the supervisor, Kaitlyn, who was Bowie's current PO, and a muscular Black man, Malik, who would be taking over for Kaitlyn due to pending maternity leave. There was a representative from Behavioral Health Court, the diversion specialist from Northwest Outpatient, Dr. Hildebrand, the psychiatrist Bowie used at Northwest, two social worker trainees, Lola Dopinger from Mockingbird, and on speakerphone, listening in and saying absolutely nothing, Bowie's care manager from his insurance company.

Eden felt all eyes watching him as he entered behind Bowie and Magdelene. Lola watched him astutely while making introductions. After she had introduced everyone, she looked at Bowie. "Bowie, will you introduce us to the people that you have with you?"

"Huh?"

Sitting in the seat beside Bowie, speaking in a low tone just for him to hear, Eden said, "She wants you to introduce us."

The parole officers sat peering at Eden from the table in the middle of the room. Magdelene crossed to the other side of the table and said, "I am Magdelene St. Charles. I'm Bowie's mother. And of course you should all know Bowie, I would hope. And this is a friend of the family that I asked to be here today, Mr. Cross."

Lola sat on the opposite side of Bowie. "Do you have any credentials, Mr. Cross?"

Eden hoped his voice did not sound as tremulous as it sounded in his own ears. "What sort of credentials?"

"Are you a therapist, nurse? Social worker of some sort?"

"I'm a friend."

Lola's lips turned up into an amused smile. "Okay. Well, as you all know, we are here to develop a plan in response to Bowie's ongoing legal issues and his recent violation, which resulted in his being placed on house arrest."

Bowie snapped, "I didn't violate no rules. What did I violate?"

Kaitlyn said, "There are reports of episodes of exposure while in treatment at the partial program."

"That's a lie!"

Eden placed his hand on Bowie's arm, trying to remind him to remain calm. Lola observed him.

"Has the partial program documented these events? Do we have some sort of tracking form that records episodes of this nature?" Eden asked.

Lola said, "We don't document these occurrences. Because of our program description, these events, which happen all the time, are not considered to be incidents. Therefore we don't track them."

Magdelene leaned forward, her hands on the table. "So we just have your say-so?"

"My say-so, as Bowie's therapist, is the only one that matters."

"That's some bullshit," said Magdelene, looking at Bowie.

Bowie said, "So you're saying what I say doesn't matter? Isn't this my treatment?"

Magdelene said, "This is how all this started anyway. Some word-of-mouth shit that nobody can prove! It seems like you want to keep my child locked behind bars."

Bowie watched her intently. Eden could see that he was matching his mother's state of agitation. He tried to re-direct him. "Why don't we let Bowie speak for himself."

Bowie looked at him, then seemed to struggle to find the words. "I don't know. I need some help. I talked to you, Dr. Hildebrand, about my meds. I don't want to take those meds anymore. They're making me sick."

Kaitlyn said, "Remaining med compliant is a stipula-tion of your probation. If you don't stick to it, you will be in violation."

"I didn't hear you."

Eden again put his hand on Bowie's arm. "He's not re-fusing to take meds. He's saying some of his meds might de-serve reconsideration. He's been on some of them for a very long time and perhaps they have lost their efficacy."

Bowie leaned forward. "I had a rough life. My dad. I don't talk to my dad. I was raped by my stepdad when I was a kid. And I don't have any friends. Kids used to make fun of me in school. That's why I hate people my own age. I don't trust them. I always been able to make friends with people older than me. I don't know why I got put on house arrest. I just want Dr. Hildebrand to take me off Abilify."

"I don't think that's necessary," interjected Dr. Hildebrand. "You haven't really been taking Abilify for very long. Especially considering you've been noncompliant much of the time, and only recently have you been switched to the monthly intramuscular shot."

"I take my meds. Who says I don't take my meds?"

Magdelene spoke up, wary that her lie explaining Bowie's legal problems, med noncompliance, was about to be exposed. "You need to take those meds. They work, so there's no reason to try something else that might not work."

Eden said, "But I thought the psychiatrist monitors and observes drug effectiveness and interactions? So why wouldn't he be able to try other meds if he is under supervision by this very large team, all of you sitting here?"

Dr. Hildebrand said, "It's just not warranted at this time."

Bowie slapped his hand on the table. "I'm not taking something that's getting me into trouble and getting me locked up! I have a lawyer, you know. I will sue your ass! This is malpractice or something."

Malik swiftly stood up, walking toward Bowie. Lola

stopped him with a look. "That won't be necessary. Bowie will be able to control his outbursts."

Magdelene said, "Calm yourself down. Are you getting sick? Are you okay, or do we need to end this meeting and go get an evaluation."

"I don't need a fucking evaluation. Why don't you get an evaluation?"

"Hey," said Eden, "why don't you explain, in a calmer fashion, the reason you want to get off of this drug? The lawsuits related to this—"

"You want to blame medications," Lola said, "for your current circumstances, which means that you're still in denial about your problem. The reason you were in jail is not because you take Abilify. You were in jail because you took your dick out in public." Lola saw Eden flinch at her mention of the word *dick*, and took some pleasure from regaining control of the room.

When he regained his composure, Eden said, "Are you aware of tearooms? Of social interactions and patterns used by gay men?"

"I don't think so."

Magdelene said, "That has nothing to do with what's going on here right now."

Eden wondered if he was imagining the smirk on the male PO's face. "Are there any gay male therapists at this program? I'm assuming that there is programming there for LGBTQ."

Lola said, "We don't have much familiarity with that

population."

Dr. Hildebrand ostentatiously looked at her watched as she stood. "Well, I need to excuse myself, as my allotted time is done."

Bowie sneered, "It's all about them billable hours, right Doc? Don't think I'll forget. My lawyer will be getting back to you."

Eden cast him a hard glance, willing him to shut up.

Lola said, "Yes, it does seem that time is winding down."

Magdelene said, "But we haven't reached any resolution. What the hell was this meeting about?"

Lola looked across the room at her. "This meeting, really, was to let Bowie know that this is the last chance we are giving him. If he continues to break the rules he will be discharged back into the custody of the county jail."

Malik cleared his throat, "Yes. And with that being said, we need to make sure you're aware of the expectations."

Not hearing clearly, Bowie leaned forward. "The what?"

"You must appear every day at Mockingbird. No signing out early, no coming in late. No use of cell phones or social media while at the program. No social media at any time. If you engage in any sexual activity, you need to contact the probation office to inform them."

Eden was stunned. Too stunned to say anything.

Bowie said, "How'm I going to have sexual activity when I'm on house arrest?"

Magdelene stood up, draping the strap of her handbag across her shoulders. "There will be no problems, here. And we thank you very kindly for your time."

As the attendees drifted from the room, Eden lingered, so that he could follow Lola into the hallway. He walked behind her and cleared his throat. "I just wanted to ask you a question." She turned, swaying her hair over her shoulder. "Sure."

"There is a problem related to gambling. All of Bowie's issues stem from this gambling problem that all his family uses as their form of socializing. Is there some sort of treatment that you could recommend to help him with that?"

Lola crossed her arms, looking to be sure no one was within proximity. "That problem is secondary to the sexual problem. I've been doing this a long time. Believe me when I tell you these people have all set up an intricate house of cards that hides years and years of deviant behavior."

"Deviant? If he were a white female with schizophrenia and he stripped at the supermarket or the library, would he have been arrested, or would he have been taken home and everything written off as a side effect of his diagnosis?"

Lola smiled sadly. "I can't answer that for you. Except to say that he is not a white female."

David Jackson Ambrose

FROM THE OFFICE OF
DR. JANET HILDEBRAND
NORTHWEST OUTPATIENT SERVICES

Dear Mr. Long,

We regret to inform you that Northwest Outpatient Services will no longer provide medication management services for you.

As you acknowledge on our Consent for Services Agreement, signed by you last year, Northwest provides medication management and administration of intramuscular medications only for members that are participating in our outpatient or individual therapy programs. As you have not been a part of those services, and have been receiving them through another provider, all services through this facility have been suspended effective today.

We recommend that you contact your partial program administrator as soon as possible to arrange for medication management. As a reminder, the intramuscular administration of medication mandated by Behavioral Health Court is due this week.

We thank you for your participation with the Northwest community. You will always remain a valued citizen as you move on to greater independence and recovery.

If you are ever in need of services in the future our door is always open to you.

Thank you,
Dr. Hildebrand

The participants of Accountability group session were milling about talking to one another. They were unaccustomed to the facilitator not being the first one in the room for group, so they kept a casual eye on the vacant chair in the circle.

"So you say you like the old heads, huh?" Kenny Mack, the senior member of not just the group, but the entire facility, asked Bowie. As one of the longtime participants of both the partial and residential program, he was looked upon as the group elder. The men looked to him as the barometer of what was accepted and what was not. Bowie gauged the man to be around sixty years old. He was tall and cocoa brown with a sandy gray afro and nappy tufts of hair sprouting on his jaw. He leaned one arm against a wall, towering over Bowie with a grandiose smile.

Tugging the threads of an old sweater, Bowie eyed the man's paunch, then looked up. "I said the old heads like me."

Kenny Mack laughed, showing yellowed teeth. "Ain't that what I said?"

"It's very different from what you said. What you want

from me, old man?"

"It's like that?"

"Just want to know what you want."

NoBueno moved over, leaning on the wall behind Bowie. "You know what he wants. Everybody knows what he wants. What you need to be asking is what he got."

Bowie laughed. "I can see what he got. You live here. You ain't got shit to offer me."

NoBueno said, "You act like the people living here are in a homeless shelter or something. We got the same things anybody else got."

Bowie laughed. "That's some bullshit. You got to stay here twenty-four seven. You can't go nowhere unless you got a one on one on your ass. I get to go home every day and live my life."

Kenny Mack stood upright, glared at them. "You think you got it better than me? You stupid."

The room quieted as Lola Dopinger entered, clapping her well-manicured hands. "Okay people, let's take our seats, we are already past time."

Bowie watched her, nodding in approval. "That's a bad bitch, right there." She wore a narrow, black skirt, black hosiery and leather stiletto pumps. Her hair was pulled back into a bun, and she wore gold glasses, low on her nose. She sat, crossing her legs, waiting for everyone to be seated before she spoke. "Kylie has taken a job elsewhere, and so I'm going to be your facilitator for today."

Someone started singing "Another One Bites the

Dust," and there was laughter all around.

"That's enough of that. Let's get focused, gentlemen."

NoBueno asked, "So we got you now?"

She laughed. "I don't think so. I am filling in in a pinch, but you will have other therapists filling in until the position is filled. Now, let's get down to it. When I walked in here just now, I saw three of you gentlemen cozied up in a corner over there. You want to tell us what the topic of discussion was?"

Bowie felt her eyes peering at him. He shrugged.

Kenny Mack said, "The young bull think he better than everybody because he don't live here."

Lola crossed her arms, looked at Bowie.

"I didn't say I was better than nobody. I feel sorry for the people that got to stay here, for real."

"How come?" someone asked.

"What?"

Lola said, "Fred wants to know why you feel sorry for the people living here."

"I don't know .... I ... it's like, well you can't go outside in peace, you can't take a shit without somebody knocking on the door asking if you beating your tallywacker."

Lola interrupted, "Let's not use kiddie words, here. Part of the problem for men with issues with sexual boundaries is the way they substitute cutesy, playful words with the terminology that they should use. You don't have a tallywacker. It's a dick."

Bowie covered his mouth and laughed into his hand while laughter erupted through the room.

"I know that's right," said NoBueno.

"Alls I'm saying is y'all might as well be in jail. You don't make your own food, you eat what they tell you to eat. You can't even have sex. Or you want me to say fuck?" He smirked.

Lola said, "I know you think you're funny. You're smarter than everybody else with that slick mouth, right? But here you are."

Kenny Mack said, "How you any more free, young bull? I see your ankle bracelet winking like a drunken whore. You in jail, too."

"Yeah, but that's coming off one day. You will be here till the day you die."

Lola said, "Don't be so sure it will come off. If you can't learn that there are rules and expectations in this world, you will be living like this the rest of your life."

NoBueno said, "I know what you mean, Bowie. But we have it better than what you think. This program has saved some people from living in a real prison or even worse. Some people lived in places nobody accepted them. Some were threatened every day and beaten up. Tortured for not being like the rest of them. It's not that bad here."

Someone laughed. "You got to be shitting me."

NoBueno shook his head. "Serious. Look, I got three hots and a cot. I ain't got no bills, no landlord trying to evict me and whatever. It's a beast out there on them streets. You ain't got no education, you ain't got no GED, don't nobody want to give you no job."

"Especially if you got jail time on your record or you served your time, paid your dues, but now your name's on the list for sex offenders, who gone hire you? You can't even get in McDonald's."

Lola said, "It's not hopeless. There are places out there willing to give people a chance, if you are really doing the work, and not just playing the game. You have to make real recovery your goal and stick to it. That's what this program is here to help you do. Give you the tools to live differently."

NoBueno said, "I got friends here, too. People in here got lives too, you know. We are more than what you can read on a docket sheet."

Lola said, "But that is why you are here. The things on those dockets are crimes you cannot pretend don't exist."

"It's more than that," NoBueno snapped, then spoke on calmly. "Like, say you're here for killing somebody."

Kenny Mack laughed. "This ain't no place for killers. Ain't nobody like that here."

"Just saying," NoBueno said. "So, take somebody like me, right? Say I was here because them docket sheets got all these offenses, saying my whole life I was exposing myself to little girls, but really I took off my clothes during a manic episode and some kids were around. Now I'm known as the pedophile. THEN, one day, when I'm fifteen years old, I find my pops buggering my kid brother in the basement, right? So I snap. Boom! Knock that fucker over the head with a coal bucket. And he dies. Courts know it happened by accident, but they also know I'm the local pervert, so instead of state prison, they 'do me a favor' and put me here. Now society is safe, they don't have to see me no more."

Kenny Mack said, "Is this fairy tale corner or group?"

Lola glared at him. "Let me just say this to you, Jose: If I find out you have somehow been reading things you're not supposed to, been acting like a social worker, you will be out of here so fast your head will spin."

"I'm just trying to make a point to Bowie."

"What is your point?"

"It's like I said: This place is not as bad as he thinks it is. We are a community in here. We watch out for each other. I got friends here. Even though some of them homophobic as fuck, they still cool."

"Homo who?" said Bowie.

"People that have an aversion to or are afraid of gay people," said Lola.

"Fuck that. I ain't friends with nobody that can't accept me like I am."

"How about your mother?" Lola asked. "Does she accept you like you are?"

"Say that again?"

"Your mother," said NoBueno.

"What about her?"

"Never mind," said Lola. "Let's move on."

Bowie said, "Me and my mom are cool. She gets on my fucking nerves sometimes, but I know I got a place to lay my head."

NoBueno said, "But you say she don't give you privacy,

right? So how you sitting here talking about how we don't have no privacy and we can't do this and we can't do that and you more restricted than we are?"

"Look, don't nobody talk about my mom. I don't play that shit."

Lola said, "No one is saying anything about your mother, Bowie."

"And I don't got no GED. I graduated." The room erupted in laughter.

NoBueno laughed, nodding his head. "I know we ain't known each other long, but you're my friend, too. I like you a lot."

Lola said, "Did you tell him what you are here for, Jose? How you groom people so they do things for you and take the fall for your shit? You like Bowie because he's got a big dick."

Bowie felt his ears burn with embarrassment as laughter filled the room. He barely heard NoBueno shouting, "That's not fair! That's not fair!"

Lola said, "As I said earlier, let's not hide behind pretty words and false narratives. Say what you really mean. If you can't be honest with others, at least be honest with yourselves."

At the close of group, Lola stood by the door as the men filed out. NoBueno sauntered past, rolling his eyes angrily. As Bowie passed, Lola flagged him. She was waving the letter he had given her earlier at him. He looked at her. "Our doctor has agreed to write you a script for your intramuscular. He was not too pleased because we do not provide med management unless you are receiving residential services."

"But he sees me every month. Asks me dumbass questions just like they all do. So why does he do that and can't write me prescriptions?"

She ignored him. "Here is our script for Abilify. We don't have a nurse in the program, but you will need to have a professional administer this for you."

"Wha? Where am I supposed to get that done? Northwest won't see me now. You saw the letter."

"If you are unable to provide evidence that you have received your shot, you know you will be violating—"

"What am I supposed to do?" he shouted.

"Lower your voice. Do I need to call your PO?"

He snatched the papers out of her hands. Lola yanked them back. "You don't snatch shit from me. You must be out of your motherfucking mind."

"I'm sorry, Lola. I got hype."

She nodded and handed the papers to him. "I'll give you an extra day to take care of this, but you better handle it."

Where u at

am waitng outside mockingbird 30 minutes now

u went me to go the fuck to jail

are u coming to get me yes or no

Eden grunted as he lifted his foot onto the bed to cut his toenails. Damn. He wondered if it had always been this much of a struggle to reach his foot or if this was the first sign of old age.

He looked over at the screen of his buzzing phone.

am going to call u in a minute baby

His phone rang.

"Why did you send a text that you were going to call me instead of just calling me in the first place?"

"What you say?"

Eden sighed. "Never mind. How can I help you?"

Bowie laughed. "You are funny, boo. What you doing?"

"Sitting on the toilet."

He laughed. "No you're not."

"I could be. What are you doing?" Eden heard voices in the background. "Are you not home?"

"I'm at this dumbass card game. Ain't nobody winning shit. And they ain't give up a spot at the table."

Eden looked at his watch. Six o'clock. "What do you mean you're at a card game? You are supposed to go home after you leave partial."

"That bald-head bitch didn't pick me up, so I had to walk. Probably at the slots somewhere."

"What the fuck is wrong with you, Bowie? Why didn't you just walk home? It's not that far."

"Why are you cussing at me? I didn't cuss at you."

"Would you fucking listen? You know you're going back to jail, don't you?"

Bowie sucked his teeth. "They ain't paying attention to this."

Eden trembled with anger. He didn't know why he was so angry. "Yeah, okay. Whatever. Talk to you later. Or not."

"Don't say that, boo. I'm asking you to come pick me up."

"Why should I pick you up, Bowie? I have my own shit to do here."

"I know you do. I'm going to get locked up anyway because I can't get my shot and that bitch says I'm violating."

"You have a call on line two."

Lola huffed angrily and stretched back languidly in the creaking chair. "This late? It's after hours. Who is it?"

"An Eden Cross."

She picked up, speaking in a clipped voice, "This is Lola."

While Eden drove through the narrow streets, Bowie held the phone out toward him so that he could hear via speakerphone.

"Hello. This is Eden Cross. We met at Bowie Long's team meeting."

She said nothing.

"I'm here with Bowie now. We went to pick up this medication, the Abilify. But he has no way of getting the injection. Northwest has discharged him. He tells me you have a doctor there. Why can't he receive the shot while he's there?"

"I'm sorry, we don't administer meds at our partial program. We're not licensed to do so. I've explained to Bowie."

Eden looked over at him, frowning. "Well how is he

supposed to stay in compliance if no one will give him the shot? That's something that's beyond his control."

"Can't you give him the shot?"

Eden pumped the brakes. "Excuse me?"

"It only has to be done by a medical professional if it's administered on site."

Eden looked over at Bowie. He nodded.

For deep intramuscular deltoid or gluteal injection by healthcare professionals only. Do not administer by any other route. Inject full syringe contents immediately following reconstitution.

Eden and Bowie looked at the sturdy white box, at the vial holding a white powder, at the glass container with a plunger at the top holding a clear liquid.

"That lying bitch," Bowie whispered.

"What?"

"She said it didn't need to be given by a medical professional."

He looked at the neatly wrapped needles. There were different gauges. According to the directions, the smaller one was for the deltoid, and the longer one was for gluteal injection.

"What's a gluteal?" Bowie asked.

Eden was reading the instructions. He answered absently, "Your ass. This fucking needle has to be three inches long. I can't do this."

"Stop being a pussy. You acting like you're getting the needle, not me. All you got to do is give it."

"How do you usually get this? Your arm or your ass?"

He rapped a song, "Ass, ass, baby."

"Shhhh! I'm trying to read these instructions!"

"Well you asked me a question!"

a) Push plunger rod slightly to engage threads. And then, rotate plunger rod until the rod stops rotating to release diluent. After plunger rod is at complete stop, middle stopper will be at the indicator line.

b) Vertically shake the syringe vigorously for 20 seconds until drug is uniformly milky-white.

"Wow. Look at that. It's chalky white. It looks kind of pretty."

Without further preamble, Bowie dropped his trousers and lay across Eden's lap. Eden, seated on the tub in the narrow bathroom, yelped and pulled him up.

"Don't rush me, would you."

"Just do it. It's cool." He once again lay across Eden's lap.

"It's supposed to be given in a standing position." He rubbed Bowie's ass, kissed the small of his back as he pushed him off. He grabbed a large grip of muscle. "You ready?"

"Would you come on!" Then he added, softly, "Baby."

Eden watched the needle descend into the mass of muscle, making sure to insert the syringe all the way in, at a forty-five-degree angle, as the instructions specified.

Bowie felt that familiar sharp brilliance of pain followed by pressure, which slowly released. He heard the familiar sound of tearing and smelled the antiseptic waft of alcohol as Eden dabbed a prep pad at the small spurt of blood that rose on the dark flesh. He felt the warmth of Eden's whiskers as he kissed him on his ass, then lightly smacked it as he stood up, making sure to cautiously place the remnants into a plastic, red bio-waste bag, tying it carefully. Bowie pulled up his pants while Eden moved past him in the tight space to get to the sink to thoroughly wash his hands. He then turned and pulled Bowie close, leaning back against the counter.

"Did it hurt?"

"Fuck yeah it hurt. It's a needle." They both laughed. Bowie said, "Thank you, baby. I love you."

Eden said, "I love you, too." Then he panicked, wished he could take it back, then let the thought of it, the possibilities and the potential consequences roam around in his mind. He liked the feel of it, the way it spread a warmth through his soul and heated the tight confines of the room.

Eden had been sitting in Mockingbird's sparsely furnished waiting room for over an hour, and he was growing increasingly annoyed at the wait. The windowless room was cool. There was a table large enough for four wooden chairs and a dusty plastic palm tree at the corner of one of the green tiled walls.

Eden once more took a slip of paper from his folder resting on the floor beside his monk strap boots and dialed the number.

This time, finally, there was an answer. A clipped, terse voice said, "Hello."

"Hello, Miss Stenger?"

"Who is this?"

"My name is Eden Cross. We sort of met last month at the treatment team meeting for Bowie Long. Well, sort of, I mean, you participated by phone."

"I don't recall the name."

"You are the care manager that represents complex case presentations for his insurance company, right?" Even though he posed this as a question he did not need an answer. The line was silent, so he went on, "I'm calling to get your help with an issue we've been having. There have been studies recently and news reports with concerns over side effects of a certain medication that Mr. Long has been taking for many, many years. There are reports of compulsive behaviors, gambling, sexual preoccupation, increased duration of manic phases."

"Who is this, again? You're with a treatment team? Are you with Behavioral Health Court?"

"I'm advocating for Mr. Long and helping him to advocate for himself. He has requested to be taken off of Abilify, but due to legal requirements, it has been hard to do."

"How did you get my number?"

Phone numbers to direct employees were not accessible to the public. Customers were patched through to a general customer service line. It had not been easy to get the number, but embedded within the voluminous reams of papers insurance sent each year to members, the name of Bowie's care manager had been listed. Eden called the corporate number, pretending to be a family member in a state of emergency.

"We were wondering if Bright Line Insurance is aware of these studies, and if you might be able to provide us with a letter of support that Mr. Long can use in the event that he is deemed to be in violation of his requirements with Behavioral Health Court." Eden looked up as Magdelene rushed into the room, spewing apologies for being late. Eden signaled to her that he was on the phone. She sat down across from him.

"I am unable to talk to you. It would be a violation of

privacy rights."

"As I stated before, I was present at Mr. Long's team meeting. If you look at the attendance sheet for that meeting you will see my signature as p—"

"If we don't have a release form signed by the member we are unable to give you information."

Eden grew angry at the indignation in the woman's voice. "I'm not asking you to give me any information that violates privacy. I'm not asking questions about Mr. Long's treatment. I am asking you if you can provide a letter for him to assist in his self-advocacy."

"Bright Line provides no information without the express permission of its members. I need to end this call now."

The line went dead. Eden shook his head in disbelief. "This bitch."

Magdelene rummaged in her handbag for her crushed pack of cigarettes, then, when Eden frowned at her, remembered that she was in a nonsmoking facility and cursed under her breath.

"I told you you wouldn't get nowhere. Ain't nobody trying to do no extra work. Especially not for some little Black nobody."

"This shit really annoys me. People are hiding behind this HIPAA shit so they don't have to do any work. I went through this same nonsense when I first tried to get help for my father.

"Nobody would talk to me. I called Aging and Adult, they acted like I was some thug trying to exploit him. I tried to get an assessment done, people just kept giving me the run around."

"What I say? The only person that's going to give two shits is me. That's all he's got."

"Even if what this woman said was true, you'd think she'd offer to email a release form to me or something. Just fucking lazy."

A dark figure flashed past the doorway, then returned. Bowie stood there with his hands on his hips, eyeing them in amazement. "What you doing in here?"

Magdelene watched him walk around to sit next to Eden. She made note of the change in Eden's demeanor, the way they both grinned stupidly at one another.

"I told you we were going to come with you to your next psych appointment to help you advocate for coming off that crap."

"I didn't think you meant it. Thank you, baby."

Eden shifted uncomfortably. Magdelene witnessing her son's endearments made him hyperaware of the differences in their age, of how different they were from each other.

Magdelene said, "I told you I think it's a bad idea to come off his meds. He's been taking them, and they work. It's stupid. Y'all going to run him back to the hospital."

"Mom! Can't you stop always being negative?"

"Well, they are not working if they are the reason that he's been getting into trouble with the law."

"And trying something else isn't coming off meds. It's just trying something else. You can be so dumb sometimes."

"Who are you talking to like that?"

"I'm talking to you."

"You must want to really be sent up to the hospital if you think you can talk to me like that."

"You think anytime I say what you don't like that I'm supposed to go to the hospital? I think maybe you need to go there your damn self. You got issues way bigger than me."

She snorted in derision. "You think? I'm not talking about the psych hospital. I'm talking about Jefferson, because I'm going to knock the shit out of you in around about a minute."

The both of them laughed, Bowie loudly smacking the table. Eden looked from one to the other in confusion, shaking his head.

Dr. Alcatraz looked upon the group in consternation as they filed into his expansive office, lined with shelves of textbooks he had never bothered to read.

Magdelene mumbled a curse about the scent of an expensive cigar floating through the room. "Guess smoking privileges are selective in this motherfucker."

"What is all this?"

As they all sat down, Magdelene fixed an officious smile on her face, clicking her dentures resolutely. "I am Bowie Long's mother, Mrs. St. Charles, and this is uh . . . a family friend."

Eden looked back at the secretary as she seated herself behind them, close to the door. "Is there a reason that the receptionist is sitting in on this consult?" Eden asked.

"It is our policy that we have a third person sit in on psychiatric reviews. Mr. uh?"

Bowie said, "I don't want her here."

"Mr. Cross, and you are?"

"Dr. Alcatraz. I am the lead psychiatrist here at Mockingbird."

"Nice to make your acquaintance." Eden made notes on the tablet on his lap. Dr.

Alcatraz also made a note. "Mr. Long has made known that he would prefer the young lady not be present."

"As I stated."

"And, if I am to understand HIPAA privacy rights, wouldn't she need to have had a release signed by Mr. Long?" Eden smiled kindly. Bowie watched his mouth move, trying to hear the words that he could not read from profile.

The doctor looked up, nodded to the woman, who collected her things and exited the room with a quiet click of the door.

"Is there an explanation as to why so many people are here for this routine consultation?"

Eden looked at Bowie and nodded, encouraging him to talk. "I want to come off Abilify."

The doctor hoped he had masked his exasperation sufficiently. He hadn't. Magdelene took a very particular pride when she noticed, smiling ferally.

"I have explained to Mr. Long that would be an unwise decision."

"Why?" Bowie asked.

He struggled to find words, made a notation on the tablet in front of him. Eden also made a note on his own tablet.

"It's just unwarranted. You see, Mr. Long has been stable with the current regimen, so it would be ill advised on my part to risk his stability when he has been making progress."

"Aren't there comparable medications that can be substituted," Magdelene asked. "Does he have to be on that one? And if he does then we understand."

Eden said, "You can talk to him. He's right here."

Bowie said, "I not only told you about what's happening when I take this, I told Dr. Hildebrand at Northwest, I told Dr. Herrera, but nobody gives a shit."

Eden looked at him sharply, warned him with a look to remain calm.

"I'm just using my rights to have the treatment I want. It's in the consumer rights policy I signed when I started here, right?"

Eden gathered a stack of papers, and standing, placed them in front of the doctor. "Here is a list of studies, done by reputable, peer reviewed experts, from Johns Hopkins, Columbia, Penn. There are reports of alarming issues related to its use, from loss of massive amounts of money for gambling compulsions to incarceration and violence. I think, if you read these, you will see that Mr. Long has a very valid concern that should not be disregarded. There has been talk of class action lawsuits."

Bowie said, "I got a lawyer."

Eden glared at him again.

The doctor took the papers, skimming the first page. "Okay. I will take a look at these and give this some thought."

Magdelene stood up, preparing to go, elaborately adjusting her shoulder strap. "That's all well and good, Doc. But how about we make this change now and read the papers later?"

Then she mumbled, low enough that the doctor probably didn't hear, but Eden and Bowie did, "Motherfucker."

David Jackson Ambrose

FROM THE OFFICE OF
DR. ALEX ALCATRAZ

To Whom It May Concern:

As Abilify Maintena does not require tapering or weaning off, Bowie Long can begin taking Seroquel after the third week of the month, by which time the effects of his monthly IM of Abilify will have eliminated itself from the body.

He will receive three prescriptions for the medication Seroquel for the next month. This medication requires a titration period—meaning your new medicine will start at a low dose and be raised each week to maximum effective dose. This is done for patient safety, to limit side effects and allow the Doctor to assess the body's reaction to the new medication.

Seroquel has been documented to have a sedative effect, particularly at the beginning stages. Be assured that as you move to higher doses the sedative effects will diminish.

By signature of this document Bowie Long consents that he is aware of the side effects and will comply with commitment to taking this medication through the titration period. If at any time after the titration period Mr. Long wishes to continue with his IM of Abilify he has the right to do so.

Dr. Alex Alcatraz

*N*ow we got to write every day in this jornal for group. I
think it's dumb. We got three questions to answer and then
read to the class.

Name three things you like about yourself.

I can dress nice. Everybody like my cloth the way I dress.
Everybody nows am a good dancer.
I got a good man.

If you can change something about yourself what would
you change?

I went live somwhere else.
I went to come off house arrest.
I don't went a P.O.

Draw a picture of yourself.

Name something that frightens you.

My dick.

When he spotted Bowie walking with the lunchtime rush toward the cafeteria, he tried to signal to him. "Pssst!"

That didn't work. NoBueno then whispered to Kenny Mack and signaled to him to signal to Bowie. Kenny Mack tapped Bowie on the shoulder and nodded his head back toward the doorway of the reading room, where NoBueno popped his head out. Kenny Mack put his hands in his pockets and leered knowingly.

"Uhmmmmhmmmm."

Bowie wondered why NoBueno was turning his head this way and that, acting like he had a big secret. He laughed as Jose tried to hide his bulk in the shadow of the low bookshelves. "What's wrong with you, man? Why you acting all funny?"

NoBueno shushed him and waved him over quickly.

When Bowie approached, Jose whipped open his voluminous sweater, like a flasher on a New York subway. Inside, there was a walkie-talkie. It looked like one of the devices the floor techs used to keep track of one another and track the participants. Bowie shrugged, not too impressed.

"Where's your one on one? And why you got on that hot ass sweater in here? You making me sweat just looking at it."

Refusing to give up the aura of covertness, NoBueno continued to whisper, "Are you kidding me? It's lunch time, honey. That nigga broke for lunch. Smoking in his car. And I don't mean smoked gouda. And why do you have on that hot ass jacket, if it's so hot?"

"Say that again? Goo what?"

Jose huffed, "Never mind, chile. You know it's very hard to be witty with a man that has hearing . . . shall we say challenges? And especially if they are so uncultured that they don't even know what gouda is."

"What you want, buddy?" Just then Bowie's phone vibrated, "Yeah? Yeah I got my lunch. You at work? Now how am I going to go somewhere? Didn't you drop me off this morning? She got a game today? In that roach motel?" Bowie laughed. "Okay. Later."

"You know you're going to get into trouble if they find you using that thing in here," NoBueno said.

"Fuck them."

"Was that your husband?"

"No. My stupid ass mom."

"Anyway, we have to hurry. *The Young and the Restless* is about to come on and I don't want to miss my story!"

"How you going to watch TV in here?"

NoBueno yanked the walkie-talkie from his sweater

and waggled it in front of Bowie's face. "We can watch it in my boyfriend's room. That's why I got this walkie-talkie. So we can hear when they are coming back from lunch and we can skedaddle on back up to the unit."

Bowie leaned forward, placing a hand on Jose's forearm. "What was that? I didn't hear you, buddy."

Jose shook him off and quickly walked away, crooking a finger at Bowie.

"Never mind. Just follow me. The show will be halfway over, waiting for me to smoke signal messages to your ass. Come on!"

As they walked through the lower passageway, Bowie took out his phone to text.

do you went to come over to see me today baby

do you need a ride home today? just say so.

no I don't need a ride I went to see my baby

i'll see what I can do

ok baby

what are you doing? did you learn anything today?

like what they dont teach you nothing am going to watch tv I miss you

I miss u 2. have a good day

On their way past the unlocked provisions closet, Jose grabbed a roll of paper towels, and put a finger to his lips with a light giggle. Bowie stared at him and shook his head.

The man was sitting in the same location as last time. He wore a powder blue pair of hospital scrubs and dark blue slides with an orange swoosh on the front.

"You wearing the slippers I got you. They look good on you."

The man looked up as they entered, nodding to Jose slowly. Bowie entered on an air of hesitancy. He looked at the large man with thick tufts of dreadlocks sprouting from his head like lava from a volcano. The man smiled at him. He looked as comfortable as an old blanket to Bowie, but Bowie looked behind him, up away from the sunlight spraying into the room.

The first time he had entered this room, it had been a black pinprick at the crook where the ceiling met the wall, but this time, when he stepped over the threshold, he heard a light inhalation. It sounded expectant and surprised. The pinprick undulated, began to glow like a gas flame.

Bowie couldn't be certain it had changed at all. It was a black and orange sunspot on his cornea, but it seemed to flicker like his eyes were playing a trick with the light.

The man's smile invited Bowie in. He walked forward, nodding at him. NoBueno had already flicked on the TV, and he moved to open the top drawer of a highboy dresser from which he pulled a bag of Wendy's sandwiches, three paper cups, and three cans of soda. Bowie eyed the stash hungrily, moving past the man toward Jose. "How'd you get that in here?"

"How you think? I paid a bitch to bring it in. It wasn't that complicated. Me and Dough have lunch together at least once a week. Whenever I can get free. Right Dough?"

The man nodded, his locks swinging about his head

like animate beasts. He stood and approached, casting the two of them in the shadow of his size. NoBueno opened the paper on a burger, placed it on a sheet of paper towel and handed it to Dough. He ignored it, reaching for a can of soda and quickly drinking it.

NoBueno laughed. "He loves soda. It's like crack. I think the caffeine gives him a little energy to fight all that shit they keep pumped in his body."

Jose pulled a chair over so he could sit close to Dough while they watched the soap. Bowie sat on the bed, his head nodding into his chest, a stream of saliva unfurling from his mouth, the hamburger in his hand slowly drifting away and rolling onto the floor.

Dough watched him with a slight spark behind otherwise dull eyes. NoBueno noticed where he was looking, sprung up and picked the burger off the floor, lightly pushing against Bowie's shoulder. "Wake the fuck up."

Bowie sniffed, rubbed his nose in surprise. "I'm sorry, buddy. I'm wasting your food, and you and Dough been so nice. Here I am slobbering on the man's bed and shit." Bowie shrugged off his jacket and folded it on the bed. "Since I been taking this Seroquel I sleep all goddamn day."

"Yeah. I noticed you snoring in group."

Bowie laughed. "Fuck you. I don't snore."

"Yeah, okay. And I'm not the first lady of Mockingbird."

Bowie frowned at him. "Lady my ass. I talked to Dr. Alcatraz about all this sleeping. He talking about that when he gives me more next week, it's going to get better. Now how the fuck is taking more of this shit going to make me sleep less?"

NoBueno shrugged. "I don't remember it making me sleep during the day. But I only take it at night, and I'm glad I do."

"How come?"

"It keeps the voices at bay."

"You hear voices?"

"Uh. Everybody hears voices. But some voices say some fucked up shit."

"I don't hear voices."

"Youse a damn lie."

"I don't."

"Sure. I believe you. Why are you even here? I mean, you're totally normal." NoBueno leered at him.

Dough stood from his chair and went to pick up the last cola on the dresser. He poured the liquid into a Styrofoam cup and crossed over to Bowie, handing it to him.

NoBueno gasped, "Oh, shit. Dough must really like you. He don't give up his Pepsi to nobody, not even me."

Bowie smiled and nodded a thank you. Dough put out his hand toward him. Bowie placed his hand inside and felt the warmth as the man squeezed tight and shook.

Bowie said, "I don't hear voices. I see stuff that's not there."

"Like what? Demons wearing Balenciaga ball gowns and shit?"

"What?"

NoBueno laughed, shaking his head.

Bowie nodded his head in the direction of the thing in the corner. "Right now. Off in that corner, there's something sitting there, looking at me. It's like this . . . shining . . . these . . . all these different colors and light spinning around and around."

"The shimmer."

"Huh?"

NoBueno approached and sat next to him. Dough lowered himself to the floor in front of them, leaning against the dresser, looking up. "I call that the shimmer. It's really pretty, you know, the violet, and cerulean. But sometimes, yeah, that shit is scary. Like it turns red like it's bleeding, or it starts turning, turning, turning. Or it starts to say things. Things you don't want to hear."

Bowie turned to him, grabbed his hands, looked at the words forming on his lips. "You see it, too?"

NoBueno laughed. "Everybody sees it. All of us. Only most people pretend they don't see it. Those people are called civilians. The ones that admit they see it are called schizophrenic. Or bipolar. Histrionic. Back before they made changes to the DSM, it was the 'sexual deviants,' too: gender dysphoria, homosexuality. That's why I'm here. I deviate from the civilians."

"So you're saying everybody sees it? Do you see it in here right now?"

NoBueno pointed languidly toward the pearlescent

throb slowly taking over the corner of the room. "Now you tell me that's not just the most beautiful thing you've ever seen."

"So like, what about Lola?" Bowie asked.

"What about that bitch?"

"And my mom. So you think my mom can see tha—see the shimmer?"

NoBueno stood up, stretching with a groan, and went to lower himself by Dough, who reached out a massive arm and placed it around his shoulder. "Let me tell you a story. Have you heard of fady?"

"Yeah. That's when a nigga got a big ass."

NoBueno rolled his eyes. Dough gave a low, keening moan from deep inside his chest. Bowie realized he was laughing, and smiled at him. Jose looked over at him in surprise.

"No, stupid. Fady is law. When you break fady, you are showing your disrespect for the ancestors. When you piss off the ancestors you unleash all sorts of karmic shit on not just your ass but out into the world."

"What? What the fuck are you talking about, fatties and dead folks. They don't even go together." Bowie looked over at his phone, blinking on the bed.

Why didn't you call me? you're supposed to let me know you're okay at lunchtime.

He sent an automatic text: *am driving.*

Keep your shit up. I don't have time for your games. Are you at the program, yes or no?

am driving.

Okay. I got something for your ass. You'll see

"When I was a kid, I remember my grandmom telling us to be sure to respect the memory of those that came before us. The shimmer is the spirit of the dead that shows up when we don't show honor. Pointing at a grave, fucking in a graveyard, disregard for a woman when she in the lifegiving stage, mocking a newborn, like saying a baby is ugly, murder. But sometimes babies do be ugly, though!"

Bowie struggled to follow what Jose was saying. He looked to the shimmer, beaming from the shadows, and pointed. "That's the pissed off spirit of somebody that died a long time ago?"

Jose shrugged, leaning on Dough's shoulder as he stood. "I guess. Dead people ain't always from a long time ago, you know. People die all the time. Some people are dead while their bodies are still breathing, eating, shitting. Their souls have left the building; they didn't want to be in that body no more or got driven out. Fucked up things are happening all the time. Babies killed, raped, men going to war, women abused. Some of us can't take that trauma. For some, checking out is the only way our body can survive."

As if on cue, the forgotten walkie-talkie began to squawk with static. Jose jumped from the dresser, snatching it from on top of the TV and turned up the volume, holding it to his ear. Bowie stood, wiping crumbs from his pants.

"We gotta go."

Dough stood up as the other two scrambled from the

room in a clatter of footsteps and whispered curses. They left in such a hurry they didn't bother to close the door behind them. Dough watched as they quietly skulked down the narrow hallway, then he closed the door to his room.

He walked back to the bed, where Bowie had left his windbreaker neatly folded upon the coverlet. The fabric was light in his hands. It tumbled loose from the folded shape, the sleeves flapping down past Dough's wrist as he lifted it toward his face. The blue color careened close to his eyes, blocking out the light as he brought it close, covered his face with it. He could smell something clean, like fabric softener and linen, but beneath that, if he let his mind wander, he could smell the buttery sweat of shea butter, the bright notes of bergamot melding with the earthen scent of hair.

Beneath the layer of actual scent, he could smell subliminal odors. The dirt of nail clippings and the smell of scaled epidermis, fallen free, atomized into the fabric. The smell was comforting to him. It was familiar. Like his own, but also different. He let his mind expand like the shimmer. The smell of burnt tobacco a starburst behind his eyes, the crackle of nicotine an explosion in his ears, the subtle scent of detergent and fabric softener filling the corners of his being. In this space, suffused in the smell of the familiar, he relaxed his mind, allowing the olfactory to unfurl and become memory. In memory, his heart ached for the things absent from him now.

He dropped the jacket in surprise at the sound of a dim vibration. He looked down at Bowie's phone, throbbing from his bed. He lifted it to his ear.

On her end, Magdelene heard a silence full of meaning. She spoke into the phone. There was no answer. She spoke again. There was no answer, but she heard a sound. She couldn't tell if it was the sound of nothing or the sound of breathing before the phone went dead.

He lay back on the bed with the phone on his chest. He was satisfied. The ache in his heart subsided a little. Memory exploded. The shimmer burned bright.

E den sat in his car in front of the double doors to Mock-ingbird for thirty minutes before he realized the panic in his chest had been there from the time he had first parked in the lot. He climbed out and rang both bells on the gray intercoms.

He realized that he now had a sense of panic whenev-er Bowie was not where he was expected to be. Whenever he was even a minute late, scenarios developed in his mind: Bowie off with some unidentified stranger, or in jail for some infraction, or raging in the psych ward of some crumbling Victorian-age building. The realization of this sense of panic angered him. He resented Bowie for making him feel this way.

"Mockingbird."

He pressed the button to speak. "Yeah, I've been wait-ing to pick up Bowie Long."

"He left at three. Like he's supposed to."

"You let him out without verifying that his pickup was here?"

"We're not a babysitter, sir. We are a day program."

Eden swore under his breath as he climbed back into his car and veered out of the drive, spraying gravel in his wake. He tried to remember which houses on the west side of town he had dropped Bowie off at for card games in the past, driving through a yellow light as car horns blared in admonishment. As he zipped up past the park, he saw a familiar form sitting on a bench by the street.

He parked and approached Bowie, who was sleeping on the bench, snoring lightly. Eden touched his shoulder. Bowie looked over at the hand lazily, then looked up with hooded eyes.

"Hey, baby."

"Why did you leave? I told you I would come get you."

Bowie stood up and hugged him. Eden looked around self-consciously.

"I got tired of waiting." He darted across the street, causing cars to jam their brakes.

"Come on, baby!" He came back across the street to grab Eden's arm and guide him through traffic as if he were an invalid. In the car, Eden watched as Bowie's eyes drooped. Bowie adjusted the seat to a near reclining position.

"When are you going to tell the doctor you've been sleeping too much?"

"I told him. He said some shit about it's going to go away once I start the higher dose."

"What kind of shit is that?"

"That's what he said."

"He's out of his mind, then."

Bowie laughed.

"Seriously. You have to advocate for yourself. Remember what I told you about the code switching? Use your 'white' voice. If they give you some bullshit, you just keep stating what you want in a calm voice."

"I don't got no 'white' voice, Eden. I'm not like you." As they pulled onto Maple Leaf, Bowie sat up. "Take me to the Marriott."

"What? Why would I take you to the Marriott?"

"That's where my mom is. Her friend had a fire and so she's been staying at the Marriott all month. When she picks me up we been staying over there."

"You're on house arrest, though."

"My PO knows. He's cool with it. He said he rather me be with her than by myself."

"Why? Like you are some kind of imbecile that shouldn't be alone?"

He shrugged. "At least I get out of the house. That bitch stays there all night."

Eden did the math. "They're playing cards?"

"You know it. All damn night. It's boring."

"You know you are there playing right along with them."

"With what money? I play a couple hands then I just sit around doing nothing. You want to go to my house for a minute? Then you can take me up to the hotel. I want to change clothes. Take a bath." He leered at Eden.

"Don't try to bullshit me. You know you ain't thinking

about no bath," Eden protested, but he parked right in front
of the house and hurriedly killed the engine.

The difference in medications had been noticeable almost
immediately. When Bowie had been able to ejaculate for
the first time, Eden felt as if some sort of huge victory had
been reached. He thought just that mere fact would create
an entirely different person, and that all the hyperactivity, the
constant movement, would just miraculously disappear. And,
to a degree, it was a victory. There were moments of calm between the storms. But Bowie still called him repeatedly, still
sent lewd texts and requests for obscene pics. He still danced
around, loudly clapping over conversations he did not want
to have.

Eden was ashamed to admit to himself that he kind of
missed the Abilify Bowie. He was relieved that Bowie was
able to ejaculate. It had always been a whisper in the back
of his mind that he had not been able to because of something lacking on Eden's part. But he loved the sexual energy
that Bowie had then. The insatiable, almost lunatic drive. The
erections, though not constant, were able to be obtained intermittently all night long. The tensile strength of his dick
had been something out of some pornographic fantasy. He
had been able to find satisfaction in just holding him in his
hand, warm and satisfyingly heavy. Or lying on him as he
radiated heat and energy, whispering loving obscenities into
his ear. Or holding him while he slept, his dick rising and
falling in Eden's cupped hand all night, almost as if it were

breathing.

As they lay there amongst the post-sex funk of mangled sheets, Bowie pulled him on top of him, whispering, "I love you."

"What do you mean when you say you love me? What do you love about me?"

"You got a nice ass. Good dick."

"That's love, then? Ass and dick? You know you don't have to equate everything with sex. It's like men only exist for you for one thing."

"What do you like about me, then?"

Eden gripped the back of his head, whispering in his ear, "You are kind, even though you've gone through some rough stuff, you still have a positive outlook. Which is, like, the total opposite of me. You were honest with me from the very start about who you are. You are proud about being gay, you never try to hide it." Eden rolled over, pulling him close. "Your skin. The way it grabs the light, takes it all in. You are the most beautiful thing I've ever seen. The shape of your head. The way you sing off-key and loud, and you don't give a damn how loud you are. Your beautiful nose. Your legs. Black men don't usually have calves like that."

Bowie licked his chest. "You know you like this dick."

He laughed lazily. "I'd be lying if I didn't say it's part of the package. You're perfect to me. You are all the boys that never paid attention to me when I was younger, because I was too light skinned, so the dark-skinned boys never bothered with me, and I loved them so much. Or the straight boys I loved who thought I was too feminine. You're just natural about who you are."

Bowie smacked him on the ass and hopped out of bed, lunging for his underwear on the floor. "We got to get going, baby. Take me up to the hotel. Or you want to do it again?"

Eden shook his head, sitting up and reaching for his clothes.

Lola sat tapping her French tips on the desk, watching him through the glass that separated her office from the common way. He rushed in spewing apologies, turning down the volume on his earbuds.

"Sorry I'm late. I fell asleep in the dayroom," he sat opposite her, grinning.

"Tardiness indicates that one is not yet fully committed to recovery. You know that you are scheduled for therapy with me on Fridays at eleven."

"We didn't meet last Friday."

"You know I had to attend a conference. You were given notice, weren't you?"

"Friday before that."

"I was out sick. People get sick."

"That's why I wasn't sure we was going to meet today."

"I am not the one that has an obligation to meet, here. You are. Now do you want to get started or do you want to keep with this game?"

Bowie laughed. "I'm just telling you what time it is."

"Don't try to bullshit me, Bowie. You should know by

now that I know all the games, all the tricks."

"You think I'm playing games? I got too much to lose to play games."

Lola sniffed. "I'm glad you recognize that. So. Have you been writing in your journal?"

"Kind of."

"This is not an optional goal. You and I have developed the goal of daily entries in your journal to help you . . . well, I shouldn't have to tell you the reason. How will writing in your journal help with your recovery?"

"Say that again?"

"You heard me. *Recovery.*"

"No, I really didn't hear you."

"So more of the games, Bowie? Is that what you want reported to your PO? Because that's not a problem for me. What are the benefits of writing in your journal?"

"I can't remember. That's written down in my treatment plan, right? Can I get a copy of it to take home? My friend wants to see it."

"I've told you before. I will get the new one to you as soon as I have Keisha type it up. What does your friend want to see it for? This is treatment for you, not your friend."

"No, I need it, too. To help me remember what my goals are. I can't remember that shit. You know I didn't get my treatment plan the last quarter neither, so it's hard to remember if there's new stuff on it or what."

She crossed her arms over her chest. "Why don't you read me your last entry."

Bowie dug into his backpack, making a big show of digging out a spiral-bound notebook, ruffling the pages loudly while Lola rolled her eyes.

"I'm tired of sitting in this fucking hotel room all night waiting on this b—on this woman."

"Your mother is still helping with the caretaking of your neighbor?"

"Caretaking? OK. Yeah, we still at the Marriott. Every day I got to sit up there with nothing to do, bored out of my mind."

"Have you told your mother you don't like staying at the hotel for such long periods of time?"

"You kidding? When's she listen to what I want?"

"Well, you could help your mother out."

"Help her out of what? She ain't doing nothing."

"Your mother does plenty. She's taking care of her friend, who's been burned out of her house. She takes care of you, with your mental disabilities and your legal troubles. She takes care of a household, works every day."

Bowie snorted. "Uh-huh."

"You show a lot of disrespect toward your mother. A lot of the people here don't have anyone still in their corner. You're very lucky, you know."

Bowie kept reading. "I am a kind person. I have gone through a lot of bad things, but I am still happy about myself."

She watched him astutely. "Did someone say these things to you?"

He shrugged. "Huh?"

"Tell me what you mean when you say you are happy about yourself."

Bowie leaned forward in his seat. "I'm proud to be a Black gay man."

"This is good. You should be accepting of who you are."

He nodded. "Yeah."

"What are the bad things you talk about? Can you name one of those things that you think of when you say bad things? Do you write down these things in your journal?"

He seemed to retreat into himself. His eyes became blank. Bowie saw the shimmer. Not really there in the room with them, but in his mind. He saw it radiating yellow and pearlescent blue, curving up into a malevolent grin. "I don't know."

Lola sighed in exasperation. "Fine. We can approach this another day."

Bowie looked into his lap, tears dropping slowly, his shoulders slumping. Lola stood, walked around the desk to sit on the edge in front of him. "Are you all right?" She reached behind her, grabbed a tissue, and held it out to him. Then, he began to cry, loud, keening sounds of anguish. Full of despair. He reached up and covered his face with his hands, wiping tears back with a stifled cough. Lola spoke gently, reaching out to place a hand on his shoulder. "Do you want to talk about it? What's going on?"

"Talking about it doesn't make it stop." Abruptly, the wailing stopped. He reached for the tissue, wiping his face as he stood. "I'm sorry about that. I don't know why that happened."

"You never have to apologize for showing your emotions. You're in a safe space."

Bowie flopped back down into the chair, laughing maniacally. "There are no safe spaces, Lola. This is America."

The Marriott lobby was like most hotel lobbies, filled with pseudo opulent touches intended to make customers feel they were in a place better than their homes, with overdone chandeliers and plush furniture arranged into separate islands where you could read magazines, or watch CNN, or help yourself to an exotic blend of coffee.

Bowie walked out of the room, packed with seven people playing a raucous game of Pitty Pat, and drifted down the hall looking down at the screen of a cell phone. A burst of noise came from the room as Magdelene quickly darted out behind him.

"Where the fuck you think you're going?"

"I'm going to sit in the lobby. Where else can I go until you take me home?"

"You don't need to be sitting in that lobby. And bring me back my phone."

"I don't need to be sitting in that hot ass room with all them funky ass niggers, neither. But I got no choice. I'm just calling Eden."

"Where's your phone?"

"I don't know. I lost it."

"You can't hold onto shit. You keep talking about how you want to move out and you can't even keep track of your house key. You need new keys and phones every damn month."

"Say what?"

"You damn well heard what I said. You hear what you want to hear."

Bowie smirked. "Say what?"

"You make sure you don't go nowhere but that lobby. And I'm going to check my phone to make sure you didn't call no other numbers but Eden."

"Mom, go back in the room!" he snapped, dialing Eden's number. He knew Eden wouldn't pick up a call from a number he didn't recognize, so he called him five times in a row, then texted.

am trying to call you baby its your men

He called again.

"Whose phone are you calling from?"

"I'm at the hotel, still," Bowie said.

"It's midnight! Tell her you have to get to sleep. You have to be at Mockingbird at eight. Doesn't she have to work in the morning?"

"She don't need no sleep when they playing cards. She's a vampire. You saw her. Only, she takes her teeth out at night."

"Stop it." Eden laughed. "Where's your phone?"

"I don't know. I'll find it."

"Why don't you call it and see if it rings? I don't hear

any card game going on."

"I'm in the lobby. I got tired sitting in there all fucking night."

"I know. There's nowhere for you to go to sleep in there?"

"I don't know these niggers like that."

"Have you ever thought about maybe getting your own place?"

"How am I going to do that? She said I won't ever make it out there. I'm not good with money."

"Is she any better with money? Lots of people aren't good with money and live on their own, Bowie. They learn to become good with money. Or get put on the street."

"I don't know how to cook."

"YouTube can teach you anything you need to know. As long as you can boil water you can make pasta. You can make sandwiches, can't you? And your finger can push the buttons on the microwave."

"Yeah, but she said she's afraid I would burn down the house. I can't hear when the food's burning."

Eden laughed. "You can't hear when the food's burning. Did you just say that?"

"Say what?" Bowie laughed. "What did I say?"

"Those aren't reasons. They're excuses. Nobody moves out one hundred percent ready. You learn as you go. Would it be any worse than what you're living with now?"

"I love my mom. She just has some fucked up ways."

"It's not about loving your mom. It's about loving yourself enough."

"Maybe we can get an apartment together."

"Are you crazy? I've done that before. I'm good with living alone. That gives me the chance to miss your ass. Anyway, I'm here taking care of my dad. I'm trapped here, for now. But you're not. But in the meantime, tell her to take you the hell home. If you don't let people know what you want, you can't get pissed off that they don't know what you want."

"Look at this motherfucker. What you looking at?"

"What?"

"This man staring at me like I'm crazy."

"How does that look? How can somebody look at you like you're crazy? Maybe he likes what he sees. You are a beautiful man."

"I don't do white niggers."

"Cut the shit, Bowie. If you think I believe you don't fuck around with white men, you are mistaken. I don't believe that for one second. No Ma'am."

Bowie laughed. "Yes, ma'am. You better believe it, ma'am."

"No ma'am, Pam."

Bowie barked a laugh. "Let me call you back."

"Wait."

The phone went dead. A few minutes later, Eden's notifications pinged.

hey baby what are you doing

if u wanted to know what i was doing you wouldn't have gotten off the phone so fast. what are you doing?

don't be like that baby i love you ok i love you because you make me believe in myself and you dont talk down to me. you show me to speak for myself. i like your lips and your smile i like the way you look at me like you really see me i like the birthmark on your neck couse it makes you special. plus you are a fine ass gay Black man and you now it.

if you are in those tea rooms over there i suggest you get back to your room before them white folks call the police

B owie was already in a state of agitation, but when he walked into Dr. Alcatraz's office and saw the secretary, seated with steno pad at the ready, he grew increasingly so. He sat heavily in the seat in front of the doctor's desk.

"I thought we talked about not having her in here listening in to report back to Lola. She been here each time after my family said it's my right not to have her here."

Dr. Alcatraz steepled his fingers, peering over his spectacles. "This is more of a safety measure. You know, so that people feel safe, that no untoward actions have taken place. Now why don't we just get you taken care of as quickly as possible, shall we? So you won't be unduly stressed by Keisha being here."

"I'm already unduly stressed."

"Have you had any thoughts of self-harm? Harming others?"

Bowie waved a hand in front of his face. "We don't need to do all that, Doc. I want to talk about why this medicine's making me sleep all damn day."

Dr. Alcatraz began scribbling on a pad. "As we discussed, those side effects will soon dissipate as you get to your full therapeutic dose. Which will be soon now that we have finished titrating and there have been no problems. You can have this script filled for next month with no changes to your dosage."

He took the paper from the doctor's outstretched hand and read it. "You want me to take three hundred milligrams in the morning and three hundred more at night? I'm taking two hundred now and sleeping all day, and my therapist keeps threatening to report me to my PO."

The doctor flashed a benevolent smile. "I can speak to your therapist and explain that things will even out in another month or two. You just have to be patient."

"I don't want to sleep like this. My friend says I should talk to you about just taking it at night and see how that goes."

"Has your friend gone through medical school? Because he seems to be interfering in efforts designed to improve your situation."

"What? He . . . no."

Dr. Alcatraz stood, beginning to move around the desk. "You just trust me. I have many years' experience dealing with people with challenges similar to yours. I have only your best interests in mind."

Bowie slammed a fist on the desk, causing the other participants in the room to jump. "What challenges are we talking about? How the fuck would you know what my best interests are when you meet with me for ten fucking minutes each month. And I've only known you for four months."

The doctor turned and went back behind the safety of his desk while Keisha stood and opened the door, eyeing the tech standing in the hallway. "I think you need to perhaps go and cool off. Practice some of the strategies in your crisis plan so that you can regain control of your emotions."

"I don't need a fucking crisis plan. I'm not out of control just because you don't like what I'm saying. I'm not taking all these drugs. You're not making me a zombie. And you can let Lola know, let the PO know. I don't give a fuck."

"We are done here." The doctor nodded to the two techs that swiftly entered.

Bowie looked back at them, laughed, clapping his hands loudly. "You got that right. You have a good day, buddy."

MEDICATION REVIEW

PATIENT: Bowie Long
CURRENT MEDICATIONS:

Depakote 500 mg BID
Luvox 150 mg BID
Seroquel 300 mg BID
Naltrexone 50 mg AM

PSYCHIATRIC NOTES: Mr. Long presented today for monthly medication consult in a state of agitation. Body language was combative, fists clenched in rage throughout the session. He demanded that administrative staff not be present and refused to acknowledge reasonable explanation for her presence. Mood was labile.

MENTAL STATUS EXAM: Short, slender build; young African-American male. Good ADL. Responses very vague. Speech is misdirected. Confused thinking. Denies auditory and visual hallucinations. Denies suicidal thoughts. History of poor coping skills to control aggression. Patient was verbally and physically threatening, requiring intervention of support staff to remove him to an area where he could be closely monitored/supported.

Bowie's cell phone began to throb. Dough could feel it languorously shimmering beneath the pillow where he had hidden it. He reached under to grab it, rolling on his back and swiping the screen to answer, holding the phone to the side of his face. He could hear Bowie.

"Hello. Hello? Who's this?"

Dough licked his bottom lip, wetting the dry spot at the middle as he listened.

"This ain't your phone, motherfucker. I'ma get this shit turned off quick fast and in a hurry. If I find out who took my shit I'm going to kick your ass!"

Dough stared at the blank screen as the light dimmed. He held the phone at arm's length, wondering if she would call.

He thought if he just heard Magdelene's voice one more time, he would be able to hold that with him for the rest of his life. He reached beneath his pillow and pulled out Bowie's jacket, brought it to his face. If he concentrated really hard, he could smell the earthen tobacco from her cigarettes, the dark musk of Bowie's sweat. He could imagine the time before, when there were three, and he could hear the echo of her rasping voice, almost as though she were standing right before him. He didn't want or need to see her. This would be enough.

FROM THE OFFICE OF
LOLA DOPINGER

Good Afternoon,

Dr. Alcatraz has decided that he will put Bowie back on the Abilify at his original dose and discontinue the Seroquel. This will take 10 days. Dr. Alcatraz has decided he will no longer prescribe medications for Bowie. By law, he is required to be available to the degree that he would normally be available for 30 days from today or until you find a new psychiatrist. Whichever comes first.

Lola Dopinger

To: Dopinger@Mockingbird.org
From: gardenofeden@gmail.com

Dear Ms. Dopinger,

I would ask that you kindly request that Dr. Alcatraz reconsider his decision to discharge Bowie from medication management. The reasons are as follows:

- Bowie is in treatment at partial hospitalization program to receive active treatment within the framework of a multidisciplinary team.

- The team requires the involvement of a psychiatrist.

- The team involves Bowie's community support network as appropriate. As part of his community network, I am a nonclinical participant and my role, as well as his mother's role, is to offer an alternate, nonclinical perspective.

- We also see how treatment is affecting the individual outside of the therapeutic milieu. Bowie requested he be weaned off Abilify because of recent findings of possible correlation to increases in compulsive behaviors and gambling.

- During the time Abilify has been decreased, there has been a corresponding decrease in Bowie's desire to gamble as wells as decreased focus on sexual urges. When the doctor began weaning back the Abilify and replacing it with Seroquel, he indicated that Mockingbird would be aware to expect certain changes in behavior likely to occur i.e. excessive sleeping, and would be accordingly supportive.

- Bowie reports that he has been warned that

sleeping during treatment will be reported to his probation officer, which seems punitive rather than supportive. The pharmacist filling orders for Seroquel informed Bowie that sleeping more than usual would occur, but that sleeping for over fifteen hours every day was more than warranted and advised Bowie to discuss with his doctor. Bowie has done this. It is reported that he has done this in a manner that was confrontational and accusatory, which led the doctor to discharge him from his care and reinstate the original doses of Abilify and discontinue Seroquel within ten days, beginning immediately. This also seems punitive and responsive to Bowie not behaving in a manner the doctor finds acceptable. I am alarmed that a doctor that works with people with pervasive psychiatric issues is put off by a person in treatment being suspicious and angry. Put off to the point that he refuses to continue to treat. Bowie has been confused about what the meds are supposed to do versus what they are actually doing. Part of the confusion may be related to his hearing loss and how he processes information because of that loss. I do not know.

I am also unsure how it is that a doctor employed by Mockingbird is able to deny treatment to someone in treatment there. Placing him back on Abilify risks returns to behaviors that have led to incarceration. I ask that Bowie not be penalized for making attempts to advocate for himself.

Thank you,
Eden Cross

Magdelene scrolled through the history on her call log, calculating the number of days that had passed since the day Bowie had used her phone.

Finding the unfamiliar number she had been searching for, she hit the call button and waited for Eden to answer.

Seeing an unfamiliar number, Eden wondered if Bowie had lost yet another phone, and picked up, expecting to hear his voice.

It was a jolt hearing Magdelene's lower register. "Bowie needs your help." She did not bother with salutations.

Eden leaned on the shopping cart, tossing in a can of tuna. "Is he with you? It's the middle of the day."

"He's at the program. But he has to take a polygraph this afternoon. It costs three hundred dollars and he doesn't have it."

"A polygraph for what?"

"That's what I said. The Black bitch at the program says it's a standard requirement for everybody there. That they test to find out if they have a history of predatory patterns they are lying about. So they can get the proper treatment.

But really it's so they can keep on feeding people into the machine. The crazy houses and the prisons."

"What?" Eden felt a knot in his stomach. He wondered, not for the first time, what was at play concerning Bowie that he didn't know about. Was this some kind of *To Catch a Predator* situation that he was entangled with. "What's been going on with Bowie? I mean, I thought I knew him, but I didn't know about all this stuff that's coming up. Is he some kind of predator?"

"You know Bowie, don't you? Have you seen him act like a predator?"

Eden tried to remember every moment he had ever spent with Bowie. Tried to deconstruct every word ever said, every gesture made. He re-evaluated Bowie's undressing in the car, his suggestive dancing, how he performed when they were in bed together. Was it possible he had misread sexual predation as just sexual? Had he been so self-centered, so consumed by his own desire that he ignored signals of something more debased? He wondered if he had been so desperate and lonely he had pushed his misgivings aside.

"Didn't he know this was coming up? Why didn't he hold onto the money to pay for it?"

Magdelene snorted. "He can't hold onto three dollars, let alone three hundred. He would certainly pay you back. Just like he did that bail money."

"Can't he reschedule for next month? And you hold onto the three hundred for him until then?"

She began talking before he even finished the sentence. "If that boy knows I got his money he will just badger me and badger me every day until he gets it all. He has no self-control."

Apparently, he wasn't the only one, Eden thought. He huffed, "Well, I'm in the middle of shopping right now. I mean, I could write a check. But could you meet me somewhere and I can give it to you? What time is the appointment?"

"It's at noon. And I'm at work." The sounds of music and ringing slot machines in the background belied her words. "Plus, he needs a ride over there, so if you could swing by to pick him up, you could take him to the place. It's here in Valley Forge."

So, she was in Valley Forge, at the casino, most likely.

"I don't know . . . w—"

"He can tell you the address when you get him. And I would feel so much better knowing you were there with him. Somebody that knows their shit, so them crackers don't try to railroad him with their bullshit."

"I don't know how much help I would be. I wrote a letter to his therapist about them putting him back on Abilify and I haven't heard a peep out of them since. She won't take my calls anymore."

"And likely won't take your calls here on out. Are you surprised?"

"Yes. I am. I don't see how they talk all this talk of a team approach and community connections as being important to recovery but they don't give a shit what anybody says if you don't have credentials at the back of your name."

Eden heard a loud ringing and shouting.

"Look, I gotta run. But thank you so much for helping out. I appreciate you. And Bowie definitely appreciates you."

"Listen, I—" The phone went dead. "Hello? Are you still there?"

Bowie beamed like the sun when he burst from the doors of Mockingbird to see Eden waiting by his car, and Eden couldn't help but beam back. He thanked Eden the entire drive to the office center where the testing was to be done.

They sat together in the cool of the reception area, Eden looking over his shoulder as Bowie completed the battery of intake documents. He began to get nervous, thinking about the implications inherent in a polygraph test.

"Listen. You are going to have to pay close attention here. You can't just act like you have heard what's being said, like you do at home. If you don't understand the question, didn't hear it, there's nothing to be ashamed of if you tell them you didn't hear the question. This thing could get you into some big trouble if they document something that's inaccurate that you just nod along to. You understand what I mean?"

"I look retarded to you? Yeah I understand you. They already asked me all this shit before I came in Mockingbird, so I don't know why I gotta answer the same shit now. And pay three hundred on top of all that."

They looked up as an official looking stocky man came

into the room smiling at them. "Mr. Long?" Bowie stood, reaching out to shake his hand. "Hi, buddy. That's me."

"I'm Josh. I'll be conducting the polygraph this afternoon." He looked at Eden. "You are?"

"A friend. Can you tell us what the purpose is for this test?"

"The Office of Probation requested this be done to discover if there is a history of predatory behavior that has up to now been unknown to the courts. It's pretty standard."

Bowie looked over at Eden. "What did he say?"

Josh said, "There's nothing to be nervous about. Just answer all the questions honestly, and quickly, with the first answer that pops in your head, and we'll be done here in about two hours."

Eden said, "Josh, I think it's important that you know that he's partially deaf. He chooses not to wear hearing aids, but primarily reads lips to understand full sentences. So it might be helpful if you make sure that he understands the questions you ask so he doesn't answer what he *thinks* you've said instead of what was actually said."

Josh frowned. "Not a problem. Come with me."

Eden watched them leave, his heart lurching. He sat down and opened the paperback he had brought with him. He had not even finished one page when a shadow loomed over his shoulder. He looked up. Eden and Josh were back in the room.

Josh said, "I don't feel comfortable giving this test at this time. I asked Mr. Long if he would prefer to have an interpreter from the courthouse here on his behalf. That is his right. The courthouse must provide whatever he needs so that he is one hundred percent competent with communication."

Bowie nodded. "I want an interpreter."

Eden stood up. "Will this be a problem, that he didn't get this done?"

"I can't speak for the Office of Probation, but I'll send them an email explaining what went on here. We can re-schedule when the courthouse provides translation services. That might take a while, if past experience is any indicator. It's not as easy to secure translation services as they'd have you believe. But there's no rush. We aren't going anywhere. I assume neither is Mr. Long."

Bowie again shook the man's hand. "Thank you for your help, sir. I appreciate you."

"Just doing my job. We'll see you soon."

Walking from the building to the parking lot, Bowie was silent. He walked behind Eden, dragging his feet. They got into the car, saying nothing.

"I think my PO's going to have a problem with this."

"You have a right to hear what the fuck is going on. This thing could follow you, label you as something you're not, for the rest of your life. Don't you want to get it right? You won't get a second chance"

Bowie was silent.

"I'm sorry. I should have stayed out of it. I don't know anything about any of this."

Bowie put his hand on Eden's knee. "It's okay. Thank you for caring about me."

"You don't have to keep thanking me. You've said thank you ten times since I picked you up. And you definitely don't have to thank me if you think I put my nose in where it doesn't belong. It's your life, not mine. I don't want to gamble with your life."

"It feels good to know somebody cares about me. I'm happy."

"You are not happy, Bowie. I know when you're happy."

"It's a different kind of happy. This is the kind that you want to cry."

"Do I take you back to Mockingbird? It's only one thirty."

"Fuck no. I'm out that bitch for the day. Take me up to Oak Street. There's a card game going on since four this morning. I'ma see if I can get a seat for a quick couple games."

"I'm not doing that. You are on house arrest. Why aren't you taking this more seriously? You can go back to jail if that thing shows you not being where you are supposed to be."

"This thing is a fucking joke. They don't give a fuck where I'm at. And anyway, the thing ain't even active during the hours I'm supposed to be at Mockingbird, plus the hour they give for me to walk home from there. So I got me a couple hours before I need to be worried. And if I'm a little late, I'll just tell them bitches I missed the bus home or something."

David Jackson Ambrose

Eden stared at him. "You think this is a joke? Aren't you scared of anything?"

Bowie thought of the shimmer, tossing amber iridescence with a golden leer. "Yeah. Just not stupid crackers and their stupid rules. If you don't want to take me I'll just walk over from my house. I don't want you doing anything you don't want to do."

Eden shook his head. "If I take you home we could do a little something before your mom gets there." Bowie smiled at him. "Maybe later. I feel lucky right now."

*t*hank *you for helping me man I love you*
      u don't have to thank me. but do me a favor and go home
before you get yourself arrested.
      am going home now boo I didn't wen shit no how
      u have a good night and I'll talk to you tomorrow.
      am going to call you tonight
      that's okay. I have a lot to do. Just call me tomorrow.
      ok baby

Eden knew, just as Bowie knew, he would be calling him as soon as he got home.

But he didn't call Eden later that night. And Eden was angry with himself for feeling nervous when he didn't call. Even more angry that he had been expecting a call that never came. He resented this feeling of worry that now seemed to loom whenever there was a gap of more than a few hours without getting a call or at least a text. The silence was no longer peaceful, but one that shouted scenarios of Bowie in jail or in the hospital.

Even more worrisome, now there were other scenes, created by the knowledge gleaned from reading psychiatric evaluations and court docket sheets. Now he also saw Bowie standing in shadow with unidentified men, saw the body he had coveted being coveted by others, imagined the freedom with which Bowie gave his body to him being given with the same abandon to someone other than him, and it caused a feeling of bleak emptiness inside.

He wanted to call Bowie, to alleviate his mind of these feelings of misgiving, but he was too afraid of what calling might reveal if Bowie didn't answer. So instead, he sat with his feelings, went through the motions of his banal existence with a great emptiness weighing upon him like stone.

And the hours turned dark.

And Eden lay there in the dark, unable to sleep, as time faded into dawn, and the silence screamed, and dawn moved to morning, to afternoon, to midday, and when his phone buzzed, his heart lurched, and he made himself wait, let it ring three times before answering. And when he answered, there was an explosion, a cacophony of sound. He was speaking fast, so rapid fire, Eden had to ask him to slow down.

"Just get out of my room, Mom! Go downstairs. I'm on the phone."

"Who are you talking to?" Magdelene asked.

"Why do you want to know? Just leave. Please!"

"Is that Eden? Let me talk to him."

"I'll tell him myself."

"Tell me what?" Eden heard a rustle of noises, cursing, then she was speaking on the phone.

"They coming to get him today. For not taking that

polygraph."

There was more noise, and he heard a thump before Bowie then spoke.

"My PO called Lola to talk to her about me not taking the test. They said it was noncompliance."

Eden heard Magdelene shout in the background, "Didn't I tell you to give me the phone?"

"I told them the man didn't want to give me the test without somebody from the court to represent me, and they say I'm just trying to get out of taking it. I left out of there and came home. They not taking me to no jail. I'm not going."

"Bowie. I'm so sorry. Why didn't you tell them you just asked for an interpreter? You weren't trying to get out of doing anything."

Bowie was crying. "I told them. He don't care about that. He said I ain't never had no trouble hearing before so why do I now have a problem all of the sudden."

Magdelene cursed. "You should have just taken the fucking test like I told you to. Now you got no choice. You're going to jail. And they'll probably send you upstate and let you sit up there for the next three years when you could have just taken it and been done with it."

Eden leaned back against the wall, looking up blearily. This was his fault.

Bowie said, "Can you get out of my room and let me talk, please."

"What good is talking now? You might as well come

downstairs and let me take you to the hospital. You're hysterical. You need to be evaluated. This is really making you sick."

"Stop saying that. No, you are making me sick. You won't let me alone to think."

"Think about what, Bowie? You don't have nothing to think about. You just get your jacket and let's get out of here before the police come through here and drag you out in front of all these people and make me look bad. Now come on. Now."

"Can you come to the hospital with me?" he asked Eden.

"Why are you going to the hospital? Do you feel like you're getting sick?"

"I will if she keeps at me like this." Bowie started shouting.

Eden could tell that he no longer held the phone in his hand.

Magdelene spoke. "I'm taking him to the ER. They have a psych unit. He can get evaluated there."

Eden was able to follow the sounds of shouting voices to get to the room where Bowie lay in a hospital bed screaming at Magdelene to get out. There was a burly security officer standing with folded arms at the door who nodded curtly as Eden approached.

He heard Magdelene rasp in an agitated voice as he entered the room, "I'm not going anywhere. I'm your mother." A nervous looking nurse stood connecting monitoring machines and taking pulses.

When he saw Eden, Bowie tried to get out of the bed, but the nurse, with Magdelene's help, pushed him back into the prone position. It seemed to Eden that Bowie's agitation decreased when he saw him. "Hey."

"Hey yourself," said Bowie.

"You feeling alright?"

"No. I don't want her in here." He glared at his mother.

Magdelene put up her hands in defeat. "No problem. I can go smoke a cigarette. I know you won't cut up while Eden's here."

"Eden don't have nothing to do with it. It's you that's my problem. I'm sick of you."

Magdelene yelled, "Look, don't put all this on my back. You are the one with the problem. Every time I try to get you some help you act like I'm the one that needs the help instead of being grateful I'm even here."

"You are the one that needs the help. You're crazy."

The nurse looked at Eden askance. "We're just running a few tests to make sure his vitals are normal. We have a call in to mobile crisis. They are the professionals that would be able to ascertain whether there are . . . nonmedical issues going on."

Bowie said, "You don't have to talk in code. You mean find out if I'm going bonkers. I'm not bonkers. I just need to get the fuck away from that bitch there. Always nagging and busting in my room like she's CSI Miami. I hate her guts."

"Fuck you, Bowie." Magdelene stormed from the room.

The nurse said, "Are you his father?"

Bowie brayed with amusement. "He's my daddy. Yup."

Eden smiled uncomfortably. "I'm a family friend."

"Okay. Well. If it's okay to leave you two here, I've got rounds to do. I'll be back once mobile crisis arrives."

When she left, Bowie leered at him. "Come over here, daddy."

Eden approached, cupped the back of his head in his hand, kissed him, letting his hand drift down to hold his neck. "Why are you here, Bowie? You look okay to me."

He laughed. "She brought me here so they won't take me to jail."

"So you're going to fake a psychiatric crisis instead of talking to your PO like a sensible human being and explaining yourself? Why?"

"You ever been to jail? You ever tried to talk to a judge, the public defender, when they know you're bipolar? You think they listen? You think they take me seriously? They don't. The only time they give a shit about anything about me is when I show them the crazy."

Eden held his hand, nodding. "But how are you going to ever get out of this whole cycle of running in and out of hospitals and jails if you keep doing things that keep putting you back in there? Your mom might mean well, but she's running around telling these people you have all these different diagnoses, then she says you tried to kill her, you're hallucinating, or you have a learning disability. Anything to keep you from getting in trouble with the law. But you're still in trouble with the law. And now you have to fight against all these misconceptions."

Bowie shrugged. "It works. I might spend some time at the county or in the hospital, but at least I'm not locked in the state prison. I would never make it up there. I would die."

"Your mom is doing the same thing my mom used to do. She's hustling these bureaucrats, running game on them so that she can get what she needs. My mom did the same trying to get my dad treatment when nobody wanted to take care of him. She would say he tried to kill us, or tried to kill himself when everything else failed. But then there's my dad, looked at like this violent animal by the powers that be."

"Say that again? I didn't hear you."

A shadow fell in the doorway. They looked up to see Lola standing there. Bowie gasped. "What's she doing here?"

Magdelene stood behind her. "I called the program to explain why you left early. How you always run off when you're starting to get sick because you automatically go home when you're sick. I didn't expect her to show up, though."

"I don't want her here!" he shouted.

Lola looked at him with a concerned expression. "If my being here agitates you, Bowie, I will step out. I just wanted to make sure you were okay. And to let you know it's okay you left program against medical advice, even though it is technically a violation."

"I don't want to talk to you!"

Magdelene brushed swiftly past her, seeking to console him.

Eden locked eyes with Lola, who nodded. They both stepped into the hall. She stared down at him with arms folded as he spoke. "I just want to say I take full responsibility for where all this ended up. All I meant to do was to make sure that Bowie was able to fully understand the questions, the gravity of the circumstances of the polygraph."

"Well, you shouldn't take responsibility for any of that. This is Bowie's life, and he makes his own choices. Bowie's low self-esteem leads him to create these scenarios where he needs to be saved by others. It's the only way he feels a sense of self-worth."

Eden frowned. "I don't know if I agree with that."

"He creates situations where he expects people to come to his rescue: me, his mother, his PO. Some of us are trained to identify these ploys, but others are sometimes foolishly pulled in. No offense intended."

"Bowie is partially deaf. He has the right to hear and to adequately represent himself. Particularly in a circumstance where there is a clear attempt to label him as some sort of sexual aberrant."

Lola smiled, "I've been doing this a long time. This population is very smart, very calculating. They've spent all their lives hiding this thing from people close to them. While they keep creating all this subterfuge, really they are relieved when they are finally able to admit to themselves that they need help. I have no other intention than to give Bowie the help he needs."

Magdelene, who had been listening from the other side

of the doorway, stepped into the hall. "You don't care about giving Bowie help. He ain't nothing but a per diem to y'all."

Eden looked back, startled. Turning to Lola, he said, "Taking all the experience you have into account, have you ever thought that you could be wrong sometimes? Every case is not the same."

"Every case is not the same, but there are similarities in pathology. I have never been wrong."

"What are your credentials?" Magdelene barked. "What makes you the expert on my child? You don't even have a degree. I looked you up."

Lola's tone remained cordial, but the steel beneath matched that in her eyes as she sized Magdelene up. "My credentials are not in question, here, Mrs. St. Charles. Your son's criminal behavior is."

Magdelene stepped close, whispering, "You're not Black. You're shit colored. In here doing the white man's work. Making more Black statistics. Shame on you." Magdelene stormed off, walking back into Bowie's room, and Eden turned back toward Lola.

"I apologize for her. She's worried about her son."

"You don't have to apologize. I'm used to it. I'm also used to these ploys at distraction. Bowie is not in crisis. He's trying once again to avoid the repercussions of his actions. I've spoken to his PO. He will be here shortly to remand Bowie to the county correctional facility."

"So he doesn't have the right to hear?"

"I don't think further discussion from me is helpful."

"You're his therapist! Do you have any experience with people like Bowie? With the LGBTQ population? You think going to jail is in anyway helpful to him? With his history of being taken advantage of by adults? How is he going to fend for himself as a gay man in a place like that? There should be at least a partial program at Mockingbird that educates about healthy boundaries and rituals in gay environments. These rituals are often, if not always, misinterpreted by heteronormative standards—"

She cut him off, "We don't really deal with the gay population at Mockingbird."

"Then how can you be helping him? Do you know about public sex for gay men? How cruising works? Any of that?"

"Why is any of that important at this time?"

Eden snapped, "Because you're navigating him through a world that's systemically homophobic. The evaluations are based on police reports written from a heteronormative view. He was arrested for cruising men. That might be illegal technically, but it's standard socialization for gay men. If you guys don't know anything about that, you pathologize it, and then here he is, forced into treatment that might not be what he needs. Cruising behavior isn't predatory or pathological. Or is it? I guess it depends on which edition of the DSM you read, right?"

"Bowie has told me he is gay. I've never judged him or based his treatment from a negative point of view based on that information."

"No? Listen, you can admit it or not, but we know Bowie is on house arrest for being gay. That female PO he had heard he had spent the night with a man, panicked thinking about how this convict was out on the streets screwing men and wanted to be able to put some controls on him ASAP. Right?"

Lola said nothing, so Eden continued, "One of the stipulations for his probation is that he is to call his PO to inform him when he's intending to engage in a sex act. Is that even legal? I've never heard anything so monstrous in my life. I wonder if that is something the American Civil Liberties Union approves." They heard the electronic swish of the doors leading out of the emergency room and looked up at Bowie's probation officer as he approached. Lola excused herself and walked toward Malik, asking to talk to him in private.

Eden went back into the room, where Bowie was nodding off, his head lolling onto his shoulder. He smiled lazily. "Why you leave me by myself? Come sit with me." Bowie was patting a spot beside him on the bed. Eden took his hand and sat beside him, nudging him with his hip.

"Malik is out there talking with Lola. She says you're faking all this just to get out of violating."

Bowie shrugged and listed over to rest his torso against Eden, who reached around to pull him into the warmth of his own torso. "I guess I'm going back to jail anyway. I'm going to miss you, Eden. Can I call you while I'm there?"

Eden leaned his head against Bowie's. "Of course you

can call me."

"I don't want you coming up to see me. I don't want you seeing me like that."

Eden whispered, "You don't have to be ashamed about being there, Bowie. At least I can lay eyes on you and make sure you're okay."

"No. I'm not the same person, then. You won't even recognize me."

"What are you talking about?"

"I have to be somebody else up there. If I'm going to make it through to get out on the other side, I'm not the same person. You come find me when I get home."

Eden couldn't talk. The lump in his throat threatened to burst into a torrent if he did. So he just nodded his head against Bowie's neck, and they sat there, holding hands, listening to one another's hearts thumping in their chests. They had both almost fallen asleep, lured by the warmth of the other's heat, by the time the probation officer tapped on the door. Eden self-consciously rousted himself, attempted to rise from the bed, but Bowie tightened his grip, holding him fast in place.

"Hi, buddy."

Malik eyed them awkwardly, nodded curtly and entered the room. "Sorry for the delay, Bowie. I've been on the phone with my supervisor. So, after consulting with your therapist, we've decided, pending approval from the judge, that Monday morning, you come down to the office and we'll take the ankle monitor off. Nine a.m. sharp. If you're late, you can stay on house arrest until further notice."

Bowie sat up, and Eden stood up from the bed. "You mean I'm off house arrest?"

Malik said, "You weren't taking house arrest seriously anyway. You been going where you want to go: up at the hotel half the night, walking home from program. Now you're up here. So what good's the ankle monitor been anyway?"

Bowie reached out his hand toward Malik. "Thank you, man. I appreciate your help. Thank you so much."

Eden watched Malik look down at Bowie's hand as if it held a live cobra, then nod to him. "Also, your polygraph's been rescheduled for the following Monday, three p.m. If you do not take the test, if you do not have the payment for the test, you will be remanded to the correctional facility until further notice."

Eden said, "The courts have been able to secure an interpreter that fast?"

"They have not," Malik said curtly.

Eden wanted to protest, to say more. But he was terrified that his self-righteous anger would only result in Bowie having to deal with further repercussions. He folded his arms, looked down at Bowie and said nothing.

"I'll be there man. I appreciate your help, so much. I'm so grateful for you and for Lola being in my corner and trying to help me when I been fucking up. You guys are my friends, man. I appreciate y'all, man."

Eden simmered with fury. Malik nodded curtly. "Show us how much you appreciate all Lola has done for you by

showing up for your appointments next week. And stop letting us down. We expect better. Show us you can do better."

"I will, man. I will."

Eden glared at Malik's broad back as he turned to leave
the room. Malik was caught up short as Magdelene rushed
forward, hands jabbing at the air in front of him. "What are
you doing? You can't take him off house arrest this soon."

"Why not?" Malik asked, but his question was echoed
by both Eden and Bowie.

"He's not ready for that. How am I going to keep track
of him if he doesn't have the monitor?"

Bowie jumped out of the bed. "Keep track of me for
what?"

Malik said, "Bowie will still be under obligation to report for probation for the next two years. He is still a part of
Behavioral Health Court, and so while he won't need to come
in to our offices, we will arrange weekly home visits until he
graduates from the program. After that he will report to the
office, just as all the other participants are required to do."

"But Bowie's not like the other participants. He has to
have supervision."

Malik dismissed her. "He will have that. As much as
has been dictated by the courts. The rest of the work needing
to be done will be done through his partial program."

"This is bullshit."

Bowie shouted, "What are you talking about? This
don't have nothing to do with you."

Malik nodded, as if in agreement. "Bowie is an adult,

ma'am. This is a situation he alone has responsibility for. Bowie, I'll see you in the office next week to sign some papers and we'll set you up then."

"Set him up for what?"

"Mom!"

Malik nodded curtly and walked out of the room. As soon as he was out of sight, Bowie bellowed, "I want you to stay the fuck out of my life. You want me to be locked up in that house all day with you like I'm a little kid or something. I'm not a kid."

"If you fuck up again you will be going back to jail. I'm just trying to keep you safe. You don't make wise choices, Bowie. I been stuck watching over you all your life and you give me your ass to kiss when I'm only looking out for you."

"Keeping me safe? You didn't keep me safe when your husband was fucking me while you were out at the casinos all night. Were you watching over me then?"

"You have to stop living in the past. I told you I was sorry that happened to you. But you should have said something to me then. Do you think I would have let that go on if I knew?"

"You knew," he spat. "You knew it. Lilith knew it, too."

"You have to stop feeling sorry for yourself. You're not the only one that suffered as a kid, that went through some shit. Everybody has a fucked-up childhood. Get over it."

Eden gasped. He walked toward the door, but Bowie grabbed his wrist. "Don't go. You don't have to go. I want you to hear this. Listen to her talk about keeping me safe in one breath and to get over it in the next."

Eden felt an acid-like knot in his belly. The accusations, the fury, it all cast him back to his own childhood, all the unresolved issues of his own family. He felt as if he were sitting in on an event he should not be privy to.

Magdelene walked to the door to close it, then leaned on it and turned to face him with eyes glittering with fury. "You think you being taken advantage of is a reason for you to act like you do? Did you ever think maybe the same thing happened to me? You don't see me running around here like you, running in and out of jail, mental institutions. I don't have the luxury of running to the psych ward when life is too much. I just got to keep going every day. Every day. I don't get to pop pills and hide away from this fucked-up life. I have to deal with it."

"I'm dealing with life, too," Bowie said. "Nobody gets to get out of that. There ain't a pill the white man can make that can stop that. These pills ain't nothing else but a prison on my brain, so my mind can be just like my body, locked the fuck up and sitting in the hole." There was a knock on the door. Magdelene opened it to face two blond women standing there tenuously, smiling uneasily, their hands folded in front of them. "Excuse me . . ."

Bowie said, "Who the hell are you?"

"Hello. Are you Bowie Long? We're from Mobile Crisis. We're here to do an evaluation."

"I don't need no evaluation. I'm just fine. Are you going to force me to take it? Are you trying to 302 me?"

"No, no. Not at all. We're just responding to a call."

Magdelene said, "Well I think you need to do the evaluation because he's clearly not in his right state of mind. Sitting in here accusing me of things and disrespecting me."

"How am I disrespecting you? If you get out of here you won't feel disrespect. I told you I don't want you here but you won't listen to me. You aren't respecting my wishes. Why should I give you respect?"

Eden said, "Maybe you just need a little time apart, right? Why don't I take Bowie with me and you just go home and relax?"

Bowie leaped from the bed, yanking the hospital gown from his torso, totally oblivious of his nudity. He reached for his jeans folded on the table and signaled for Eden to hand his sneakers to him. He excitedly put them on. He whooped and clapped his hands like a boom of thunder, causing the two crisis techs to jump in surprise.

"That's right. All y'all can be gone now. I got my freedom papers. Massa done set me free." Eden laughed. Bowie, watching him, laughed too. He grabbed Eden around the waist and lifted him from the floor, spinning him, spinning them both until they lost balance and fell onto the bed, still laughing. "I'm a free man."

"Hardly that," snapped Magdelene, reaching into her bag for her cigarettes and turning to leave.

O ver the next few days Bowie found that freedom and captivity had a lot in common. After he had been deemed competent by mobile crisis he was able to return home without the weight of a tracking device on his ankle. But freedom was spent in a locked facility between the hours of eight to three p.m. Freedom was waiting to be picked up by Magdelene and driven to the Marriott Hotel, where he sat in a smoke-filled room crowded with people he had known since his childhood, where he remained until midnight most nights. Then he would go home, where he would sleep until it was time to rise in the morning. Or, some nights, when Magdelene felt lucky, they would leave the hotel and spend the early morning hours in local casinos.

During this time, Eden sat at home, conducting Google searches while keeping his father company in front of the television, contacting various psychiatrists, attempting to find one that accepted Medicare, trying to locate someone to prescribe something, anything other than the Abilify that Bowie was now being forced to take.

In three weeks Eden was unable to locate a practice

accepting Medicare.

Bowie requested permission to leave program early, walked across the campus to the inpatient building, and requested to meet with Dr. Herrera.

After many appeals, he managed to convince her to go against company policy, and he left her office with a prescription of antipsychotics even though he was not in treatment at the facility.

Walking through the intake lobby, Bowie recognized the bedraggled woman that sat rocking in the plastic chair bolted to the floor. "Mom Birdie. What you doing here?"

The woman looked up at him quizzically. "What you think I'm doing here, fool?"

He laughed, kept walking toward the metal detector that canopied the exit. He turned back, watched her. "You want to pray with me?"

"Why the fuck I want to pray with you for?"

He shrugged. "God told me you might be in need of a prayer."

The woman stood up, hugging herself. "What you got, then?"

He moved close, reached his hands out toward her. "I'm asking God to keep his humble servant in his hands, keep her safe and make her suffer no more. Let her feel your love and to know that she is loved, and that I, too, love her, God. Because she is my sister, and we do not seek to do my sister harm but to build her up in love and prayer. Please guide her,

Lord, and keep her comforted in your love."

She nodded and rocked back and forth, whispering, "Yes, Lord. Yes."

The woman behind the plexiglass partition banged on the glass, screaming something unintelligible. Mom Birdie loosened her grasp, but Bowie held firm, as though he did not hear the woman or the banging. "Would you have words for me, Mom?"

She squinted, squeezed her eyes tight in concentration. "Therefore if you are offering your gift at the altar and there remember that your brother or sister has something against you, leave your gift there in front of the altar. First go and reconcile to them, then come and offer your gift.

"Bowie, I remember you when you was nothing but a little baby. You was always special. You and your mom and your dad and your brother. Then there was just three."

"What?"

She shook her head. Dust motes fell from her cowrie shelled locks, dancing in the light like pixies. "Everybody knew that monster was touching you. But what could we do about it? They whispered about that all the time. 'Don't send your kids round lest they get teched.' Only he twisted things around, said it was Hendryx doing the touching. Well, where'd you think a boy like that learned dark things?"

Bowie jabbed a finger toward her. "What the hell you talking, crazy old woman. Didn't I just speak blessings on you? Stop that 'flicted talk."

The woman turned from him as if a switch had been

flipped. She started yelling, "Hendryx no more. He gone. He's dead to you and he's dead to me. Now it's just John Doe, John Dough! Who the fuck is Dough? Baby fucker mother fucker father killer!"

She laughed, loud and screeching. Bowie looked at her quizzically.

The woman banged on the glass again, ringing a bell of alarm. Bowie rushed toward the door, standing there until the woman opened the door, allowing him to exit. He looked back through the glass, where the old woman now stood waving and smiling beatifically, resplendent goldenrod hovering around her.

hi eden what are you doing

Google searching for a psychiatrist. This shit is very annoying.

I got a doctor to gave me screpts

What do you mean? How did you do that?

your men knows what he is doing

Are you shitting me? Did you really find somebody? Did you make sure they take Medicare?

i know what am doing

i hope you're right. if you mess this up you will be in a world of trouble

do you think i should were hearing aid

What do you think?

I went to know what you think will you like me batter if i got hearing aid

I like you fine Bowie, with whatever you feel is best for you.
You have to make those choices for yourself. I love you whatever
way you are.

    I love you to and i went to be your man
    cut the shit, Bowie. you got a man already.

Walking home he saw a sign that read HELP WANTED
on a low standing storefront. He walked in and completed
an application.

*g*uess *what baby your men got a job*
    What are you talking about?
    I got a job i start tommorow
    People don't get jobs that fast, Bowie. Stop the bullshit.
    okay you well see .... you coming to get me tonight
    will let you know later

His phone rang. "What, Mom?"

"Where are you? You got me out in front of this nut-
house waiting and you ain't even there."

"I told you I had to take care of something."

"What the hell you have to take care of?"

"I got a job."

"You what!"

"You deaf?"

"You don't need to be working. Why would you want to
mess up your disability? That's free money."

"Ain't nothing free about that money. And anyway, I
can work and still get my disability."

"You aren't ready to work, yet. You need to finish your treatment first. If those people find out you're schizophrenic they going to get rid of you anyway."

"How they going to find that out?"

Magdelene laughed. "You think you can hide it?"

"You know what? You don't give me credit for nothing."

"I'm happy for you. I am. I just don't want you to put too much on yourself. That's how you got sick before, remember?"

"That was a long time ago. You know what? I don't want to talk about it." Bowie hung up. And even though Magdelene called him over and over for the twenty minutes it took him to walk home, he resisted the urge to answer his phone. He put the phone in his pocket where he could not hear it ring, but he knew, from experience, that his phone was ringing repeatedly.

At some point during his walk home, Magdelene located him. She pulled up close to the curb, spitting gravel in her wake as she screamed out the window, "There you are. Get your ass in here." Bowie kept walking, moving blithely around the car to cross the street. "I'm not fucking around with you. You get in here. You can't be running around the streets like a wild animal." Bowie turned back in the direction from where he came, walking faster.

Magdelene swung the steering wheel sharply, skidding a U-turn in the middle of the street, oblivious to the car horns blaring and brakes skidding in her wake. "Don't have me call the PO about this shit. You think I won't but you are sadly mistaken!" Bowie began to sprint, taking off down the first alley he came to, jumping a fence and running through the back yard of a tiny house, laughing maniacally.

He called Eden and told him what had just happened. Eden laughed, too. "So you're running away from your mom? And she's chasing you?"

"I'm still running!" His voice jumped as he ran at a steady pace along side streets.

"I want to know what she thinks is going to happen. Why is she so worried about you being outside the house. Does she think you are a flasher? That you're doing these things they say? There's a reason she's like this."

"I got caught in the car having sex before, with my first boyfriend. I should've never told Lola about it. Now I supposed to go take a polygraph because they say there's more times I exposed myself in public." Bowie stopped running, leaning against a fence to catch his breath. He sat in the dirt.

"But why didn't you just explain the difference between what they're saying you did and what you were really doing? Why don't you defend yourself?"

"I defend myself every day. Nobody listens to what I say. They believe the words on those test papers faster than they believe me. And I do have a problem. I tried to tell them about my racing thoughts to get off that Abilify."

"I think it's ridiculous that a grown ass man is running the streets hiding from his mom. Tell her to back off."

"You met that bitch. You know she don't listen. Now she's saying I can't go to work because I'll get sick again.

And I'll mess up my money. She really means I'll mess up her money. I got to spend my money soon's I get it, or she'll spend it first."

Eden didn't want to travel down that line of inquiry; it made him sick to his stomach. "I gotta go now. I want you to know that I'm proud that you took care of your business. Finding a doctor to take care of your meds. I see you starting to take charge of your life."

"Thank you, Eden. Thank you for helping me. Oh look, here comes that bald-head bitch now. Driving like a bat out of hell. I'll talk to you later." Before the call disconnected, Eden heard Magdelene demand to know who was on the phone and Bowie shouting back.

The rest of the evening, Bowie and Magdelene sat in that cramped hotel room. They ordered food from the Jamaican Hut. Magdelene informed him it was her treat, so she bought him oxtails and curried goat with rice, watched him approvingly as he heartily ate every morsel on the Styrofoam plate.

She gave him change to get sodas from the vending machine in the lobby, and then gave him money to play a few rounds of whist. She knew he wouldn't be playing for long. He was a terrible card player. People liked to have him come to their card games because he was an easy mark, very seldom leaving with any wins, usually quick to tap out.

As the sun went down, Magdelene continued to play, almost by rote. Smoke clouded the room, lulling Bowie's eyes closed. At eight, he snapped them open, reminding her that he needed to go to the pharmacy to pick up his new prescription. She assured him that she would pick it up in the morning. At nine, he reminded her that he needed to go home to take his evening meds. She assured him that he could just take them when they got home later. At midnight, as they walked to the silver hatchback in the parking lot, Magdelene reached into her handbag and gave him eighty dollars. He counted it swiftly, efficiently. "What's this for?"

"I want to go to Valley Forge right quick. I'm feeling like I might do a little something tonight."

"You know I can't go in there. And what's eighty dollars going to do, anyway?"

"We can go to Chester, then. I got you. Let's just see what you do with that first. I feel you going to do a little something tonight, too."

"I'm supposed to start work in the morning."

"So what. I got to work tomorrow, too."

His eyes began to flash. He grinned at her. "I'm better at Sugar House. We should go there."

She shrugged, turned the ignition, and they were off.

When Eden did not hear from Bowie by eleven that night, he had a suspicion of what was amiss. He hoped against hope he was mistaken and shrugged it off. Maybe Bowie's nighttime meds had kicked in before he could call. He knew how quickly they took effect once taken. When his phone rang at one a.m., he knew it was him before he even looked at his screen. Bowie was shouting at Magdelene when Eden picked up.

"She's lying. I don't care what she says."

"Lying about what?" Eden asked.

"I don't know what she got to lie about, but she's lying."

Eden spoke calmly, "What's going on?"

"I didn't do it. It's a fucking lie."

"What? Wait, hold on, what's happening? Where are you?"

"We at the mini market on Main Street."

"Why . . . what are you doing there at one o'clock in the morning?"

"They got a machine here. She wanted to play the machine when we got out the casino, 'cause she didn't win nothing there. This bitch is in here from around the way looking at me crazy, so I told her stop fucking staring at me. She says 'fuck you faggot. You a faggot. Everybody knows you go to that place where the perverts go.' Fuck that bitch. I didn't pull my dick out. That's a lie."

"Who said you took your dick out? Did she say that?" Eden could hear Magdelene in the background: "I've known Gracie since she was a baby. She told me 'I wouldn't lie to you, Miss Magdelene. He was staring at my boyfriend at the train station, and we had to chase him out of there.'"

"That bitch didn't chase me nowhere. I left. I only went up there to see who was up there."

Magdelene said, "And I told your ass to stay right here with me until I was finished. Didn't I tell you that?"

"Why do I have to stay up under you all night. That's

what I want to know."

"That girl didn't lie to me. She called you a pedophile."

"That dumb bitch don't even know what a pedophile is. She probably thinks it's what you use on your fingernails."

Eden said, "Listen, Bowie. Did you hear the girl say she saw you do this? Did you hear her call you a pedophile?"

"She called me a faggot, and I cussed that bitch out."

"Bowie, listen to me. Did you hear her say this, or did your mom tell you she said it? Is the girl there now? What's she saying?"

"No that bitch ain't here. If she was I'd kick her fucking ass."

Magdelene said, "And go back to jail for assault. That girl ain't got no reason to carry tales back here. Why would she come in here and just say those things to you?"

"I don't know why. I know how bitches are."

"You're not listening to me," Eden said. "What did you actually hear the girl say?"

Bowie was too distraught to listen. "Y'all believe her instead of me and you don't even know her. I don't give a fuck. I know what I did and didn't do."

Magdelene took the phone from him, spoke to Eden, "I know this girl's family. She wouldn't just come in here and make shit up. And even if she did, how would she know he's a pedophile?"

"He's not a pedophile. Where is this coming from? Why are you guys even down there when he has to get up in the morning?"

"That's another thing. I told him he's not ready to go back to work yet. This just proves it.

"Where you going, now? You stay right here, Bowie. Hear? I'm going to leave out in a minute. If you go to work and this happens while you're there, you're going to just go right back to jail."

Eden heard Bowie shout from far away.

"Bowie can't go to work in the morning. He has to go to Mockingbird, so the job is a moot point."

Eden felt the electricity in the air diminish slightly. "Oh, that's right. I forgot about that."

"He's left the store, so let me go after him."

The call ended.

To: gardenofeden@gmail.com
From: Dopinger@Mockingbird.org

Dear Mr. Cross,

I would not normally reach out to you, but I wanted to inform you that Bowie did not show up for program this morning. As you know, attendance is part of his agreement with Behavioral Health Court. I have attempted to contact both Bowie and Mrs. St. Charles, but neither has answered the phone.

I was hoping you might be able to let us know whether Bowie is safe. I will not contact his probation officer unless I do not hear from you or Bowie by the end of the day with an explanation for why he has been absent.

Cordially, Lola Dopinger, Senior Assessments and Intake Coordinator

To: Dopinger@Mockingbird.org
From: gardenofeden@gmail.com
Dear Ms. Dopinger,

Thank you for reaching out to me. Bowie was scheduled to have a dental appointment today. It slipped my mind that you needed to be informed. I will be sure that he reports to the program as soon as his appointment is completed. Of course he will have a doctor's note to present to you.

Best,
Eden Cross

Eden called Bowie's phone several times, knowing it was unlikely he would answer. He would not hear the phone if he were asleep, which Eden assumed he was, since he and Magdelene had spent most of the night playing slot machines at the convenience store. He tried Magdelene's number but she didn't answer, either.

Between calls, he opened up his laptop and crafted a believable dentist note, including a masthead and emblem. He inserted the phone number from his father's government-issued cell phone, which was never used, and crossed his fingers that Lola would be too busy to call the number for verification. On the third attempt, Magdelene answered with a sleep hazy voice.

"Bowie overslept. He's late for program, and they emailed me that they are going to contact his PO unless they hear from him. Can you get him up?"

"What the hell is wrong with those people? Can't he even be sick or take a day off?"

"But he's not sick. Why would you keep him up all night when you know he has to get up in the morning?"

"Shit, I have to get up, too. I overslept. Bowie's an adult. It's not my responsibility to get him up in the morning."

Eden gritted his teeth and counted to five before answering. "Can you get him up? Ask him to call me. If you can't take him in, just let me know and I can scoop him up real quick. The visiting nurse is here, so I'm free."

Magdelene said nothing, just hung up the phone.

"Bitch," he whispered.

Eden decided he should just drive over and take him to Mockingbird. He grabbed his keys and went out to the driveway. While driving the short distance into town, his phone rang. There was chaos as soon as Eden answered the phone. He heard shouting, then silence. "What's going on over there?"

Bowie spoke in a low voice, "I can't be here no more, man."

"Well then move out. What's keeping you there?"

"I'm terrified."

"What do you mean you're terrified? Of what?"

"I'm terrified of being here. Of this house. Of her."

"You mean you don't like living there. Your mother is very domineering, but you don't have to give her that power. But that's not terrifying. What are you saying? What do you feel?"

"I'm terrified every time I walk past that empty bedroom, with that blue door, where everything happened. I hate every time I have to walk past that door. And she's in here doing stuff. She pulled down her pants to shit in a fucking bucket in the pantry."

Eden shook his head, as if it were filled with cobwebs. "Wha?"

"I told her use the fucking bathroom like a human being. I don't want to see that shit."

"Why would she do something like that?"

"She said she can't hold it to get to the bathroom. But I don't care, I don't need to see that!"

"In that small ass house? It took as many steps to get to the pantry as it would have to go up the stairs to the bathroom."

"That's what I'm saying!" There was a slight scuffle, then Bowie was shouting, "Why you down here like that, Mom? The door's open. Go upstairs and put on some clothes!"

"I just came down to bring up the laundry basket, Bowie. You act like you ain't seen bra and panties before."

"You're my mom, I shouldn't have to tell you how to act."

"You don't tell me shit."

"I'm going to talk to the court about this shit, because I'm not supposed to live this way."

Eden pulled up in front of the house, noticed the door standing ajar. He could see Bowie's dark form standing at the foot of the stairs, shouting up into space. As he opened the door, he heard Magdelene shout from upstairs, "Throw these clothes in the washer, then." A ball of clothing sailed through the air, landed at Bowie's feet.

"You still standing there like that? Close the fucking

door!"

"Fuck you, Bowie."

The door slammed shut, shaking the stair railing. Eden heard chips of paint fall from the jamb to the floor. He stepped in and quickly closed the door behind him, hoping the neighbors didn't hear the commotion. Bowie turned a face of dark fury toward Eden. "Let's get the fuck out of here before I snap on this woman. I'm trying to get my life right and she's doing the same old stupid shit."

"Bowie, just like Lola said, you can't just put the blame for everything on other people. Your mother didn't force you to stay out all night and miss the program. You did that."

"No. She did that shit on purpose. She was so scared of me going to work she made sure I couldn't. She wants me to stay up in this house till the day I die because she can't stand her own company."

The door upstairs creaked open and Magdelene pounded down the stairs clutching a robe closed at her neck. Eden saw the flash of white underwear as she descended, noticed it was the same robe she put on that morning he had found them both sleeping in the same bed.

"Don't flatter yourself. I'm not the one that needs taking care of."

"You are. You need to be in a hospital somewhere. You put your shit off on me, but that's done. I'm going to get my own place even if I got to rent a room in a whorehouse to get away from you."

Magdelene snorted. "A whorehouse would be right up

your alley, too, wouldn't it? Don't fool yourself. You're not ready to live on your own."

Eden asked, "Why not?"

She started. "What? He's just not."

"But why not?"

"He can't do it."

"You've said that already, but what is it that makes you think he couldn't live on his own? There has to be a reason?"

"Are you serious? Knowing all that you found out recently? The jail time, everything. He can't hold on to a fifty-cent piece, so how's he going to pay his bills?"

"You don't pay your bills either, but you doing it," Bowie snapped.

Eden said, "Plenty of people are living on their own and have to learn to budget their money."

"He can't hear. If the smoke alarm went off that boy would burn to a crisp."

Bowie laughed. "I can burn up here just as well as I can burn up somewhere else. Lola told me about service pets and stuff like that to help me, so I can live on my own."

"You want me to just come out and say it? You're special needs, and you won't ever be able to live like everybody else. I love you. You're my child, and I don't want to hurt you, but that's how it is. You want a normal life but you're not normal."

Eden slowly shook his head, not believing his ears. "Don't do that. Why would you say that to him? I don't understand you at all. Mothers are supposed to encourage their kid to be the best he can be."

"I don't give a fuck what you think about me. I've lived this life, taking care of Bowie since the day he was born. I'm used to the looks, to people thinking shit about me. You walk in my shoes before you look down your nose at me. You think you're doing so right by Bowie, but you're taking advantage of him just like everybody else has. Would you be so willing to help him out if he wasn't sexing you up?"

"What are you talking about?"

She laughed mockingly. "What am I talking about? Like you don't know. You're the one that should be in that program. You're the predator. Taking advantage of somebody confused about sex."

"How do you feel he's confused? Being gay doesn't mean you're confused."

"He's not gay!" she screamed. "He's confused. And it's you people that created that. Fucking a boy that didn't know no better, making him think that shit is normal. You brainwashed him."

Eden shook his head, laughed. "You are some piece of work. Is this how you twist things for him? You are a fucking bitch."

Bowie shouted, "You don't call my mom a bitch!"

He lunged forward, shoving Eden back. Eden fell back in surprise, his shoulder knocking into the sheetrock, creating a large hole. He stumbled as he stood, brushing the debris from his shirt as he stared openmouthed at the both of them. Then, he smiled a little and walked away. The keys jingled in his hand as he unlocked the car and climbed inside. He tried to insert the key into the ignition but kept missing. So he just sat there, staring out at the road in front of him. The tension in his shoulders lessened, and he slumped over in his seat, leaning his head onto the steering wheel with his arm folded over the wheel. He heard a click, then the door on the passenger side opened, and he felt the weight of the car shift as Bowie climbed inside. Bowie sat there, watching. Eden sat back up, in case he needed to protect himself.

"I didn't mean to push you, Eden. I'm sorry."

Eden said nothing.

"You accept my apology? Please."

"I don't know what else to say to you, Bowie. I don't know what you want."

"I don't want nothing."

"You're making a fool of me. I don't even know who you are. You got all these diagnoses. Every single person has a different impression of you."

"What do you think about me?"

"I don't know anymore. It's hard. I keep trying to re-member the guy I thought I knew. I keep reminding myself who that person is, but all these other stories keep clouding my mind, telling me what I thought I knew was bullshit. All I wanted was something easy. Something simple to take me away from the boredom of my life. And you were that before. You used to make me light up just seeing you. I didn't want all this work."

"What work? I didn't ask you to do any work."

"Are you fucking kidding me? I've been spending so much time trying to get your shit together I barely have time to concentrate on myself. Representing you at meetings, lying to people, advocating for you, trying to fight your battles with your mom because you don't have the balls to do it yourself."

Bowie shouted, "I didn't ask you to do none of that, did I? I never asked you to do one thing for me!"

Eden shouted back, "Then what do you want from me?"

"All I wanted was you to love me. I never asked you to do one thing for me. I don't need you to save me, Eden. I'm not your dad. You can't make up for all the things you didn't do for him by putting me in his place. I don't need saving. I need you to see me right now, for who I am."

"I do see you."

"Do you? You're trying to cure me. Make me better. You think one day I can stop taking these pills and the bipolar or schizophrenia or whatever they say it is next week will just disappear. But what if it doesn't? What if who I am right now is all I can be? Can you accept that, or do I have to pretend to be normal? Go out and find a job, go live on my own, get off the meds? All that will make you see me?"

Eden turned to him. "I told you before, Bowie, I love you right now. Who you are right now is the person I fell in love with. I only want you to be the best you you can be. I don't know if you believe enough in yourself to try to do that. Not for me, but for yourself."

Bowie leaned over, laid his head in Eden's lap, wrapping his arms around his torso. "What about you, Eden? Do you believe enough in yourself to be the best person you can be? It's easy to talk it, but can you do it, too?" They were both silent for a moment. Then Bowie spoke so low Eden almost missed it. "Are you giving up on me, Eden?"

Eden rested his hands on his head, on his neck. His voice was thick with emotion. "I'll never let go of you, Bowie, until you want me to."

Acknowledgments

Thank you Townsend Montilla and the Jaded Ibis team for helping to bring my vision into the light. Jennifer Natalya Fink: a true warrior and friend. And Mom. Always.